Natasha Mostert

Dark Prayer

portable magic

Jacket design by Asha Hossain/Stefan Coetzee
Photograph: *Entwined* © Daria Bulavina
Author photograph by Mark Andreani.
© Natasha Mostert

ISBN 978-1-909965-20-1

www.natashamostert.com
www.portablemagic.com

PRAISE FOR
NATASHA MOSTERT

'One of the most original voices on the literary scene. A master wordsmith.'

Glamour Magazine

'Bedtime reading for the brave.'

The Times (London)

'Dazzlingly clever and original ... one can only marvel at the author's own witch-like power to enchant her audience.'

Daily Mail (London)

'Intellectual meets Paranormal. Mostert has a knack of blending science and the paranormal in interesting, "it-could-happen" ways ... The story, the science behind it, and its mysticism will leave readers thinking (and discussing) long after the story is over.'

Graffiti

'(Mostert's) heady fiction doesn't so much push at the edges of the genre as ride roughshod over them.'

Observer (London)

For my mother, Hantie:
artist, seeker, free spirit

*For ease of reference the terms 'parkour'
and 'free running' are used interchangeably.*

'I longed to embrace my dead mother's ghost. Thrice I tried to clasp her image, and thrice it slipped through my hands. Like a shadow, like a dream...'
—*Homer, The Odyssey*

PROLOGUE

The little girl was not a sound sleeper. In the early morning hours, she would often open her eyes and look calmly and unafraid into the near darkness. After a moment of staring at the far ceiling above her, she'd dangle her feet out of bed, tuck Mr Cuddles under her arm and pad down the passage towards her mother's room.

She never stepped inside. For a few heartbeats she would wait at the door, watching the soft shape asleep inside the big 'princess and the pea' bed. If she listened carefully, she could hear her mother breathing. This would be enough to satisfy her and she'd yawn once, twice – and return to her own bed.

Tonight is no different. There is the door to her mother's room. There, hazy in the gloom, the first glimpse of the dressing table with her mother's red scarf trailing from a post, its gypsy fire muted by the dark. The air is scented with the familiar fragrances leaking from the perfume bottles reflected in the mirror's shadowed face. The little girl pauses at the threshold and turns her head in the direction of the snowy bed.

The bed is empty.

The little girl looks at the undisturbed sheets and the plumped-up pillows. Her head droops to one shoulder as it does when she is puzzled or feeling shy.

Hesitantly, she steps back into the passage.

'Mama?'

The word stops in the air, the thick carpet and velvet curtains keeping the sound from carrying.

She starts walking towards the staircase, Mr Cuddles dragging at one hand. Her other hand clutches at her pyjama bottoms, which are slipping.

Down the staircase and past the fan-shaped window framing the glossy blackness outside. Through the living room, with its tall bookcases and its many books, which seem to glow even in the dark. Past the piano with its exposed keys and sheet music trailing on the floor.

Against the wall the old-fashioned clock tings softly. The big numerals and filigreed arms glow, coolly phosphorescent. The little girl is only five, but she can tell the time. She stares at the clock face and holds up her left forefinger and thumb in a wobbly L.

'Mama?'

The kitchen door is closed but there is a yellow slit of light at the bottom. As she turns the handle and pushes the door open, she smells lemons.

Black and white tiled floor, bright in the electric light. Water drip, dripping into the sink. The woman lying on her back, her right leg forming a startling triangle, her mouth smiling and her eyes hidden in a sticky nest of hair and blood. There is blood on the floor, and on the cricket bat clutched in the hand of the man who had turned around as the door opened.

He holds out his other hand. 'Come with me, little girl. I will make you forget.'

'Only the hand that erases can write the true thing.'
—*Meister Eckhart*

CHAPTER ONE

Memory was a funny old thing.

Jack watched his father lean towards the interviewer, his face taking on a nicely self-deprecating expression. Jack could tell his father was about to launch into an anecdote about his past: an anecdote that would tell of bravery under fire and a young man's courage tested. Each time his father told this story, the battle became a little fiercer, the danger a little greater, the bullets a little closer. His father sounded sincere; because he was sincere. He wasn't consciously embellishing: each time he wheeled out this chestnut of a story he truly believed he was accurately recounting what had happened.

His father modestly inclined his head as the interviewer gushed her admiration. Jack smiled. You had to hand it to the old guy; he knew how to milk the moment.

As he flicked off the TV remote, he wondered idly at what point unreliable memories started affecting one's sense of self. If you remembered the earlier you as braver, stronger, more concerned for your fellow man than you actually were, would this souped-up recollection determine how you acted in the present? If you were born a lowly Ford Focus but started remembering yourself as a Shelby Mustang, would you become one? Maybe, after all these years of building a legend in his

own mind, his father had indeed turned himself into the kind
of man who would selflessly race to the rescue: rushing into
fiery buildings, jumping into fast-flowing rivers, dragging limp
survivors out of burning cars.

'Finished?'

Chloe Quindlen, his father's personal assistant, stepped
into the office. Chloe was attractive, smart and hopelessly in
love with her boss. 'Smart' and 'foolish' were not mutually
incompatible.

'Yes. Thanks for showing it to me.'

Chloe pressed her finger on the player's eject button and
removed the CD, her expression reverent. 'Great interview,
wasn't it. Mr Simonetti is a wonderful man.'

'Yes, indeed.'

His tone of voice was not to her satisfaction. She frowned.
'I hear you've been naughty.'

Naughty. He tried desperately to think of a response to
this accusation that would be even remotely appropriate.

'Your father is rather disappointed, Jack.'

'I know. Very sad.'

'How can you laugh about it?' She glared at him.

Contrition was clearly called for. 'I'm sorry, sweetheart.
I'm behaving badly. Will you forgive me?'

She sniffed, slightly mollified. 'He shouldn't be long. Can I
get you anything while you wait?'

'No, I'm good. Thanks.'

She walked out the door trailing L'Air du Temps and left
him to his own company and his father's collection of contem-
porary art. Leon Simonetti had recently begun to see himself as
New York City's answer to Charles Saatchi and the vast walls
of his office were covered with canvases vibrating spiky angst.

His father's desk was exceptionally neat. Apart from a
leather blotter and a telephone, the only other object on the
slab of polished mahogany was a tripod-shaped piece of steel
engraved with the words *aut vincere aut mori*: either to conquer or to die. Very macho. The Latin wasn't an affectation,
though. His father had a genuine love for the classics and had

insisted on his reluctant son acquiring a nodding acquaintance with both Latin and Greek. As a teenager, the value of studying a dead language had never made sense to Jack although he found it paid off in unexpected ways later on. Girls, he discovered, were surprisingly impressed by a guy who could drop a casual quote or two from the *Ars Amatoria*.

The sound of voices in the outside office, and the next moment his father strode into the room, his shoulders belligerent and his eyes snapping behind the steel rims of his spectacles. He waved impatiently at Jack, who was getting to his feet, and slapped a newspaper onto the desk.

'What the hell were you thinking?'

Jack looked at the grainy black and white picture and winced. The photographer had certainly captured the moment. It showed him with an unholy grin on his face, holding a chair above his head, which he was clearly about to crash down on the head of the wild-eyed individual facing him. The caption read: 'Tycoon's son in brawl.'

'I was helping a lady in distress.'

'You were looking for a bar fight and you found it. The woman was just an excuse.'

Jack sighed. 'I'm sorry.'

His father jabbed a vicious finger at the photograph. 'And this is out there for everyone to see!'

It probably wasn't the time to tell his father that he had become quite the celebrity on YouTube as well: 2,300 hits since the previous night and counting.

'I don't understand you. You have a brain but you waste it. I've given you an education. I've given you all the tools you need to make something of yourself but you take nothing seriously. You are not a child any more. Is there anything you care about, Jack? Anything you truly want?'

'A long cool woman in a black dress …'

His father's nostrils flared.

'No, sorry. Of course not. World peace. That's it – world peace.'

A long silence.

'Well, I've had enough.' His father's face was set.

Jack looked at him warily. He had heard these words before, but this time they sounded different. Something told him he wasn't going to like what came next.

His father opened the drawer of his desk and removed an envelope.

'Here. An e-ticket to London. You have a seat booked on the late flight to Heathrow.'

London. Well, that wasn't so bad. If his father wanted to banish him from home and hearth, he could think of worse places to hang than London. Jack pushed his hand inside the envelope and removed the ticket. Economy class. Still …

'An English friend of mine has a problem. He thinks you might be able to help. His name is Daniel Barone.'

The name stirred a recollection. In his father's study at home were dozens of tastefully framed photographs showing his father glad-handing the rich and famous. Pushed into the back row was a picture of three men and two women. They were a striking group: young, beautiful, confident. In the photograph his father still had a shock of black hair and a jaw as planed as Clark Kent's. Next to him, a handsome man with dark blond hair was looking into the camera with hooded eyes. 'Barone,' his mother had told him years ago when he had asked her about the photograph. 'He was a friend of your father's when they were both at Oxford. He was a famous scientist. I met him once. Charming man.'

'And the girls?'

His mother frowned. 'I don't know. When your father moved to the States he said he lost touch with all of them except Daniel.' She had frowned again, touching her hand thoughtfully to the glass, her fingers hovering over the young faces.

Jack replaced the ticket in the envelope. 'What kind of problem are we talking about?'

'Daniel's ward disappeared.'

Ward. To Jack the word tasted old-fashioned. Like something from *Jane Eyre*.

'Surely this is a matter for the police?'

'You don't understand. His ward disappeared but she has been found again. But there are … complications.'

'I don't see how I can help.'

'This is not open for discussion, Jack. You will get on the plane tonight and when you arrive at the other side; you will place yourself at Daniel's complete disposal. If you refuse – or if you make a mess of things over there – I will cut you off. No allowance. No apartment. No trendy little art gallery for your friend, Nicola. No more funding for your mountaineering expeditions or that ridiculous stock-car racing. And this time, I mean it. You will come back to New York to nothing. And don't go crying to your grandmother – I've discussed this with her and she finally agrees with me that the time has come for you to get on track.'

Things were looking grim. 'How long will I have to stay?'

'You will stay until Daniel no longer has any need of you.'

Leon Simonetti reached for the phone. Jack knew he was being dismissed but for a few moments he simply stared at his parent. People always remarked on the strong resemblance between father and son and he supposed it was true. He had inherited his father's Roman profile and they had the same colouring: black hair, blue eyes. They shared the same long-limbed build as well, although his father's body had a softness to it which his own had yet to acquire. Maybe, thirty years from now, he too would have a fleshy roll around his middle and a crumpled jaw like a Caesar gone to seed. And, who knows? Maybe he had inherited other traits as well. Perhaps, with the passage of time, he too would become a destroyer of worlds.

His father looked up and lifted his eyebrows – an impatient, 'is there anything else?' expression on his face. Jack shook his head and stood up from his chair. But as he reached the door, his father spoke again.

'Life is what you make of it, Jack.'

He turned to look at his father across the wide expanse of the Aubusson rug separating them. Ordinarily, he would have shrugged off these words as just another platitude. But his father's voice sounded strange: small, cold.

'The choices you make determine the life you lead. Remember that.' Still that small, faraway voice. 'You live with those choices ... and die by them.'

CHAPTER TWO

Free running can be exhilarating. It can be like flying. But if you miscalculate, nothing can make you feel more clumsy and earthbound. This was not going to be pretty.

She had started off well enough, running strongly and maintaining good momentum, but as she hit the wall with the ball of her foot and tried to gain distance by kicking off and out, she realised she had kicked too high and her body was far too upright.

Desperately, she twisted from the waist but her foot slipped under the downward force. Instead of a fluid, accurate touch-down, she flopped like a flounder.

Shit.

Beside her, Jungles completed his own effortless tic-tac, bouncing dynamically off the brick wall and speeding smoothly ahead like a stunt man in a James Bond movie. Running straight at the handrail blocking his path, he grasped the metal bar with bent arms and pushed his lower body through the gap without any drop in speed. The next moment he was running down the alley, a shadow disappearing among shadows. She couldn't even hear his foot fall.

She knew she should follow him immediately. Never slow down. If a movement doesn't work out, don't agonise over the recovery; just move your body forward. *Movement is life.* That was what parkour was all about. Never look back. Find another way.

Get your butt in gear, girl.

But she felt sluggish and she could still feel a pull in her groin muscle from the injury she sustained three weeks ago when she had dropped from a wall onto a loose piece of sheet metal. The echo of past pain made her hesitant and she knew she should have stayed at home tonight. If Jungles knew she was trying to work her way through an injury while on a night run, he would be furious.

Jungles was no longer anywhere to be seen. The concrete towers on either side of the alley loomed dark and silent. This part of the City emptied at night, the investment bankers and money men deserting their offices for the wine bars, restaurants and theatres of the West End. Tilting her head back, she looked straight up at the night sky above her. It was hazy with light and pollution – reddened – as though the city was burning.

And as she stood there, swaying slightly on her feet, suddenly feeling a little lightheaded, a little high ... it happened. Everything became white at the edges and the stark lines of the world around her – brick, mortar, concrete – started to slide out of focus, the outlines wavering and rippling as though the tall buildings were about to dissolve and drown.

Still she continued to stare at the sky, and watched as they started to fall towards her. Books. They tumbled from the bleeding sky like wounded birds. The spines snapping open and the pages fanning white. Black letters slipping off the slanted pages and falling, falling to the ground where they ...

Shatter.

No! Not again! She pressed her hands hard over her eyes and felt the panicked movement of her eyeballs against her palms. Desperately she tried to shut out the image of the books, but inside her closed eyelids, numbers were starting to form, crimson and bright, like a cipher written in secret ink: (3/207/-7/3) (4/98/-5/12) (2/55/-1/99) ... And now she could hear the voices softly whispering, and she knew if she opened her eyes, she would see figures moving at the periphery of her vision.

An ugly sound left her chest.

Stop it! Take control. She dropped her hands; took a deep breath.

Keeping her eyes resolutely ahead of her, she pushed off the ball of her back foot and began to run – haltingly at first but then with greater fluidity. As she picked up speed, she continued to breathe through her nose. Kill the panic. Focus. Think of nothing but the movement. *Become* the movement. When she reached the handrail, she launched herself into a lateral vault and cleared the obstacle effortlessly, landing on the other side softly and with control and balance. Without breaking step she continued to run.

Run.

She ran – skimming off walls, leaping gaps. Her mind was still, her body flying. The world had snapped back into focus. The phantom books with their poisoned pages were left far behind. She could no longer hear the voices. All she needed to do was to go forward always and to keep running, running, running towards escape.

CHAPTER THREE

'Well, me old mucker. Good to see you.' Charles Esquith leant bonelessly against the door frame of his London flat and grinned at Jack. He flipped back a lock of flaxen hair from his forehead. 'Do you want to come in?'

'No, Einstein. I like standing in the hallway.'

Esquith grinned again and opened the door wide. 'A wee bit irritable, are we? Must be the shock of slumming it at the back of the plane. Let me guess: your old man made sure the seat was next to the toilets as well.'

Jack pushed past him into a room filled with watery sunlight, shabby furniture and faded Qums on the plank floor. The Esquiths owned half of London but Charlie liked to play bohemian. Through the window was a view of the cinnamon-coloured dome of the Royal Albert Hall.

'Enter the Warrior.' Esquith closed the door and looked at Jack critically. 'You look like shit.'

'Thanks.'

He nodded at the bandage around Jack's forearm. 'How serious is that?'

'Not serious. A few stitches.' Truth to tell, the wound on his shoulder where the bastard had bitten him was of more concern. The doctor in the ER had kept up a running commentary, and Jack now knew more about what lived inside the human mouth than he had ever wanted to.

'Hmm. Well, take a load off. I'll make us a cuppa.'

Esquith disappeared into the kitchenette. Jack sank into an over-stuffed armchair and glanced around him. Stacks of paper, piles of books, Charlie's vintage collection of rude seaside postcards: the apartment appeared almost exactly the same as he had seen it the last time he visited about eighteen months ago. The tray with rocks was new: it must represent Charlie's latest passion. Esquith was a perpetual student, moving from one subject to another – psychology, astronomy, alternative religions, butterflies – his voracious curiosity ran wide. He reminded Jack of the gentlemen scholars and explorers of the Victorian era with their vast fortunes and stately homes who turned their hobbies into treasure troves of knowledge: cataloguing the flora and fauna of the West Indies, translating fairy tales from exotic cultures, seeking the origin of the Nile.

They had met in Goa five years ago. Jack had made the pilgrimage to the land of trance and stoner happiness, hoping for what, he did not know – some kind of freak dream of self-knowledge and spaced-out bliss, maybe – but Goa had turned out not to be his thing. He felt no connection with the retro hippies, cyber gypsies and curious European backpackers looking for nirvana, cheap drugs and techno overload.

In fact, after a week of constant, repetitive electronic soup drifting from houses, apartments, cafés and rave nights, Jack had felt homicidal, not enlightened. On top of it, he found himself rooming with a bona fide nutter who kept muttering, 'there are links in silence' and 'your brain is a drum' while staring at him with unblinking intensity. When Jack woke up one night to find the man on his knees next to the bed, his face disturbingly close to his own, he had had enough.

His next roommate was a lanky Brit with a slightly effete drawl whose laconic attitude hid a mind keen as a razorblade and a burning curiosity about the world. It was a fortuitous encounter: two rich boys slumming it together. Under Charlie's tutelage, Jack had managed to develop, if not a fondness, at least some appreciation for the shabby paradise in which they found themselves. Goa was now little more than a psychedelic-hued memory, but his friendship with Charlie had endured.

He looked up as Esquith entered the room, bearing an enormous teapot. 'Here we go.' Esquith poured the tea competently into a thin-rimmed cup. 'One lump or two?' he asked solicitously, his hand hovering over the sugar bowl.

'The hostess with the mostest.' Jack brought the cup to his lips and swallowed. Not bad. Charles knew his way around a pot of English Breakfast.

'So fill me in. Your email was cryptic, to say the least.' Esquith leant back in his chair and lifted his long legs onto a footrest. 'It sounds as though you have to play the detective? Someone's disappeared?'

'The girl is no longer lost. They found her. But there are problems – don't ask me what. And why the hell this Barone guy thinks I can help, I have no idea.'

'Daniel Barone. Now there's an illustrious name.' Esquith pursed his lips. 'While you were tucking into your microwave meal at 30,000 feet I did some googling on your behalf and I tell you – I'm impressed. The man is a genius – of the Stephen Hawking kind. Everyone thought he would be a sure bet for a Nobel Prize one day. But two decades ago he dropped out of academic research almost overnight.'

'What was his field?'

'He's a neuroscientist. He was trying to identify the memory molecule.'

'I thought that had been done.'

'You're talking about the work of the Sackler Lab and the identification of PKMzeta. Yes. But there is talk that Barone made his discovery all of twenty years ago. And, on top of it, that he has perfected the manipulation of this molecule. Most scientists believe such a breakthrough to be some way off.'

Jack lifted his eyebrows. 'Over the years my father has invested millions into research on memory. He is convinced it is going to be the next big success story in pharmaceuticals – bigger than Viagra, he says.'

'The population of the West is greying. An astute man, your father.'

Jack frowned. 'I don't understand, though. You're telling me this Barone had cracked the memory puzzle decades ago and hadn't shared with my beloved parent? I'm amazed they're still friends.'

'Well, it's all rumour.' Esquith waved a languid hand. 'Who knows if Barone really managed to pull it off? If he did, he never shared his findings with the world. The man's become a bit of a recluse. He had a car accident and is not well.'

Jack drained his cup and glanced at his watch. 'Is this the time? I need to catch a train. Is it OK if I use your shower first?'

'*Mi casa es su casa*. You'll be staying with me, won't you?'

'Thanks, but I don't know how long this whole thing will drag on for.'

'Is Daddy footing the bill for the Mandarin Oriental? No? Well, then the choice is a B&B in Acton or my spare bedroom.'

'You're a good friend, Charles.'

'I'm a goddamned saint.' Esquith picked up Jack's suitcase.

'At any rate,' Jack said, as he followed his friend down a narrow passage, 'I won't have to make use of your hospitality tonight. Barone wants me to stay over at Whiteladies this evening.'

'Whiteladies.' Esquith nodded his approval. 'The name has possibilities. I can picture it already – battlements, crenelated towers, a dungeon. Where is it? Cornwall? The Moors?'

'Oxfordshire. Somewhere on the Thames.'

'How disappointing.' Esquith opened a door. 'Here's your room. You like?'

Jack surveyed the walls, which had been tastefully decorated with sepia-coloured images of nineteenth-century porn: a veritable bouquet of powdered bosoms, bloomers, dimpled cheeks, pin curls and coquettish fans.

'I will sleep well.'

'Excellent. By the way, I should mention that Alice cannot wait to see you.'

Jack turned to his friend with foreboding in his heart. 'You told her I'm in town?'

'Of course. What kind of brother would I be if I didn't tell my little sister the object of her young lust is visiting the Big Smoke?'

'Dammit, Charlie ...'

'Tsk. Tsk. Saint, remember. ' Esquith lifted an admonishing finger.

'Oh, man. I knew this trip was going to be a disaster.'

'Cheer up.' Esquith grinned callously. 'Right, then. I'll leave you with the ladies. Fresh towels are in the cupboard over there.' Another grin and he closed the door softly behind him.

CHAPTER FOUR

The light was fading when Jack disembarked at Whitley train station. The station itself was quaint, with tubs of pink and lavender blooms and a carpet of autumn leaves covering the walkways. He had hardly stepped off the platform when a strongly built man waiting outside a maroon and chrome Jaguar approached him and introduced himself as Scott, Mr Barone's chauffeur. Scott was polite but not what one would call the chatty type. Jack stared at the square, impassive shoulders of the man in front of him. Twenty minutes and not a word from our Scott.

But it seemed they had reached journey's end. As the car passed through a pair of automated gates, Jack peered at a house that showed itself in glimpses through the dark trees crowding the driveway. It was an enigmatic house with thick stone walls and leaded windows glowing amber in the gathering dusk. Stone caryatids, their graceful drapery smothered in ivy, supported the double front door on either side. There was nothing as overtly Gothic as turrets or a widow's walk, but Jack decided Whiteladies exuded enough gloomy glamour to appeal to even Charlie's extravagant sense of romance.

The car sped up a slight incline, cleared the wooded drive-way and came to a hushed halt on the gravel sweep outside the front door.

While Jack waited for Scott to remove his backpack from the car boot, he looked around him. On the left was a formal walled garden – he glimpsed a fountain and a marble seat through the filigree of a wrought-iron gate – and the house itself faced an expanse of unbroken lawn that ended at the river's edge. A magnificent willow trailed its denuded branches in the black water. And there were swans. They floated pale and ghost-like in the fading light.

Behind him came the pointed jingle of keys: Scott was holding open the front door and trying – not too subtly – to gain his attention.

Maybe he was simply tired, the jet lag playing with his mind, but as Jack stared at the open door, which allowed a view of a curled banister and buttery pools of light soaking a parquet floor, his skin was suddenly prickling. In some secret recess of his subconscious, he sensed that this was a defining moment. He could choose to walk over the threshold and his life would change irrevocably. Or he could turn around right now and the door would close – literally – on what could be the next chapter in his life.

The moment passed. A sudden breeze blew in from the river, carrying with it the dank scent of mud and vegetation. The wind chilled the back of his neck and sent dry leaves skittering across the forecourt. He was now only aware that he was cold and hungry and that he wanted nothing more than to get out of the chill and wrap his hands around a generous glass of Scotch.

Without further thought, he stepped inside.

Forty minutes later, he had a glass of excellent Macallan in his hand and his outlook on life had improved considerably. But he was also starting to get impatient. His host was clearly in no great haste to meet him.

At least there was a decent fire and Scott had left him with the drinks trolley. He sloshed some more whisky into his glass, scooped a few cubes from the ice bucket with his fingers and took a deep swallow. That was the ticket. Another couple of glasses and he'd be so mellow he might not even mind sitting here cooling his heels like an idiot.

The room in which he found himself was obviously the study. It was an impressive room with graceful, bevelled-edged bookcases and a medallioned ceiling. On the coffee table was a sparkling crystal vase from which drooped fat, creamy roses. But everything in the room seemed just a little worn. Even in the dim light of the one table lamp, he was able to see that the armrests of the sofas were rubbed shiny and that the velvet folds of the curtains were discoloured. A bald spot showed in the Tabriz rug. The place lacked a woman's touch. The writing desk was – oddly – without a chair. And the room was not heated properly: every now and then a cold draught eddied across the floor and chilled his ankles, maddeningly, cancelling out the good work done by the Macallan.

As he walked closer to the fire, Jack looked up at the large oil painting that had pride of place above the mantelpiece. It showed a white-shouldered woman in a diaphanous gown. She was kneeling next to a river and in one hand she held a lamp, while the other hand trailed in the river's black water. Usually he had rather a thing for white-shouldered women, but there was knowingness in this one's gaze, which was disquieting.

He peered at the signature in the corner of the canvas but it was practically illegible. The date said 1952 but those auburn tresses and cupid-bow mouth spoke very much of a pre-Raphaelite fantasy. In fact, Jack thought, studying the painting critically, the figure in the canvas reminded him strongly of a Dante Gabriel Rossetti painting: a woman in an emerald dress, also holding a lamp. What was it called it again? Ricordanza or some such...

'Mnemosyne.' The voice behind him was cool and dry as paper.

Jack turned around, surprised. The man behind him had entered through a side door without any noise. His stealth was even more remarkable considering he was in a wheelchair.

The wheelchair moved forward again with unnerving quiet. The man seated in it tilted back his head and looked up at the painting.

'The goddess of memory. She slept with Zeus for nine consecutive nights and gave birth to the muses. Here she is trailing her hand in the water of forgetfulness – the Lethe – where dead souls would drink so as to forget their past lives when they are reincarnated.'

He turned his head towards Jack and smiled. 'I'm Daniel Barone. Apologies for keeping you waiting.'

Jack reached downwards to shake the hand that was held out at him. The handshake was firm but not crushing, the clasp quickly released.

'Please.' Barone motioned towards one of the sofas.

Jack sat down and studied the man who was manoeuvring his wheelchair with smooth economy of movement. Despite the squat shape of the wheelchair, Barone looked elegant. He was dressed in a tweed jacket and polo-neck sweater. A tartan rug covered his legs. But it was his face that commanded attention. It was lined but still extraordinarily handsome. Strongly marked brows were set above heavy-lidded black eyes. His dark blond hair showed deep streaks of white but was thick and springy.

'I trust your trip was comfortable?'

'Thank you. Yes.'

'And your father is well?'

'He sends his regards.'

Barone surveyed him for a moment. 'You don't want to be here, do you?'

Jack blinked, taken aback. But seeing as they were being so open with each other …

'No, I don't. I'm here because my father is forcing me to be here.'

'Forcing you.' Barone paused. 'Forgive me, Jack, but why are you in a position where he is able to force you to do anything you don't want to do?'

'Because I'm a cliché, Mr Barone. I pretty much live off my father's wealth. Everything I have, I get from him. I don't work. I have no income of my own. I play.'

Barone lifted a quizzical eyebrow. 'I understand.'

Jack shrugged. 'I doubt you do. It's a game. My father enjoys the power and I enjoy seeing how far I can bait him. Every now and then I crash and burn. This is one of those times.'

'All games come to an end eventually.'

'Indeed. This game will end when my father dies.'

'And you inherit.'

'I won't inherit a cent. Upon my father's death, his money will go to several very deserving charities. I know: he showed me the will.'

Barone smiled faintly. 'And when there is no more money? What will you do?'

'Not a clue. But I'm happy to say this freaks my father out far more than it does me. Now. How can I help you?'

'How much has Leon told you about my situation?'

'Not much. He told me there's a problem with your ward.'

Barone nodded. 'Her name is Jenilee. Jenilee Gray. Her mother was a great friend of mine. When Julianne was … killed … Jenilee came to live with me.'

Jack homed in on the hesitation in Barone's voice. 'Killed?'

'Julianne was bludgeoned to death in her kitchen.'

Christ. Jack stared at Barone, who was watching him steadily.

'Jenilee was only five years old at the time. From what the police could gather, Julianne had put Jenilee to bed that night but never went to bed herself. When the cleaning woman arrived the next morning, she found Julianne dead and Jenilee fast asleep in her own room. Thankfully, she had slept through the entire horror.'

'Did they find who did it?'

'They did not. The back door was open; Julianne must have neglected to lock it. There were a few valuables missing and the police think it was a crime of opportunity which escalated into violence: a burglar who panicked when he was surprised in the act.' Still that emotionless face but Barone's hands moved suddenly, jerkily, in his lap. 'This past tragedy has nothing to do with the present-day situation, though. I take it Leon told you Jenilee had disappeared.'

Jack nodded. 'She was a runaway?'

'Not in the conventional sense. There was no friction between Jenilee and me, and she wanted for nothing. But one day she simply walked out of the restaurant where she was having lunch, without taking even her handbag with her. And then – nothing.'

'I thought you found her?'

'I did. After two years of going mad with worry. The police had given up but one of my own private investigators managed to track her down.'

'So what's the problem?'

'She doesn't want to come home.' A pause. 'She doesn't recognise me.'

'What do you mean?' Jack frowned. 'She has amnesia?'

'I'm afraid it is more complicated than that. Amnesia is caused by physical trauma – damage to the brain. Jenilee has sustained no such physical injury. She seems to be in what is called, in common parlance, a fugue state. She has taken on a different identity: in fact, she has completely reinvented herself – new name, new life – and she has no memories of her earlier self. None. But, more disturbing, she has become a different person – not only in appearance and name – but with regard to her personality as well. The woman she is now is as different as black is to white from the girl who grew up in my house.'

This was growing seriously weird. But, Jack had to admit, interesting.

'So how did she get to be in this fugue state, then?'

'I don't know. But there must have been a stressor. Something happened – something emotionally devastating.'

Barone paused, the lines at the corners of his mouth deepening. 'The problem is: fugues never remember the stressor. Whatever it was that triggered her amnesia, she has no recollection of it. I trained as a neuroscientist, Jack. My field of study is memory and the brain. If there is anyone who might be able to help Jenilee, it is me. But I can't get her to trust me. She doesn't remember me and she believes she has a fully functional, self-sufficient life. She doesn't feel she requires help.'

'You've met with her personally? After your investigator found her?'

Barone nodded. 'It wasn't easy to arrange, but in the end I did manage to sit down with her and talk to her at some length. But she seems to have no interest in reclaiming her former life.'

'Are you absolutely sure it's her?'

'She has a birthmark – here.' Barone touched his wrist. 'And her eyes – they are unmistakable. '

Stranger and stranger. Jack thought of B-grade movies and the amnesiac heroine opening her eyes gratefully one morning to a world filled with sanity and sunlight. 'Is there any chance she can … I don't know … snap out of it?'

'Oh, yes. Fugue is characterised as reversible amnesia and the memory loss usually lasts for only a few hours, days at most. It usually disappears as mysteriously as it came. But there are rare documented cases of victims who suffered protracted psychogenic amnesia for decades. Jenilee has now been in a fugue state for two years.'

From somewhere at the back of the house, someone suddenly started playing the piano. A few hesitant, try-out chords and then the notes began to tumble into each other with dreamy precision. 'Clair de Lune'. Jack wondered who it was. The chauffeur didn't seem a likely candidate.

Barone offered no explanation for the invisible pianist. He was staring into the spitting fire, his face set. After several moments had passed, Jack broke the silence.

'Mr Barone. I am sure this must all be very distressing for you, but I'm afraid I still don't see how I can help.'

Barone looked up and smiled. The smile was uncomplicated and made him suddenly seem years younger.

'I am asking you for help, Jack, because your father tells me you are very skilled at parkour.'

Jack blinked. 'You think I can help because I am a free runner?'

'Aren't you?'

'Well,' Jack tried to gather his wits, 'I suppose. But I haven't run for a while.'

'I'm sure you haven't forgotten how. Muscles have memory too.' Barone's hands smoothed the blanket over his knees and Jack had to stop himself from dropping his eyes to the man's lap and to the wasted legs showing underneath the rug. 'My private investigator tells me Jenilee has become an obsessive free runner. I still find it difficult to grasp this new passion of hers, as she never showed the slightest interest in sport or any extreme physical activity before.'

Jack shook his head. 'Many free runners don't practise free running because of the physical activity. Free running is all about increasing your self-confidence. Priming the mind to overcome barriers – not just physical – but mental as well.'

'Like a self-help tool?'

'Exactly. If you can overcome your physical fear and pain when you run, you stand a better chance of controlling your mind as well.'

'Interesting.' Barone sounded as though he meant it.

Jack shrugged. 'At least, that's the theory.'

'All of what you just said makes me even more convinced that you will be perfectly suited to the task. You know the world of free running. Its ethos. You are part of that community. Jenilee will feel comfortable with you.'

'Comfortable? We can't even be sure she'll like me.'

Barone lifted an eyebrow. 'Something tells me that won't be a problem if you set your mind to it.'

The music drifting in from the back of the house was no longer Debussy. The piano player had switched to 'The Entertainer'. The jaunty notes were muted but the pianist was playing with a sure touch at exactly the right tempo. Again Jack wondered who it was.

He realised Barone was waiting for his response. 'Let me see if I have this straight. You want me to talk to Jenilee and convince her to return home so you can help her retrieve her memory.'

'That is the long-term goal. But if you talk to her straight away, she won't be receptive. It will take time for you to win her trust. Until that happens, I want you to keep an eye on her.'

Oh, hell no. Jack grimaced. Not that he wasn't sorry for the poor girl, but there was no way he was going to become her babysitter. He opened his mouth to protest, but Barone suddenly turned his wheelchair in the direction of the desk and slid the wheels smoothly underneath its polished top. Of course: that explained the absence of a chair.

The piano music had stopped. Jack heard a door open and a man's deliberate footsteps crossing the entrance hall. Then followed the sound of the front door opening and closing and someone stepping onto the gravel driveway. From where he sat on the couch, Jack was able to see out of the window to where a man in a coat was walking towards the Jaguar. At first Jack thought it was Scott after all, but as the man opened the door of the car and slid behind the wheel, the inside light illuminated his profile and Jack saw that it was a man in his fifties. He had the face of an aesthete: narrow nose, fastidious mouth, a short beard. Strong shoulders. The features struck an elusive chord of memory in Jack's mind. He had seen this man before – he was sure of it. But where?

The man suddenly looked up and for a moment it felt to Jack as though he was looking straight at him. But then he slammed the car door shut. Jack watched as the Jaguar made a wide sweep and sped powerfully down the driveway.

He turned his attention back to the room. Barone had opened a desk drawer, extracting from it a large manila envelope. With the envelope balanced on his lap, he manoeuvred the chair so that he faced Jack.

'I am giving you these photos so that you may get a sense of who Jenilee was before she became who she is now. They may help you.'

Jack accepted the envelope without enthusiasm and removed one of the photographs inside. A baby dressed in a bright pink babygro and even brighter pink cap smiled at him toothlessly. The kid looked as though she had been dipped in Pepto-Bismol.

'I have also set up an appointment for you tomorrow with the private investigator who found her,' Barone continued. 'He will walk you through the case and give you a lead on where to find Jenilee. She now goes by a different name. She calls herself Eloise Blake.'

Jack pushed the picture back in its envelope. 'Mr Barone, I'm sorry but you can't expect me—'

'I do expect. I expect you to befriend her and to find out everything you can about her new life. And I expect you to watch over her. And when I say watch over her, I truly mean *watch* over her.' Those heavy-lidded eyes were suddenly cold. For the first time Jack felt the full force of Barone's personality. This was a man used to getting his own way.

Barone spoke deliberately. 'I am very concerned. Jenilee has had a number of accidents over the past couple of months. Close calls.'

'Free runners tend to be accident-prone. It goes with the territory.'

'No.' Barone shook his head decisively. 'We're not talking about a few bumps and bruises. Or even broken bones.'

'What are we talking about?'

For a long moment there was silence in the room. From above the fireplace, white-shouldered Mnemosyne stared down at them with her knowing gaze.

When Barone spoke again, he sounded indescribably weary. 'I think … I think someone is trying to kill her.'

CHAPTER FIVE

The street light overhead blotted out Jungles' features, but she saw him raise his hand in a goodbye gesture. She waved back. She knew he was worried about her, but she had declined his offer to walk her to her door. He was a great friend and she owed him a lot, but she did not appreciate him hovering. For a moment he hesitated, but then he turned his bicycle around and sped down the quiet street, the tiny orange reflector on the mudguard moving into the distance before disappearing.

Dropping to one knee, she chained her own bicycle to the railing. The chain was heavy and thick-linked but would probably not stand up to a determined thief. Too bad; it was a chance she'd have to take. She used to keep the bicycle with her inside her flat, but the lift was simply no longer safe. It was a large, industrial-sized model but hadn't been serviced in a long time and a month ago she had got stuck in it after the doors scarily, and inexplicably, opened between floors and into a vertiginous drop. After that experience, she was avoiding it.

She opened the small gate leading into an alley where black sacks were stacked up to one side in anticipation of the morning collection. The narrow passage smelt strongly of bleach. Old Mr Henderson regularly doused the alley with disinfectant and she was grateful for it. The two of them were the only people living at number 322 but, despite the big 'PRIVATE' sign, many other residents of the street liked to use this little layby as a rubbish drop.

Mr Henderson's window was dark: the old man must already be asleep. He was the property guardian, but deaf as a door post and his eyesight was failing. She wondered how long he would still be able to live unassisted. If he moved out, she would miss him: he had a wicked sense of humour and a big heart. Of course, once he moved out, her own position would become uncertain. The next caretaker might not be as willing to turn a blind eye to her unauthorised use of the top floor.

Number 322 was a squat, ugly building that was once meant to be part of an ambitious renovation project. The developers had bought out many of the industrial premises around here in the hope of turning the area into a new Hoxton Square, complete with edgy bars, clubs, loft apartments and trendy galleries catering to up-and-coming artists. The stockmarket crash and housing collapse had put an end to such plans and the green shoots of recovery had yet to be seen in this neighbourhood. On the ground floor of 322 a cement mixer still waited, like a stranded dinosaur. Scaffolding covered one side of the building – erected years ago, and simply left there.

A sharp scream made her whip around, her hand to her throat. Even as her mind recognised it was only the cat, which was now walking nonchalantly towards her on soft paws, a wave of adrenaline hit her body and she tasted salt in her mouth.

Dammit. She took a deep breath, angry with herself for being so jittery.

The big, snowy tom opened its mouth and gave the same harrowing scream, staring at her with glowing eyes. He was the third resident of 322 and only a shade away from feral. He allowed her to give him milk, and a few days ago he left her a dead mouse at her front door, a gesture she chose to interpret as a gift and not a hostile act, but he rarely allowed her to touch him and once left two bloody scratch marks on her wrist. Even so, she believed they had a connection.

'Hi, handsome. Are you thirsty? Would you like some of the white stuff?'

He turned his head away disdainfully but nevertheless followed her up the stairs. At the top, she unlocked the door and stood to one side. Tail held high, he glided past her as though walking on air.

She closed the door behind them and stood still for a few moments, allowing her eyes to become used to the darkness inside. She left the light switch alone. The overhead lights were monstrous fluorescent panels which, when turned on, would sputter and hum, illuminating everything with an evil blue hue, and she avoided using them as far as possible.

Not that she really needed additional light. The darkness inside was far from impenetrable. The tall, un-curtained windows allowed light from the outside to gently wash the walls and leave a butterscotch sheen on the floors. She had also invested in two soft-shaded lamps and had draped fairy lights around the concrete pillars and around the posts of her bed. She walked over and switched them on and they glowed like tiny white stars.

The single room in which she found herself was substantial and covered most of the top floor. It had long walls and exposed beams and would probably have been transformed into a fancy loft apartment if the builders had ever managed to get that far. Instead, the previous tenant – an importer of spices – had used it as office premises and storage space. The company had long since moved on, but sometimes she fancied she could smell star anise.

Bit by bit, she had made the place her own. She had a bed in here, a table, a chest of drawers, a steel rack of the kind you find in department stores for hanging clothes, and an antique, hand-carved dressing table, which Jungles had given her: an object so wonderful, it made her smile every time she looked at it. One corner of the room served as the kitchen area. Next to a steel sink was a long, narrow worktop, which held a kettle, electric frying pan and crockery. The surface of the worktop sloped somewhat: it had taken her two days and two battered fingers to complete, but there it was – functional and, to her mind, a thing of beauty. The only thing lacking from her living space was a bathroom. For this, she had to go one floor down, where there was a working bath and a toilet.

Balancing on one leg, she untied the laces of her trainers and kicked them to one side before walking barefoot to the fridge. She poured milk into a saucer and placed it in front of the cat, which immediately lowered its head.

She was still standing there, now quite relaxed, watching the cat and admiring the way its pink tongue lapped daintily at the liquid, when it happened again.

Shatter.

Her breath caught and the edges of her vision turned white. The plastered walls fractured and fissured as though the reality of the world around her was revealed for the fake construct it was. She felt the familiar sense of everything she knew slipping from her grasp. But this time, she did not fight it. She sank down to the ground, hugging her knees to her chest, and kept her eyes wide open, not even blinking as that other world pushed through.

The snowy books. The black letters spooling off the pages. The string of numbers – alien, relentless – spinning on and on through the labyrinth of her brain like a mad, never-ending ball of string: (8/137/-9/2) (5/78/-2/10) (1/44/-4/8) ...

And now came the whispering, and the figures emerging from the shadows. On the other side of the room, a woman placed her arms around the neck of a man who smiled at her with affectionate amusement.

The glow from the fairy lights was too weak to fully illuminate that far corner and the faces of the figures slipped in and out of focus. But she was able to see that the woman had pale hair and was beautiful. Pushing back her hair in a gesture at once graceful and flirtatious, she stood on tiptoes and murmured something secret in the man's ear. He threw back his head and laughed.

Shatter.

As she watched, her knees pressing tightly against her chest, the cool surface of the fridge at her back, she recognised the feeling inside her own heart. Sorrow. There was something about the sight of the two figures embracing which made her feel so sad. Had she not herself written a love letter to the man who was now tenderly brushing away a lock of errant hair from the cheek of the woman he held in his arms? It was a letter that told of music in the darkness and daffodils in the spring. The memory of it was strong. Or perhaps, she thought as she continued to stare with aching heart, it was a memory of things she never knew.

CHAPTER SIX

N.O.M

Memory image 2501

'Love is as irrational as murder.'

Anything Bella says always sounds cleverer, more enig-matic and more profound than if anyone else had uttered the same words. It is that breathy voice of hers, I always think. It invests even the most mundane idea with a kind of hidden subtext. When was it, I wonder, that I had also started to find it irritating?

She smiles at me as though she can read my mind. 'Don't you agree, Julianne?'

'I suppose so. But you know me. I'm a scientist. The irra-tional is not what interests me.'

She lifts her eyebrows and through the viewfinder of the video recorder I can see tiny beads of sweat on her forehead and the shimmer at her temple where her hair is deepest gold. It is already five o'clock in the afternoon but the heat is still intense, even here at Whiteladies where there is always a breeze blowing in off the river.

'What, then?'

I lower the video recorder and look her directly in the face.

'The deliberate. The calculating.' I pause. 'Like betrayal. Betrayal is far more interesting than love. Or murder.'

CHAPTER SEVEN

In his first year at college, Jack had briefly dated a woman in his fine arts class. Her name was Clothilde and she had worn knitted gloves with the fingers cut off and drab scarves she crocheted herself. But what he remembered best was that she had been a budding graphologist who had insisted on studying his handwriting before agreeing to date him. As someone who had endured the scolding of a succession of grade school teachers, Jack was not surprised when Clothilde castigated him for his 'sloppy' down strokes, but was greatly cheered to learn that his large looped 'g's and flamboyantly slanted vowels showed him to be sexually adventurous. Way to go, Daddy O.

If memory served, Clothilde had also told him that people who underlined their names suffered from insecurity and a fear of not being taken seriously. If this was true, then Jenilee Gray had a problem in the confidence department, Jack thought, studying the small, even signature underscored by a faint line, which curled just slightly at the edges. Eloise Blake, on the other hand, signed her name with thick, bold strokes and heavy, flyaway cross-lines on the letter 't'. He didn't need his old girlfriend to tell him that Eloise strode the earth with a far firmer tread than Jenilee. Jack thought back on Daniel

Barone's words: 'The woman she is now is as different as black is to white from the girl who grew up in my house.'

Barone's assessment was confirmed by his private investigator. Earlier in the day, Jack had spent forty minutes in the company of the rather splendidly named Archibald Fitzhenry, who looked nothing like Jack had expected a PI to look. Fitzhenry was small, rotund and very expensively dressed.

'Everything about Jenilee Gray is different now,' Fitzhenry told Jack. 'It was pure luck that I recognised her face.'

'How did you find her?'

'By chance.' Fitzhenry sighed deeply and brushed an invisible speck off the cuff of his suit. Ermenegildo Zegna. Jack had identified it immediately: an identical suit was hanging in his closet in Manhattan. The snoop business must be more lucrative than he thought.

Fitzhenry opened a folder and extracted a newspaper clipping. Next to a heading that stated 'Near-fatal accident at Victoria Station' was a grainy photograph of a girl with short dark hair that curled thick and vigorously around her face. The picture had clearly been taken on the fly by someone with a mobile phone. The girl was frowning and gesticulating towards something off-camera.

'Different indeed.' Jack studied the picture with interest. On his return journey to Charlie's London apartment this morning, Jack had taken the opportunity to flip through the photographs Barone had given him the night before. After looking at numerous pictures of wide-eyed Jenilee as a baby, gawky Jenilee at boarding school, grown-up Jenilee at Oxford, Jack now had a clear image of her in his mind.

Before she had morphed into Eloise Blake, Jenilee Gray had been attractive in a soft-focus way. She wore her hair long and neatly swept behind her ears, fixed in place with a prim barrette. Even as a young girl her taste in clothes had been old-fashioned: there were no pictures of her dressed in jeans, no T-shirts with slogans, nothing sassy at all. Gentle smile. Lovely bone structure and a soft rounded chin. The only feature that was at all unusual was her eyes. 'Unmistakable,' Barone had called them, and he was right. One eye was green; the other, brown. But it wasn't only the difference in colour that caught the attention: one eye was also set slightly higher than its twin. The effect was startling. But despite the off-kilter eyes, the overall impression Jack had gathered had been of a well-brought-up, well-mannered young woman. Placid, calm.

There was nothing placid about the girl in the newspaper picture. Her gaze was diamond-sharp and she had a whiplash quality to her. She had lost a lot of weight and you could cut glass on those cheekbones. Whereas everything about Jenilee seemed soft and pliable, this woman gave out a signal that said, 'touch at your peril'. Jenilee was pretty. Eloise was beautiful, in a stark, wild, disturbing way.

Jack started reading the first paragraph and lifted his eyebrows in surprise. 'She was pushed in front of a train? No wonder Mr Barone is worried.'

'Yes, well.' Fitzhenry shrugged. 'It was a distressing incident, of course, but the police – and the girl, for that matter – think someone had simply shoved against her: nothing more sinister than that. It was rush hour at Victoria and the platform was packed. You know what it's like: commuters jostling each other to get on the train first.'

'Mr Barone referred to several incidents.'

Fitzhenry sighed. 'She was mugged recently, but she managed to get away. And she was involved in a hit-and-run: a car swiped her when she was on her bicycle. Fortunately, that too wasn't serious.'

He paused and Jack could see him choosing his words carefully. 'Mr Simonetti. The fact is, this girl lives an existence which exposes her to casual danger to a far greater extent than previously. Jenilee Gray led a very sheltered life. Eloise Blake is street. To be completely frank, she is poor and she lives poorly. Whereas Jenilee Gray had her own car, Eloise takes the Tube and likes to cycle. Cycling in London traffic is not risk-free. And she got mugged in a part of town where you run the risk of getting mugged if you wander by yourself in the early morning hours. Are you following me?'

'Did you tell Mr Barone this?'

'I did. And I believe this is why he took me off the case. He thinks she is in danger and I'm not taking it seriously. But it would be very difficult to see why anyone would want to harm her. She lives simply. Most days she works at a street market with a friend of hers, selling bric-a-brac. Her spare time seems to be taken up with free running. Now, it is true that a few times she disappeared and I wasn't able to follow her. Mr Barone seems to think those disappearances are important, but I don't believe there is anything there.'

'She gave you the slip? She knew you were following her?'

'No. I was unable to follow her because I simply couldn't keep up. She runs … very fast. And across terrain where I cannot follow by car and which is difficult for a man of my proportions to navigate at speed under my own steam.' Fitzhenry pointed ruefully at his ample stomach.

Jack thought for a moment. 'Mr Barone said there must have been an incident which acted as a stressor and which was responsible for the girl going into a fugue state. Do you have any idea what that stressor might be?'

'No. But we have a good idea of when it happened. On the day she disappeared she drove into London to visit a solicitor who had contacted her about an envelope that was left her by her mother and date-stamped for release that day.'

'Do you know what was inside the envelope?'

'According to the solicitor, a single sheet of paper – that's all. But he wasn't privy to its contents. From the solicitor's office, Miss Gray went to a restaurant where she was supposed to meet friends. While she was waiting for her guests, a waiter remembers her telling him the battery on her mobile phone was flat. The last he saw of her, she was talking on the restaurant's public telephone, looking agitated and holding a sheet of paper in her hand. She must have simply walked out of the restaurant immediately afterwards because she did not return to her table where she had left her bag. Mr Barone thinks this may be when she lost contact with her identity.'

Fitzhenry paused and puffed out his cheeks. 'I should also mention that Miss Gray may have suffered from emotional problems even before her memory loss. We discovered that she had been consulting a psychiatrist for several months before she disappeared. A very well-respected consultant by the name of Derek Payne.'

'Did you talk to him?'

'For all the good it did me. Doctor-patient confidentiality, you understand. Even Mr Barone wasn't able to persuade him to hand over his notes.'

'Well, I guess I'd better go check on the lady.' Jack stood up. 'Where does she live?'

Fitzhenry pushed the folder over to Jack. 'The address is in here. But right now,' he glanced at his watch, 'she should still be at the street market with her friend. Stall 27. The details are in here, in addition to all the other information I have on her.'

As Fitzhenry walked Jack to the door, he said: 'I should probably warn you: her friend is very protective of her. His name is Jungles.'

'Jungles?'

'Real name, John Barring. He too is a free runner. Anyway, watch out for him. Rough customer. He told me he would smash my face in the next time I "messed" – his word, not mine – with Ms Gray. I have no doubt he would.'

'Boyfriend?'

Fitzhenry shook his head. 'I think he'd like to be but she's not having it. Anyway, be careful. I wouldn't like to rub him up the wrong way. He could be dangerous.'

Dangerous. Maybe so, Jack thought, watching from behind dark glasses as the man on the other side of the road lifted a heavy chest effortlessly from the ground before manoeuvring it onto a wooden pallet. Despite the chilly air, the guy was wearing a tank top, which exposed his powerful shoulders and the thickly corded muscles of his arms. A beanie covered his shaven head. Jungles. The name was apt. He looked tough and able to handle himself. In fact, Jack thought, if this character was hanging around Jenilee Gray, she was probably safe as houses.

Of the girl there was no sign. He glanced at his watch. He had been sitting at this coffee table for almost two hours. But at least he had put the time to good use and had familiarised himself with the contents of Fitzhenry's folder.

As the man said, she lived simply. In fact, she lived pretty much off the grid. She did not have a National Insurance number, which considering that Eloise Blake hadn't existed until two years ago was hardly surprising. There was no record of her paying taxes. She had a bank account with a grand total of £412. She practically lived in a squat. Jack thought of Whiteladies: the manicured gardens, the high-ceilinged rooms, the atmosphere of faded elegance. To lose all of that and not even realise what you had lost ...

Fitzhenry's file also included copied screenshots of her Facebook page when Eloise Blake had still been Jenilee Gray. Jenilee's favourite colour was peach. She liked sweet peas and pansies. She had read *Gone with the Wind* three times. She was a churchgoer and – rather surprisingly – a good tap dancer. But the overall impression was of an orderly, conventional life.

The light was starting to fail and the street market was emptying. The tourists were leaving, as were the goths and the punks with their retro Mohawks. The vendors were dismantling their stands. Across the road, Jungles had started to pack up as well: trays of cheap jewellery, vinyl records, a rocking chair, a rather beautiful chest of drawers, a chandelier – all disappearing into the back of his van. It was clearly time to go; Jack could only hope Jenilee Gray would put in an appearance the next day. It felt like an anti-climax. After immersing himself in Fitzhenry's folder, he was seriously curious to see little Orphan Annie in person.

He twisted in his seat and signalled to the waitress for his bill. But as he turned back, his hand fishing distractedly for his wallet, there she was – as though she had dropped from the sky. It was a shock. She was so close, if he were to lean forward and stretch out his arm, he would be able to touch the sleeve of her jacket.

She looked to her right, her eyes looking past him – scanning the busy traffic in anticipation of crossing the road – and he had a clear view of her features: delicate, heart-shaped face and those unsettling eyes. It was definitely her. She wore not a speck of make-up and her hair was unruly. A combat jacket hung shapelessly off her slight frame. As she stepped into the road, she held out a hand at the oncoming traffic and her fingers were pale and unadorned.

She evaded the oncoming cars with ease. When she reached the other side, she walked up to Jungles and poked him slyly in the ribs. He swung around, surprised. When he saw who it was, his face broke into a grin and he encircled the girl in a bear hug, lifting her off her feet.

All very touching. Jack tried to read the body language of the girl. She was obviously comfortable with the guy but the playful punch she threw to his shoulder was friendly, not flirtatious. As for Jungles – he was smitten, that much was clear. The girl was speaking rapidly, obviously apologising for something, but the man made a dismissive gesture with his hand. *Forget about it, sweetness; Papa Bear is happy just to see you.*

As he watched Jungles slam shut the back doors to the van, it suddenly dawned on Jack that as he had no car of his own, it was going to be rather difficult to follow the pair once they took off. He could take a taxi, of course, but he wondered how enthusiastic a London cabbie would be if told to 'follow that car'.

But he was in luck. Jungles eased himself behind the wheel of the van but the girl made no attempt to get into the passenger seat. For a brief moment the two spoke as Jungles leant out of the window. Then she stepped back and after a touch of the horn, the van pulled into the stream of traffic. The girl immediately headed back across the road and turned purposefully to the left. The Tube station. Good. This would be easy. In anticipation of the demands his new role as snoop and guardian would make on him, Jack had bought an Oyster card only this morning. Rather enterprising of him, even if he said so himself.

He followed her down the shallow steps and through the turnstiles. She walked like a dancer, her movements graceful and springy. The station was packed with commuters and as they walked down the long, evil-smelling tunnel towards the platform, she looked over her shoulder a couple of times – not as though she was expecting anyone to follow her, but as though she was scanning her environment. Street sense. An awareness of who was behind and beside her. When a big, lumbering guy accidentally bumped the side of his cello case into her, she reacted with lightning speed, placing distance between them in a flash and staring at the poor guy with far more hostility than the moment warranted. Still, after the failed mugging attempt Fitzhenry had told him about, this was hardly surprising. After such an attack her antennae would be super-sensitive. He fell back even more.

Truth to tell, he couldn't help feeling like some sleazy stalker, and he would be hard pressed to explain what he had in mind by following her. He supposed he wanted to get a feel for what she did and who she hung out with. The rhythm of her day. At some point he was going to have to introduce himself and Barone was probably correct in thinking that parkour would be the way in, but he'd have to figure out how to get to that point first.

On the platform he continued to keep his distance and positioned himself behind a couple who looked like relatives of Marilyn Manson. Not a good move, as it turned out. The white-faced boy suddenly started staring at Jack with an unpleasant glint in his eye, his lip curling and his hand hovering over his coat pocket. His girlfriend, a bleached blonde with chunky calves and a tasteful nose ring, sniggered companionably.

Jack stared back. The last thing he needed was to become embroiled in an altercation. There was no doubt in his mind that he could take out the kid, even if he had something sinister hiding in that coat pocket, but this was certainly not how he wanted to register on Jenilee Gray's radar for the first time.

Decking a guy in a public place was hardly the ideal way to go about gaining her trust. So he continued to look at the boy, keeping his face carefully expressionless but allowing enough tension in his shoulders to signal that he was willing – and capable – to do the business, if pushed. It worked. After a few moments the kid looked away.

Jack glanced over at Jenilee Gray again. Considering that she had almost landed herself in front of a train not that long ago, he was surprised to see her in the front row of heaving bodies. Still, despite her relaxed stance, he once again got that impression of contained energy as though, if needed, her stillness could explode into ferocious action. And she looked so – he surprised himself with the word – free. All the women around her were clutching at handbags and packages but she had nothing in her hands and her arms hung loosely by her sides.

A subterranean rattle, a rush of air, and the train rounded the bend and drew up at the platform. She entered the compartment at the front, whereas he stepped through the second door at the rear. He immediately turned his back but made sure to keep an eye on her reflection in the window.

As the train speeded up, it occurred to him that he had no idea where they were going. He had thought the girl might be on her way home, but against the wall was a map of the London Underground and, if he read the colourful spaghetti of Tube lines correctly, she was not going home. She was heading somewhere else. He wondered where.

CHAPTER EIGHT

The air coming through the open window had a diamond-bright chill to it and Daniel Barone tucked the rug around his legs a little closer.

Dusk had fallen quickly and thick shadows were gathering in the corners of the room. Outside the window, the garden was darkening: the velvety expanse of lawn black at the river's edge. He could see pale mist rising on the water.

The whispered call of an owl made him turn his head. Close to the house, a giant oak stretched massive branches into the air. As he watched, a dark shadow swooped down on the tree with the graceful sweep of a wing. A female owl, returning from her hunt.

There had been owls using the oak for nesting as long as he could remember. The first year he bought Whiteladies, he was delighted to discover two tawny owls raising a family. He bought a pair of binoculars and kept watch: impressed with the busy industry of the parents and thoroughly enchanted by the baby owls with their soft feathered legs, which looked like bloomers.

The others had been just as captivated, especially the girls. Bella christened the owls Heloise and Abelard. Julianne kept a picture diary, meticulously recording every milestone in the chicks' development on her video camera. When one of the chicks fell out of the nest, she had immediately climbed up the tree to return it to its parents, only to take a tumble when the male owl rushed at her threateningly. For the next two weeks she had nursed a sprained wrist, cradling the injured limb in a jaunty sling fashioned from a Jolly Roger.

Those were good memories: warm summer evenings, the girls wearing long, floaty dresses; Francis at the piano; Leon mixing extravagant cocktails. Every moment bright and shimmery and full of promise and magic. Weren't they going to conquer the world? Weren't they invincible? For a moment the recollection of it was so strong, Barone closed his eyes and felt his chest tighten.

A sound behind him made him turn the wheelchair around. Francis was standing in the doorway, his tall figure a black shape.

'Daniel? Why are you sitting in the darkness?' Francis's hand went unerringly to the light switch on the wall.

Barone blinked in the sudden shower of light. 'I was thinking of the summer Julianne sprained her wrist. With the owls. Remember?'

'Vaguely.' He walked into the room and sat down in a large, wing-backed armchair. Dressed in a velvet smoking jacket and with his hooded eyes, aquiline nose and trim beard, he made Barone think of a figure in a Renaissance canvas. A cavalier. Or a man of the cloth.

He looked at his friend with affection. He had known Francis Godine for more than thirty years and theirs was an exceptional friendship. Together they had taken journeys of the mind and the spirit: moments bright with possibilities; hours of darkest despair. If not for Francis, Barone knew he would have found it impossible to cope with Julianne's death. And when it became clear that he would never walk again after his car crash, Francis had stepped in and offered to make Whiteladies his home.

Francis was frowning. 'Why were you thinking of Julianne?'

'I was thinking of both Bella and Julianne.'

'It is no good communing with ghosts, Daniel.'

'They were so beautiful.'

'Yes. Leon used to say they were like those splendidly iridescent fish of the Great Barrier Reef – wonderful to look at but lethally poisonous.'

Barone grimaced. 'Leon is a cynic.'

'Among other things. But on this point I happen to agree with him.'

'You … you have no forgiveness, Francis.'

For a moment the two women stood as clear in Barone's mind as though they were in the room with him. Bella, with her sensuous mouth and her cool eyes. And Julianne. Small-boned and delicate, she had a luminous quality that stayed with you long after she had left the room.

Francis's voice brought him back to the present. 'Speaking of Leon. What is his son like?'

Barone tried to smile. 'He looks so much like his father it is uncanny. Interesting young man. But angry. Not comfortable in his own skin.'

'If I were Leon's son, I'd probably have issues as well. Was he willing to do what you asked of him?'

'He wasn't over-enthusiastic at first, but by the end of our conversation I think he became intrigued.'

A deep crease appeared once again between Francis's eyes. 'Daniel. Please reconsider. This is not going to lead to anything good. The girl does not want to be saved. Accept that.'

'The girl? You're speaking as though she's a stranger. We're talking about Jenilee, for God's sake. She grew up before your eyes. Don't you care?'

'Of course I care. But that girl is no longer Jenilee. She is … I don't know who she is. But she is no longer Julianne's daughter. Jenilee is gone.'

'Maybe I can bring her back.'

'Doubtful. Besides, she doesn't want to come back.'

'Francis, she is in danger, I am convinced of it.'

Godine made an impatient gesture. 'What danger? Even your own private investigator doesn't believe that.'

'I'm not going to argue the point with you. And whether she's in physical danger or not, she has obviously lost her way. I can't give up on her. I owe it to Julianne.'

'You owe Julianne nothing. Nothing! Julianne was the master of her own fate. If you make certain choices, you have to live with the consequences. She knew that.'

Barone swallowed painfully. 'I'm not thinking of her life. I'm thinking of her death.'

'My friend.' Francis's voice softened. 'Stop holding hands with the past.'

For a moment Barone didn't answer. If there was anyone in the world he could trust, it was Francis. But somewhere along the way, Francis had lost his faith. All those years ago when the five of them had attempted to touch the face of God, Francis had been their conscience, their sane voice. He had chosen as his motto the words *laborare est orare*: work is prayer. But that had been a long time ago.

He looked past Francis's shoulder to where emerald-eyed Mnemosyne looked down at them from above the fireplace. Titaness. Goddess. Mother of all inspiration.

Whore.

Suddenly, Barone felt so exhausted, he did not think he could lift his hand.

'Daniel? Are you alright?' Godine leant forward, his eyes concerned.

'I am. But I think it is time for me to see Dr Lucas again. It's been a while.'

Godine spoke slowly. 'You saw him last week.'

Barone felt the gears in his mind slip and a rushing noise filled his ears. But then he nodded. 'Of course. Of course I did.'

'I'll make an appointment anyway.' Godine got to his feet. 'Are you ready for dinner? Mrs Steward left us a casserole.'

'I'll be there in a minute.'

Barone waited for his friend to leave the room before turning his wheelchair back to the window. The garden was now almost completely dark, but for a moment he thought he saw movement right there underneath the oak tree where the grass was always patchy and the shadow deepest: five friends clasping each other's hands, their faces close together, their voices thrilling with secrets.

He blinked and now all he saw was the tree – black against the lesser blackness of the sky – and his own reflection, bright against the window pane. A man looking out with haunted eyes. He should stop holding hands with the past, Francis said. But Barone sensed that ghosts were rising.

CHAPTER NINE

Jack was cold. It was near dark and a wind was blowing. He beat his arms with his fists and pulled up his shoulders to try and shield his exposed neck from the chill.

What the hell was he still doing here? He could be in Charlie's living room right now with his feet up and a glass of something in his hand. Instead, here he was hiding behind a tree, freezing his ass off watching Jenilee Gray crawl around on all fours. Not that this didn't offer its own rewards, but after ten minutes of watching her walk backwards, forwards and sideways on her hands and feet only, the entertainment value was beginning to pall. But he had to hand it to the woman: she was a machine. He had done this kind of quadrupedal workout himself many times – it was a favourite way for free runners to warm up before a run – and knew from experience how strenuous it was.

He peered at her through the dusk: she was now doing rolls – touching the palms of her hands to the ground before rolling over her forward shoulder. All of this activity made him convinced she was warming up for a run, but it did seem like a damn odd location for her to choose.

He had been surprised when she left the train at Holland Park station – this neighbourhood was a far cry indeed from where she lived – and had followed her with some curiosity as she walked down Holland Park Avenue with its roar and bustle and ceaseless traffic. After about five minutes she had turned into a quiet, green side street that led to this exclusive residential square ringed with houses. He was even more surprised to find that her ultimate destination was a communal garden set behind delicate wrought-iron fencing. Discreet 'Private' signs warned that the garden was very much off-limits to ordinary yobs. Only the residents had keys granting them access to its manicured beauty.

Not that this had concerned the girl in the slightest. The locked gate to the garden was almost chest-height on her, but she had vaulted across it with the utmost ease. Once on the other side, she started jogging around the garden, looking for all the world as though she had every right in the world to use that exclusive patch of lawn for exercise. Anyone watching would never dream she was a trespasser.

He glanced around him. He was using a sturdy plane tree on the other side of the street to shield him from her view but he was getting worried that someone in the row of houses might notice him and be concerned enough to call the police. The denizens of this wealthy enclave of London probably didn't like shady characters loitering around.

But it looked as though she was about to wrap up. She slipped into her jacket and he saw her look at her watch. *Where are you off to now, Ms Gray?*

She exited the garden the same way she had entered and walked swiftly down the deserted street. He followed, keeping a good distance between them. The plane trees threw deep shadows but lights glittered in the windows of the terraced houses and every couple of yards the pavement was washed with yellow. A few times he lost sight of her in the shadowed patches but then, there she was again, flitting in and out of the light and dark, as ephemeral as a ghost.

She turned the corner into yet another hushed, elegant street and suddenly disappeared. After a confused moment, in which he was convinced he had lost her, he spotted her again.

She was standing inside a public telephone box only yards away. Usually these boxes were brightly lit but this one was dark and it was difficult to see her figure. His first thought was that she had become aware of his following her and had stopped to check him out from the safety of the box, but after a couple of speeded-up heartbeats, he realised this was not the case. She was looking away from him and directing all of her attention to the houses on the opposite side of the street.

He became friends with the nearest tree again. It was difficult to figure out what it was she found so fascinating. As far as he could tell, there was nothing around here that was out of the ordinary. The houses were all typical terraced houses sharing their party walls with their neighbours, and all had tall pediment-topped windows and identical lofty façades fashioned from white stucco. Doric pillars led off every front door, creating well-defined entrances, repetitive in their similarity. From where he stood he could also see the beginning of an alley running at the back of the thirty-foot gardens set behind this exclusive block of properties.

Cautiously, he peered around the tree again and tried to follow her gaze. She seemed to be staring at one house in particular: the second house from the corner. Number 44. It was fully five storeys high and had a mansard with dormer rooms on the top level – built at a time when families were large and servants ubiquitous. The one doorbell showed that, unlike its neighbours, it had not been subdivided into flats and was used as a single residence.

The minutes ticked past. Was this a stake-out? Was she waiting for something to happen? Whatever it was, he hoped to hell it was soon. She was nicely sheltered, but he was getting damn tired of hugging a tree and slowly losing sensory contact with his extremities.

The front porch light sprang to life and the girl stiffened like a gun dog scenting prey. After a few moments the front door opened and a sturdy man dressed in tracksuit bottoms and a hooded anorak stepped out. In one hand he carried a gym bag with a squash racket protruding from the zip. Lifting his other hand, he pointed his car keys at a dark green Maserati, which beeped as the alarm deactivated.

The man opened the car door and slid behind the steering wheel. The Maserati pulled smoothly away from the kerb, accelerating as it moved down the street, its engine revving into a subdued growl. The next moment it turned a corner and disappeared from view.

And still the girl waited. Even after the sound of the engine had died away, she stayed in the telephone box, motionless.

At last. The door of the phone box opened wider and he heard it click as she let it close behind her. He tried to melt into the tree but he needn't have worried. She was oblivious.

He watched as she crossed the street with that strong, graceful gait of hers and disappeared into the alley. There was no doubt in his mind that she was about to approach the house, but she had obviously decided to do it from the back. The question was, why?

He crossed the road swiftly before walking more carefully into the alley. After all this cloak-and-dagger stuff, it would be pretty lame if he bumped into her from behind.

The alley was narrow and lined on one side with low buildings, which had probably once been used as stables and workshops but which had since been converted to garages. On the other side ran a long brick wall, providing privacy to the gardens. The girl was only a few yards ahead but she had her back to him. He saw immediately that he had no need to worry that she would notice, or indeed sense, him.

She was gearing up for a wall run and her concentration was absolute. The brick wall she was aiming for was more than twice her height and Jack pursed his lips in a soundless whistle. This was a tough proposition. If she was truly going to try and haul herself up that wall, she would have to reach up a long way indeed to grasp the top and would then have to muster enough power to pull herself up and over. No wonder she had warmed up so thoroughly. This was not to be attempted with cold muscles.

She took off, approaching the wall with long, powerful strides. When she was that one critical step away from the wall, she jumped slightly, placing her foot at waist height and reaching upwards immediately.

Damn, she was good. Momentum, distance, direction – she had timed it perfectly. She reached up with one arm only, which gave her additional flexibility in her upper body. It also showed impressive strength. The girl might look fragile but she was about as delicate as pressed steel. For the briefest of moments she hung in a straight position before pulling herself up. This part of a wall run was known as the 'climb-up' among free runners, and this was where many movements broke down due to insufficient power in the shoulders and back. No problem here. She finished the climb-up smoothly and lifted her feet to the top of the wall in a beautifully coordinated movement.

He realised he had been holding his breath and slowly let it out. He waited for her to do the drop on the other side into the garden but instead she got to her feet and started walking along the top of the wall, balancing with ease. He pressed himself into the shadowed doorway of the nearest garage. If she looked up now, she would see him.

She did not look up. She was focused on her feet, as well she might be. If she lost her balance right now, she would tumble heavily.

Without warning, she stopped. She had reached the point where the boundary wall which set number 44 apart from the adjacent property intersected with the outer wall she was traversing at present. It was much narrower than the outer wall and also had a rounded top, which would make footing a challenge. Surely she wasn't thinking of going that way?

She was indeed. Fascinated, he watched as she dropped to all fours and stretched herself out in a cat balance crouch, moving along the wall swiftly and continuously in the direction of the house.

A sharp beam suddenly stabbed from a light fitting attached to the wall of the house. A movement sensor. The girl froze for a moment but then continued even more swiftly, her arms and her legs propelling her forward with smooth precision.

There was a substantial gap between the top of the wall and an open sash window set against the side of the house. The girl got to her feet, swaying slightly. Then, without hesitation, she launched herself into a cat leap and jumped across the gap, her fingers gripping the edge of the window, her feet flat against the vertical surface of the wall underneath. The next moment, she had pushed herself through the opening and disappeared from view.

Huh? Jack stared, stupefied.

He waited, half-expecting to hear outraged cries of 'Stop! Thief!' but apart from the sound of a TV drifting from the adjacent property, everything was quiet. The security light had timed out and the back of the house was once again dark.

He looked at the sash window through which she had disappeared. It was unlit. A net curtain blew fitfully in the wind.

Should he try it? More to the point, would he be able to?

He moved his shoulders experimentally. He had not warmed up. The last time he had done free running was months ago. He had stitches in his arm.

He unzipped his jacket and pushed the folder Fitzhenry had given him between his sweater and the top of his pants. Not the best solution but he couldn't think what else to do with it. Pushing aside thoughts of his father's probable apoplexy should his son be caught *in flagrante delicto*, he took a deep breath.

Here goes.

His approach was not nearly as elastically dynamic as the girl's and his climb-up was un-pretty, but he did at least manage to pull himself up and on top of the wall without much trouble. But when he hit the narrow boundary wall with its treacherous rounded top, things started getting tricky.

First, Fitzhenry's folder kept jabbing uncomfortably into his ribs. Second, he had decided to emulate the girl's cat crouch and was moving forward on all fours – it was really the only way to do it – but he was wearing Italian slip-ons with smooth leather soles that had minimal grip. Though he expected it, the intensity of the security light suddenly stabbing from the side of the house startled him and his foot slipped. He landed squarely on his crotch.

For a few moments he was quite incapable of moving. Even the knowledge that any neighbour glancing idly out of a back window would have a prime view of him sitting there hunched over, holding himself, was not enough to propel him into action. Silently he repeated to himself the three most obscene words in his vocabulary. Then, painfully, he started to inch forward again.

The gap between the wall and the open window seemed as wide as the Grand Canyon. He got to his feet, staying in a half-crouch, keeping his feet close together. He swung his arms behind him, but felt himself starting to lose his balance. It robbed him of some of his power but he did in the end manage a fairly quick, explosive push with his legs, raising his knees as he launched himself fully into the jump.

He slammed into the side of the house with all the elegance of a wrecking ball. The muscles in his back screeched and he was convinced he had popped a stitch but the balls of his feet landed firmly against the wall and with relief he felt his fingers hook securely around the bottom of the window.

For a few seconds he hung there like a clumsy monkey and contemplated his next move. The idea of catapulting himself into a room without knowing what was waiting for him on the other side did not appeal – he could be diving head first into a rack of kitchen knives, for all he knew – but he didn't quite see what choice he had.

A breath of wind lifted the net curtain in front of him and allowed him the briefest of glimpses of the room inside. It was enough. There was no mistaking the boxes of detergent, the pile of folded clothes, the washing machine. This was where the owner of the house took care of his ring-around-the-collar.

He managed to ease himself through the narrow opening without knocking over the ironing board positioned just below the sill and gently lowered his feet. Even though the light inside the room was switched off, light from the passage outside was strong enough that he had no problem seeing. On tiptoes he walked to the open door and peeked gingerly around the corner.

A long passage carpeted in crimson wool stretched ahead of him. The passage was empty except for an elegant console table carrying a Chinese vase from which drooped a spray of white orchids. The house was dead quiet. Of the girl, there was no trace.

The fact that the owner of the house – at least, he assumed the guy with the Maserati was the owner – had locked the front door behind him when he left was a good indication that except for the girl, the house was empty, but he still felt dreadfully exposed as he walked down the hushed corridor. Several open doors led off the passage. He glimpsed a determinedly masculine bedroom decorated in navy blue; a small room messy with computer paraphernalia and filing cabinets; an impressive claw-footed bath inside a spacious bathroom. But of the elusive Ms Gray there was no sign.

The passage ended in a rather beautiful staircase winding its way up another two flights of stairs and also leading downwards to the ground floor. He gripped the polished balustrade and looked down the stairwell to where he could see the chequerboard floor of the entrance hall one storey below. A pair of glossy hunting boots stood next to an old-fashioned coat stand laden with scarves and waxed Barbour jackets. To the far side he could make out two slim panelled doors with drop handles. They were open and behind them he glimpsed a sofa and a splendid Oriental screen decorated with cranes and cherry blossoms. The living room. On the other side of the entrance hall was a swing door, which he guessed might give access to the kitchen area.

Softly he walked down the carpeted stairs, his hand trailing along the wall. When he was one step away from the bottom of the staircase, he leant down and gently eased his feet out of his shoes – fearful of the sound they would make on the marble tiles – and inched forward with as much stealth as he could muster. Just before the living room came into full view he stopped and listened.

Nothing.

He turned the corner.

She was standing with her back half-turned to him, an open book in her hand, facing a row of glass-fronted bookcases that spanned the full length of the wall. Between the shelves and in the recesses of the bookcases were mirrors that reflected the dark brocaded curtains and rich leather furnishings and made the room seem endless. They also reflected a slightly stooped figure in an almost ludicrously furtive pose. Himself.

She whipped around with an audible intake of breath and stared at him, her face white with shock. God knows what his own face looked like. After all that prowling and skulking – to have it end like this.

'Who are you? What are you doing here?' She spoke in a fierce, carrying whisper.

Attack was the best form of defence. 'You're asking me? You're the one trespassing!'

The shock was leaving her face. She lifted a contemptuous eyebrow and glanced pointedly at the shoes in his hands. So much for his attack strategy.

He realised he was still poised stealthily on his toes. It seemed like a good time to straighten up. And to put on his shoes. Facing her in his socks placed him at a distinct psychological disadvantage.

For a few moments they simply stared at each other. Close-up, those off-kilter eyes of hers were even more arresting. They were framed by the thickest black lashes he had ever seen, and her eyebrows looked like the wings of a bird in flight.

She suddenly sighed, a quick, impatient sigh as though bored and irritated. She slammed shut the book in her hand. He watched as she unzipped her jacket and calmly slipped the small, leather-bound volume into an inside pocket before zipping the jacket closed again.

'I have to go now.' She was no longer whispering: her voice pleasingly low and just slightly husky. As though it was the most natural thing in the world to break into a house and waltz off with a pilfered book, she started walking straight at him, clearly expecting him to step aside.

There didn't seem to be anything else to do but to move out of her way. He couldn't help but admire the way she nodded at him as dismissively as though she were the lady of the house and he some bumbling servant. But as she walked past him into the entrance hall, there was the unmistakable sound of a key turning in the front door.

She froze and in her eyes he saw the panic that he knew must be written on his own face as well. Their escape route through the laundry room had just been cut off: there was no way they would be able to run up the flight of stairs without being seen. The front door was already opening inwards and he could hear a man speaking in the unconsciously raised voice of someone talking on a mobile phone.

Acting instinctively, Jack reached for the girl and pulled her towards him, at the same time moving back into the living room. He felt her resist for just one second but then she must have realised he was heading for the big Oriental screen. Blessing the sound-deadening qualities of the plush carpet, he slipped behind the silk panels, the girl following.

The screen was high, but placed at such an angle that it was barely wide enough to conceal them both from being spotted from the entrance hall. There was no choice but to pull her close. She didn't like it, he could tell, but she didn't fight it either. As she pressed against him, he saw her frown at the crackling sound that emanated from his manly chest. Fitzhenry's folder. There was some kind of irony there, he was sure, but he was too freaked out by the possibility of imminent discovery to be able to think what it was.

Stuck behind the screen, they were effectively blind but they heard the sound of the door slamming shut and then the voice became louder as its owner walked into the entrance hall. Now, if only the man would continue up the stairs and deeper into the house, they might have the opportunity to slip out the front door. But, infuriatingly, it sounded as though he had stopped right outside the living room.

Jack breathed shallowly. He realised he was painfully hollowing his back in an attempt to make himself smaller. He tried to relax. He could see only the top of the girl's head but her breath, soft and even, blew against his neck.

At last. The guy was moving away. He was still speaking on the phone but Jack could clearly hear his footsteps. Suddenly, the voice was cut off in mid-sentence.

He peered around the screen. The swing door on the other side of the entrance hall was moving slightly. Right. Time to split.

He nodded at the girl and stepped out from behind the screen. Keeping a wary eye on that swing door, he tiptoed his way across the black and white marbled floor, sensing the girl following close behind. His fingers gripped the gleamingly polished slip lock of the front door and then, suddenly, they were outside. The night air was cold against his face: a shock after the rarefied atmosphere of the house. Without speaking, they both automatically turned right in the direction of Holland Park Avenue, its flow of traffic a distant ocean.

They were walking fast, but not fast enough to attract attention. He glanced at her, surprised that she was still by his side. He would have bet good money that she would have tried to place as much distance between them in the shortest amount of time as soon as she could, but she showed no sign of bolting. In fact, when he followed her down the steps and into Holland Park Tube station, she did not demur and when they sprinted to catch the train that was waiting at the platform, she even stuck out her arm to keep the door from closing in his face.

He took a seat opposite her and she merely shot him an enigmatic glance from those amazing eyes. For the rest of the journey she kept her gaze lazily fixed on a spot somewhere behind his shoulder. She had her legs pushed out in front of her and there was no tension in her body. Something about her attitude was all wrong but, try as he might, he couldn't figure out what she was up to.

He discovered the answer shortly after they disembarked. As they pushed through the turnstiles and walked into the petrol-scented air, he realised that the neighbourhood in which they now found themselves was rather different. Instead of wedding-cake houses and graceful wrought-ironwork, the buildings around here were unlovely and the iron railings shabby with rust. A depressing tower block thrust into the sky, the playground at its base ugly with litter.

A block away from the Tube station, she motioned to him to follow her into a narrow, poorly lit street. The next moment, his right knee simply gave way. The unexpectedness of it took him completely by surprise and the pain that shot up his leg knocked the breath out of him. Vaguely he realised she had kicked him, targeting the exact spot that would take him down. She pushed against him – hard – making good and sure that he lost his balance completely. And then she was behind him and his head was in a lock and something sharp was at his throat.

'Now.' Her voice was calm and cold. 'Who are you and what do you want with me?'

CHAPTER TEN

Memory image 3094

Bella is telling us a story. A terrible story, because it is true. In medieval times, she tells us, when few could write, a solution had to be found to preserve records of important events: treaties between aristocratic families, important weddings, the division of land after war.

One solution was to pick a young child to bear witness to the proceedings. Afterwards the child would be thrown into a river. It was believed the memory of this event would be forever imprinted in the child's mind and he would carry it with him throughout life, its vividness undimmed even in old age.

'Ingenious.' Leon's tone of voice is admiring. 'Fear activates the stress hormones and the availability of glucose, thereby stimulating the brain system responsible for consolidating newly acquired information.'

I look at him where he stands in front of the fire with a brandy snifter in his hand. So urbane, so civilised.

'Leon, you're shocking Julianne.' Bella smiles at me from the other side of the room.

I drink deeply from my glass and hold it out for a refill. When had I started drinking so much?

'Don't be squeamish, sweetheart.' Leon's mouth is impatient. 'A little stress is good for the body and the brain. And the child was never allowed to drown.'

'It is still a child we're talking about.'

Leon pours brandy into my glass. He moves closer and his fingers trail across my cheek. I hate myself for it but I lean into his hand.

His fingers are caressing. 'Even a child can be an instrument for the greater good.'

I look up into his eyes. 'Maybe ...'

Francis walks into the room and we move apart. I sometimes wonder if I should take Francis into my confidence. But what would I say? My compass is spinning, Francis. I am sorry but I am in a twilight place where I am losing myself and what I know to be right. It is a body of black water that threatens to swallow me – and the only reed I can grasp at is the certainty that I am in love.

CHAPTER ELEVEN

'I'm not asking you again.' The arm around his neck tightened and something sharp bit into his skin. Jack froze.

'This is a box cutter against your throat. Who are you?'

A box cutter. Christ. She hadn't only lost her memory. The woman was violently unstable as well.

Jack swallowed. He was stronger than the girl and he would be able to break her arm lock, but he had seen how quick her reflexes were. No guarantee she wouldn't slice through his carotid artery before he managed to break free.

He blinked away the mental image of geysers of blood spurting from his neck and tried to keep his voice soothing. 'Listen. I'm a free runner too. I saw you on the wall back there. I was bored and what you were doing looked like fun. So I followed you.'

Silence.

He tried again. 'And you're hot.'

Wrong answer. 'Hot?' Her arm tightened around his windpipe.

'I mean cool,' he wheezed desperately. 'A cool girl doing hot stuff.'

More silence while she pondered this. He breathed shallowly through his nose, wondering how it was possible for him to be terrified and exasperated with himself at the same time. If she killed him now for being terminally lame he couldn't blame her.

When she spoke again, she sounded thoughtful. 'You're American.' For some reason this seemed to reassure her. At least the pressure around his throat eased a little. But he could still feel the box cutter's cold kiss.

'Yes. I arrived in London yesterday.'

These seemed to be the magic words. He felt her lift the blade from his throat. She straightened and pushed him away from her.

'OK. Sorry. You can go.'

'What?' He scrambled to his feet and looked at her unbelievingly. 'You're *sorry*?'

She lifted her eyebrows. 'You're upset.'

'Upset?' He felt like throwing something. There was something incredibly galling about the way in which she was patiently watching him as though he was a toddler about to throw a tantrum. 'You bet I'm upset.'

'Well, next time you're bored, remember what happened here.'

She turned around and started walking away, her hands deep in the pockets of her jacket.

'Wait. Please. I'd like to buy you a coffee.'

'I don't have coffee with strangers. Or stalkers.' She was still walking and spoke without even turning her head.

'Maybe we can go running together.'

She paid no attention, continued walking as though he hadn't spoken.

'Are you a reader? I'm a reader.'

At this she stopped and turned around. 'What the hell do you mean?'

'You seem to like books.'

She continued to stare at him and the expression on her face was not pleasant.

'I'm sorry. You're right.' He held up his hands, indicating surrender. 'What you were doing inside that house is none of my business. I won't mention it again. But I wasn't lying when I said I think you're cool. I want to be friends, that's all.'

She watched him, unblinking, for another long moment. He had the uncomfortable impression she was doing some kind of mental arithmetic – adding and subtracting plus and minus points – as she tried to come to a decision on whether he was worth the trouble. Based on the less than dashing figure he had cut so far, he wouldn't have bet on it, but to his surprise, she suddenly nodded. 'OK. I know a place.'

The place turned out to be a greasy spoon squeezed in between a betting shop and a newsagent. As he opened the door for her, he recoiled at the mixture of smells that met them. The heating was turned up so high that the plate-glass window had steamed up and there was no mistaking the body odour that mingled cosily with the tang of mustard and ketchup.

The girl seemed not to notice. She pushed past two burly men and nodded at the woman behind the counter. 'White coffee.'

The woman, whose name tag read 'Gwendolyn', turned her gaze on him without enthusiasm. 'You?'

'Do you have macchiato?'

Gwendolyn stared at him as though he had lost his mind.

He continued hastily. 'Just coffee will be fine.'

'Anything to eat?'

He glanced enquiringly at the girl, who had pulled out a chair and was shrugging out of her jacket.

She hung the jacket over the back of the chair and glanced at him. 'You're buying?'

'Of course.'

'Good. Full English.'

A full English, from what he could make out from the scribbles on the blackboard, consisted of three eggs, toast, bacon, baked beans and something called black pudding. Tasty.

He pulled out a chair opposite her. 'Do you always have breakfast at night?'

'Does that bother you?'

'No. It's … unusual.'

She shrugged as though this comment was not worth a response.

'By the way, I'm Jack.'

She didn't hesitate. 'Eloise.'

He had to stop himself from staring at her eyes. This close he could see tiny yellow flecks in her hazel eye. The left eye was a clear green specked with black.

'So what are you doing in London, Jack? Apart from following girls around.'

'I'm visiting a friend.'

'That's nice.'

She brushed the hair away from her forehead and he noticed the thick calluses on her palm.

'You don't wear gloves when you run?'

'I train with a guy who believes you need to feel your environment. If he had his way I'd train barefoot.'

'Hard-core.'

'He was the one who introduced me to parkour. He taught me it is possible to run away from your problems.' She smiled, enjoying the play on words.

'So what problems do you have that require you to run fast?'

'You ask a lot of questions, Jack.'

'Sorry.' He paused. 'I wonder what you must think of me. You must think I'm some kind of weirdo.'

'Don't worry. I have you pegged. You're a bored rich boy looking for adventure and a little bit of rough. How am I doing?'

'Rich? How would you know that?'

She smiled with a hint of contempt. 'Do you have macchiato?' Leaning forward, she touched her hand to his sweater. 'And this. Very nice. Cashmere?'

'Alpaca.'

'Ah.'

Gwendolyn approached their table with a tray and plonked his coffee in front of him. Some of it sloshed messily into the saucer. Next she placed Eloise's full English on the table. The girl picked up her knife and fork and looked at Jack.

'Would you like some?'

He looked at the plate with respect. 'I don't think so. But thanks.'

She ate with a quiet concentration that brooked no interruption. Pushing the plate away from her, she leant back in her chair. She had polished off everything – even the strange black sausage that looked like a piece of tyre.

'I only ate what I liked.' He couldn't tell whether she was being serious or trying to make a joke.

'I'm impressed.'

She got to her feet. 'Order me another coffee.'

He gestured to Gwendolyn that they needed a refill and watched as Eloise walked down the narrow passage towards the ladies room. As she disappeared behind the swing door, he reached casually for her jacket.

The book. What kind of book would be so important that she had felt compelled to break and enter?

His fingers closed around the slight volume. It had a matt black cover stained with the oils from many fingers. The inside pages were beautifully marbled and a thin silk ribbon drooped down the inside crease of the title page. *Septem Sermones ad Mortuos.* Carl Gustav Jung. The date, in Roman letters, indicated the book had been published in 1916. The paper on which the text was printed had a coarse – almost home-spun – feel to it.

He cast a quick glance at the swing door. Placing his thumb in the middle of the book, he opened a page at random.

Die Toten füllten murrend den Raum und sprachen.

German, and therefore impenetrable to him. And it didn't help that the type was set in a spiky Gothic font.

But at least he was able to translate the title, which was not in German, but in Latin. *Septem Sermones ad Mortuos*: *The Seven Sermons to the Dead*. Not exactly beach reading, then. He had never heard of it before but maybe Charlie would be able to give him the low-down: he seemed to remember

Esquith waxing eloquently, and rather entertainingly, about *Man and His Symbols* during one of their drinking sessions together. Although it had to be said that after three bottles of excellent Barolo, anything would have sounded entertaining.

The door at the back of the passage was starting on its inward swing. He managed to return the book to the pocket of her jacket just as she emerged.

She sat down at the table and brought the fresh cup of coffee to her lips. But after one sip, she pushed back her chair.

'Well, thanks for the food, Jack. And now it's goodbye.'

'I'd like to see you again.'

'I don't think so.'

He spoke urgently. 'I was hoping to do parkour while I'm in London. Maybe hook up with a tribe? But now that I've met you – would you be willing to at least tell me where the good sites are? I can't leave this city without doing a few runs.'

As he had hoped, this made sense to her and he knew that by asking her for help this way, he was placing her under an obligation. If she bought into the whole free-runner ethos and community thing, she was honour-bound to help. Free runners understood the desire to explore. Every city had its own vibe, its own challenges. Any serious free runner would literally jump at the opportunity to interact with a fresh environment. But you needed to know where you were going. Some people took a dim view of runners using the exterior of their buildings or houses as a playground. Other neighbourhoods were more tolerant. It helped to have insider knowledge.

She hesitated, but then gave a brief nod. 'There's a group of us tracing the day after tomorrow. But early, you understand? We all work, so we need to do this at break of day. Get me a pen and I'll write you the address.'

By the time he had managed to coax a pen from Gwendolyn, she had already put on her jacket and was waiting at the door.

'Here.' She scribbled something on a paper napkin and held it out at him. 'Warm-up starts at 6 A.M.' As she handed him the napkin, she hesitated. 'One thing. When you meet the others ... keep it to yourself, will you? How we met.'

'Sure.' As she still looked uncertain, he leant forward and added in a stage whisper, 'Don't worry, fair lady. Your secret's safe with me.'

His reward was the hint of a smile. He watched her cross the road and turn right, going back in the direction from which they had come. As she walked, she kicked away some dried leaves with a small, skipping movement, like a little girl. For some reason it touched him. She looked so small in that overly large jacket: vulnerable, even; far removed from the hard-assed woman who had menaced him with a sharp instrument.

At the end of the block, she turned around and looked in his direction. He lifted his hand and waved. There was a street-light right above her, which threw her face in shadow, and for a moment he thought she was going to ignore him. But then she lifted her hand awkwardly before letting it fall swiftly to her side. It was an abbreviated, uncertain movement but still, she had reciprocated. Strange how happy it made him feel.

CHAPTER TWELVE

Memory image 4001

By the age of five, a child's body has grown to only 40 per cent of what it will be as a fully grown human being. Its brain, however, has attained 90 per cent of its adult size. The hippocampus, the seat of long-term autobiographical memories, is fully operational. The child knows language and can fashion a primitive narrative.

Catholic Canon states that a child becomes capable of sin and confession at the age of reason, which is seven. Leon says the Catholic Church is wrong: five is the thin red line. The 'magic' age, he called it the other night when we were in the laboratory together. 'The best age.' He had looked at me beseechingly with those blue, blue eyes. 'Tell me you understand, Julianne. Why it has to be at the age of five.'

Jenilee turns five today.

Daniel and Francis have bought her a pink tricycle. Leon has bought her a doll with big, floppy eyes. When you turn it on its side, it says 'Mama' in a frightened voice.

'What a creepy thing,' Bella declared immediately and I agree, but Jenilee already loves it.

The birthday cake is in the shape of a fairy. Leon is cutting into the cake and I am plating it. I watch as his knife slices into the fairy's wing. He picks it up, thick with white icing and silver sprinkles, and places it directly into my daughter's sticky palm. 'Five years old, sweetheart. Imagine. You're such a big girl, now.'

He smiles at me but I turn my head away. I cannot bear to see the greed in his eyes.

CHAPTER THIRTEEN

'Rise and shine, sleeping beauty.' A hand was shaking him by the shoulder, not gently. Jack cracked open a pained eye.

'Come on.' Charles shook him again. 'Birds are a-singin', bells are a-ringin'. You need to wake up.'

Jack struggled upright.

'What time is it?'

'Ten thirty.' Esquith sat down on the edge of the bed and lifted an eyebrow. 'Rough night?'

'You could say that.'

'Your eyes look like piss-holes in the snow. And what happened to your neck?'

'What do you mean?'

'It looks like one of Count Dracula's succubae got hold of you.'

Jack touched his neck. 'I had a run-in with a box cutter last night.'

'Don't tell me.' Charles closed his eyes for a moment. 'Another bar fight.'

Jack raised his arms above his head and stretched. He was feeling the effects of the previous night's exploits. His shoulder muscles especially were suffering from that cat leap he had made when he followed the girl into the house.

'No bar fight. There was a small misunderstanding when I introduced myself to Eloise.'

'You mean Jenilee.'

'Believe me, the girl I met last night was not Miss "bland as butter" Gray. She was Miss "kick your butt" Blake. Besides, if I'm going to keep her company from now on, I'd better get used to Eloise. Wouldn't do to slip and call her Jenilee.'

'You must have made a hell of an impression on her if she stuck a box cutter into your throat.'

Jack swung his legs out of the bed. 'I need to go to the bathroom but if you go make me breakfast, dear heart, I will tell you all. Scrambled eggs: a little runny. And lots. I'm feeling weak.'

'Alright.' Charles headed for the door. 'I'll also make you a cup of ginger and dandelion tea. It will pick you up.'

In the bathroom Jack looked at himself in the mirror and winced. He didn't look too hot and that was a fact. His hair was lank and his eyes bloodshot. He peered at his neck. Charlie was right: it did look as if someone had fanged him. He hadn't realised she had actually drawn blood with that stunt of hers.

After a quick shower he felt better and when he walked into the kitchen and saw the plate of food waiting for him on the counter, he realised he was ravenous.

Between mouthfuls of egg and sips of the quite vile tea Charlie insisted he drink, he gave his friend a run-down of what had happened the night before. It was fun watching Charlie's expression. It took a lot to surprise Esquith but this morning he nailed it, no problem.

'What I don't understand is this whole thing with the book.' Jack pushed his plate away.

Esquith cocked his head. 'What don't you understand? She's obviously a thief.'

'If she was a thief, she could have found something a lot more worth her while to steal than a book. It was a posh house.'

'Don't be so sure. From what you're telling me, it sounds as though she lifted a first edition of a very rare book – in fact, it could be one of the original copies of the Black Books printed by Jung himself. *The Sermons to the Dead* was never widely distributed, you understand. Jung gave copies as gifts to friends and students only. It wasn't until the sixties, when his Red Book was finally made available to the public, that *The Seven Sermons* were included as an appendage.'

'So it's valuable.'

'Oh, yes.'

Jack was quiet for a moment. He didn't want to admit it, but the knowledge that the girl was nothing more than a common thief was a disappointment. But maybe it was just as well to look facts in the face. No use romanticising the woman.

'So what is your next step, mate?'

'Well, she invited me to free run tomorrow with a group of her buddies. And sometime soon, I also think I should have a little snoop around her apartment. Nothing tells you more about a person than her home sweet home.'

Esquith frowned. 'Another break-in. Not a good idea. Besides, I do not want to be the one to tell your father you've been arrested for trespassing.'

'Relax. I don't think she'll be calling the police on me.'

'No, but she might decide to use the box cutter for real this time. I don't like it, Jack. She's clearly not well. In fact, she sounds positively feral.'

'But she's interesting. And I'm having fun. Don't worry,' he said as Esquith continued frowning. 'She won't even know about it. I just have to figure out a way in.'

CHAPTER FOURTEEN

The first time she had extracted a book was eight months ago. Izaak Walton and Charles Cotton's *The Compleat Angler,* 1760. It had taken her almost a year of detective work to locate this particular edition. It had to be a first Hawkins edition and ninth edition overall – no other would do. Not only was tracking down such an edition not easy, but finding a copy she could realistically hope to get her hands on was even more difficult. There was a fine Hawkins sitting on a shelf in an antiquarian bookshop on the Fulham Road, but after casing the place, she reluctantly had to abandon any hope of extracting this particular exemplar. The bookstore used impressive burglar bars in addition to the alarm system, and employed too many security cameras. No, she would have to find another copy somewhere more accessible.

After scouring the internet for months, she found her baby. An estate sale in Kent. Listed among the objects offered for sale – a grand piano, kitchen implements, silverware, a dining-room suite, a ride-on lawnmower – were books. The catalogue stated that the owner preferred to sell the entire library as a set, but would entertain offers for certain individual volumes. A list of these books was provided and among them was Mr Walton's discourse of the contemplative man on rivers, fishponds and fishing in two parts. Asking price £200. The copy in the Fulham Road was valued at £1,300, she knew, which meant that the estate sale copy may not be in great shape. But that was not important to her and might just be a plus, as she probably wouldn't have to worry about an army of antiquarian booksellers storming the gates when the sale opened.

And so it proved to be. The country house in Kent was magnificent, but the sale itself a rather run-down affair. The piano was badly scratched and the kitchen implements in the open cardboard boxes looked over-big and bulky as though they had been manufactured somewhere in the middle part of the previous century. Only a few desultory gawkers strolled through the sparsely furnished rooms. Best of all was the fact that security was negligible. A middle-aged security guard had planted himself next to a tray with tarnished silverware, his face obscured by a copy of the *Sun*. The library with its shelf upon shelf of dusty books was empty when she entered.

And there it was. A sturdy volume bound in green grained morocco with raised bands on the spine; gilt edges and a blind embossed design. Most important was the copyright page: first Hawkins, ninth edition overall. It was the real thing. Without fuss she slipped the book into her satchel and left unchallenged.

The second extraction was even easier, for the simple reason that she had not had to steal this time but had enough money to pay for the book. It was a 1986 Grafton paperback of William Gibson's *Neuromancer*. The book was cheap – well, relatively cheap – £12 for a second-hand paperback with a broken spine was not exactly a give-away. But even though it was inexpensive, it was rare and it had taken her forever to find. What made the book unusual was that it was one of a very few copies that had been misprinted before the publisher caught the mistakes and corrected them. On the first page, the subtitle 'Chiba City Blues' was misspelt as 'Ciba City Blues' and page 224 was followed by page 176 and then continued on from page 228.

Whereas the value of a stamp greatly increased if misprinted, this was generally not the case with books. A misprint was considered a nuisance, and the offending volume usually ended up in a bin. Still, there were always offbeat collectors looking for the weird, if not the wonderful. In a small Clapham Junction shop called Oddball, squeezed in next to a box of six-fingered gloves, she found her dream copy of *Neuromancer* – complete with out-of-sequence pages and fractured subtitle. She had placed the William Gibson next to the Walton in the bottom drawer of her dresser with a sense of accomplishment. Two down, one to go.

Last night's extraction of the *Sermons to the Dead* promised to be straightforward as well, even though this would be the first time she'd actually have to break and enter, which made her nervous. She had cased the house in Holland Park for weeks: it was a matter of getting to know the routine of the owner and finding out when the house was likely to be empty. She had also carefully noted that the laundry room window was only ever shut when the weather was bad. If she made her move on a clear night, therefore, it would be easy. Simple. And so it turned out to be, except for the part where she ran into a bored American rich boy looking for a thrill.

He was attractive, though, she had to admit that. Probably knew it too, of course. She was sorry about the thing with the box cutter – she knew she had over-reacted – but so many inexplicable things had happened to her over the past couple of months. The accident with the bicycle. The scare at the Tube station. The aborted mugging. When he materialised out of thin air like that, it had just seemed too weird to be coincidental. But an American newly arrived in London could not have anything to do with anything. Besides, she should stop being so paranoid. Shit happened. Cyclists got bopped and people got mugged every day.

And the man in the wheelchair?

She shook her head sharply as though she could erase the thought of him from her mind. She did not want to deal with Daniel Barone or with what he had told her. Just thinking about him made her feel cold and shivery, as though she was about to lose something precious.

What Barone offered was a cage. He called it help, but she did not need help. She was following her path and dealing with the obstacles she encountered along the way in her own fashion. If she did not know exactly where she was going or how it would end, this did not matter. No looking over her shoulder. As Jungles always said, quoting the free runner's mantra: 'One step at a time, but every step forward.' Live in the moment. And now that she had all three books, maybe she would be able to figure out why she was haunted by voices and numbers and people who weren't there.

Again she found herself thinking of her stray American. He had a way of looking at her with great concentration, as though he was utterly spellbound by whatever it was she had to say. It was probably an act, but it was a good one. She had felt herself relax in his company; in fact, she ended up almost enjoying herself.

She gave herself a mental shake. No way. A guy like that – privileged, spoilt – could never be part of her world. He was trouble she did not need.

But to her mind came an image once more of those blue eyes and the grin which made a small cleft in his cheek.

She smiled.

CHAPTER FIFTEEN

The BFI IMAX on Charlie Chaplin Street was the size of five double-decker buses and could rightly lay claim to being London's biggest cinema screen. Jack had googled it the night before and discovered that the exterior site was also a playground to free runners, offering some of the sweetest training spots in the capital.

Eloise had said six o'clock, and when Jack arrived a few minutes early, he found a group of ten already gathered at the IMAX steps at Waterloo station. Like parkour tribes anywhere, at first glance they were an unassuming bunch. Most were dressed in tracksuit bottoms, T-shirts and hoodies against the cold. No fancy logos, no bling, no expensive trainers: shoes were bought with an eye on regular replacement. Guys outnumbered the girls. Apart from Eloise, there were only two other women: a cheerful, snub-nosed redhead and a leggy blonde with a purple streaks in her hair. Almost everyone present was young although there was a sinewy guy who looked to be pushing fifty at least. Parkour's unofficial motto was *être et durer* – 'to be and to last'. Parkour did not age-discriminate. If your body was sufficiently fit and prepared, you were on.

Eloise looked rested and bright-eyed. Her face was once again bare of make-up, as though it had stripped itself for action. Jack was surprised at the rush of excitement he felt at seeing her again. *Not wise*, he chided himself. *Down, boy.*

Next to her stood Jungles, dressed in dark green sweat-pants and a tank top, blithely impervious to the cold. He looked even tougher than Jack remembered, all ropey muscles and heavy shoulders. When Eloise made introductions, he looked at Jack with indifferent eyes, although his handshake was amiable enough.

Jack pummelled his upper arms with his fists. It was freezing and there were no clouds in the sky. The light was pale but golden and the air felt sharp. Sunrise, when the streets were empty and the sky magical, was the best time to free run. In the hesitant light, even soot-stained concrete assumed a rough beauty. And he loved the sense of the city awakening. These were the hours when the day's disappointments and failed plans were as yet unrealised and anything seemed possible.

As the group started on their warm-up exercises – rotating joints, stretching legs, flexing arms – their breath steamed the air. After finishing his turn at walking on all fours up and down the row of steps, however, he was starting to feel decidedly toasty and by the time the group hit the slippery blue walls, he was sweating profusely.

He had missed free running. He hadn't realised how much. This was the way the body was meant to be used: legs working explosively, arms and upper body stretching and grabbing and crackling with energy. Soon he was on a high, his exultant brain kicking out on endorphins.

A few paces ahead of him Eloise crossed a gap, knees raised, feet extended. Flying. When she landed on the other side she immediately turned and leapt back. He raised his hand in a celebratory high five and her palm grazed his. Her eyes sparkled, her cheeks had a lovely colour.

After half an hour of practising leaps, the group moved on, running past pedestrians laden down with bags, briefcases and paper cups of coffee. It was now up to every member to plot his or her own course. Jack focused, willing himself to change his perspective and spatial awareness. It was fascinating to see how quickly his eye slotted in again. Parkour practitioners saw the world differently. What was an obstacle or a nuisance for the ordinary pedestrian was an invitation to the free runner to play. Bollards, lamp posts, mounts, railings, ledges: these were all surfaces that cried out to be used. It did something to one's brain, Jack thought, the imperative to view every obstacle as an opportunity.

In front of him a stick-thin teenager called Ben affected a lateral vault, tucking his outside leg effortlessly underneath him and sliding over the railing with less than an inch to spare. This was clearly a strong tribe and from what he had seen so far, the level of proficiency of each member was high. The vibe between the members was determinedly egalitarian and they were generous towards each other. Still, Jack had yet to find any tribe where there was no hierarchy. However subtle, there was always a leader. And in this group, the alpha of the pack was Jungles, no question.

The guy was good. In fact, he was probably the best Jack had ever seen. He never faltered, his pace remaining constantly fast and dynamic. Jack watched as Jungles skimmed a wall, smoothly continuing the movement until it culminated in a stunning precision jump onto a thin railing. He was 'sticking' the jump perfectly, showing ultimate control. No overbalancing, no scrabbling – just a big guy, landing light as air. It took your breath away.

It also had the unfortunate effect of stirring his competitive fire. Jack knew he should clamp down on this impulse: most free runners considered parkour a way of living, not a sport. Expressing yourself was one thing: competition and overt showing-off quite another. But he wasn't really competing. Not really. He just wanted to see how far he could push it.

He started shadowing Jungles, mimicking his every move. Jungles was picking up the pace, though, and soon the speed at which they were moving was brutal, leaving no time for thought. They were leaving the others behind.

Jack's breath whistled through his chest. Up, over. Slam of the hand onto a concrete ledge, palm spinning, body corkscrewing. Too quick; shoulder ramming into the wall, no time for recovery, the muscles in his arm screeching. Speeding on, kong vault next, hands square, legs tucked tight, spine horizontal – and onwards again. He was blowing like a loco-motive. His fitness level was not up for this crap. What the hell had he been thinking?

They were approaching a wall. Oh, man. Jack's mind cringed at the idea of finding the necessary momentum and energy to mount. But instead of making a run at it, Jungles veered off, heading for an apartment building to their left and attacking a flight of metal stairs clinging to its side. Jack fol-lowed. He could hear the thump, thump, thump of Jungles' feet as the man bounced powerfully off every second stair. At the first landing, without a moment's hesitation, Jungles jumped, pushing himself out, clearing the wall below with a good foot to spare, dropping down on a patch of black soil and scrubby grass on the other side.

How long was this drop? Ten foot? More? Jack hesitated; first mistake. As he fell forward, he held his breath; second mistake. He could feel his shoulders tense. Wrong, wrong. For one terrifying moment he thought he was going to drop – completely out of control – on top of the wall instead of clearing it, but in the end his jump had just enough power.

He managed to place his feet in line with his knees but on the descent his body was too rigid. He immediately launched himself into a roll after touch-down in an attempt to redirect his downward energy away from his body. The rigidity of his torso stopped him from coming out of the roll cleanly and landing softly on the balls of his feet. Unable to control the drive, he found himself collapsing in an inelegant, sprawling, sideways heap.

'Are you OK?'

He looked up to find Jungles watching him, hands on his hips.

'Sure.' Jack struggled to his feet. Odd how wobbly his legs felt.

Jungles was still watching him, black eyes inscrutable, a slight tilt to his head as though trying to work out something.

'OK, then. Let's go and join the others. They'll be having a coffee at Rafiki's.'

As they started walking, Jack tried to brush the dirt off his hands. His sweatshirt had a thick black streak of mud across it where his shoulder had hit the ground. The shoulder itself felt like someone had taken a sledgehammer to it. A sloppy roll will do that for you.

Jack glanced over at Jungles and cleared his throat.

'It was a good run.' 'Good' wasn't really the word he felt like using but his pride wouldn't allow for 'excruciating'.

Jungles gave a grunt – not hostile, just uninterested. For a while back there as he was following the man, Jack had thought the blistering pace might be because Jungles was responding to his wordless challenge. But the guy had clearly not even noticed his pathetic attempt at throwing down the gauntlet. Galling.

'How long have you known Eloise?'

This got a reaction. Jungles gave him a shuttered glance from beneath lowered eyebrows. 'Why do you ask?'

'No reason. It just looks like the two of you have been running together for a long time.'

Jungles shrugged. Jack saw with disapproval that even this slight gesture made the muscles in his shoulders pop. 'Me? I can't remember not ever tracing. Eloise ...' Jungles rubbed his hand over his shaven head thoughtfully. 'Maybe two years since I started training her. She's a natural. I've never seen any-one take to it the way she has.'

'Where did you guys meet?'

But Jungles had had enough of being social. He gestured with a blunt hand. 'There's Rafiki's.'

Inside the shop, they found the group drinking coffee and exchanging friendly abuse. Eloise was standing on her own in the far corner, paging through last night's *Evening Standard*. On the counter next to her was a cup with a sealed lid. As

Jungles approached her, she held it out to him: it was obviously a routine they had done many times before.

Jack watched sourly as Jungles extracted a dripping bag of coarse-leaved tea from the depths of the cup. Green tea, of course. God forbid the guy should poison his body with common caffeine. His eyes met Eloise's across Jungles' shoulder. She lifted her eyebrows and he thought he saw an expression of amusement cross her face.

Feeling suddenly childish and out of sorts, he turned away.

'Would you like mine?'

It was the tall blonde with the purple fringe. She seemed to be offering him a very milky latte.

'Thanks, but I shouldn't take your coffee.'

'No, that's OK. I always buy two, but this morning I can't manage both.'

She introduced herself as Tracy and for a minute or two they talked backflips and vaults, but he had the impression she had something else on her mind. And sure enough …

'How long have you and Eloise been friends?' Her voice was casual but the glance she gave him was sharp.

'Not long.'

'So you're not together?'

'Together? No.'

Her expression made it clear this was not the answer she had hoped for. So much for his ego: he had assumed she was angling for a date.

'Eloise invited me to come running with you guys after we sort of … bumped … into each other.'

'Eloise seems to have a knack of doing that.' When he looked at her questioningly, she explained, 'Bumping into guys.'

He didn't quite know how to respond to this. Tracy was looking to where Jungles and Eloise were standing in the corner, reading from the newspaper together, their heads almost touching.

'Are you talking about Jungles?'

She nodded. On her face was a sad, resigned look. Well, if the girl was looking for a shoulder to cry on, he was willing and able. Jack smiled at her sympathetically to let her know he understood. 'How did they meet, then?'

The corners of Tracy's mouth turned down. 'Jungles rescued her.' Her voice was suddenly tight with frustration. 'Like a friggin' Prince Charming. She was a right mess, was Eloise. You should have seen her when she joined us. Messed up.'

'Messed up how?'

'As if she was on drugs. Tripping. Spaced. I was with her once and she started counting. Couldn't stop.'

'Counting?'

'She's still not right, you know. She looks like she's got it all together, but she doesn't.'

Jack suddenly wanted to be anywhere but here. The coffee shop felt stifling.

'If it wasn't for Jungles, she'd be on the street. You'd think she'd be grateful, right? But she's such a tease. Always playing hard to get. She'll break his heart; see if she doesn't.'

For a few moments she stared at Jack, her mouth angry. Then she shook her head. 'Sorry. I shouldn't have unloaded on you.'

'Don't worry about it.'

She gave him a shamefaced look and he wasn't surprised when she started making time-to-leave gestures. 'I have to get to work.' She bopped her head. 'Very nice to meet you, anyway.'

'You too. Thanks for the coffee.'

He watched her walk out the door, throwing him a last awkward glance over her shoulder. He crushed the paper cup in his hand and lobbed it into the waste basket.

She looks like she's got it all together, but she doesn't. Into his mind's eye came an image of Eloise the way she had looked this morning; her movements joyous, the wind whipping colour into her cheeks. She had looked beautiful, alive, aggressively *sane*.

He pushed his way over to the other side of the room.

'Eloise?'

She looked up.

'I just wanted to say thanks. I had an awesome time.' He turned to Jungles. 'You too, man.'

'A pleasure.' Jungles' voice was formal.

They were looking at him politely. Suddenly, there didn't really seem to be anything else to say.

'OK, see you around.' He started walking to the door, feeling altogether despondent. What now?

But as he placed his hand on the glass door, someone touched his arm. Eloise. She seemed wary, almost puzzled at herself.

'We're all getting together again on Thursday. South Bank Centre. You want to come?'

The relief was overwhelming but something else must have shown in his face because she continued quickly, 'Only if you want to.'

He nodded fervently. 'I want to.'

'Love is strong as death, hard as hell.'
                                    –*Meister Eckhart*

CHAPTER SIXTEEN

Memory image 9996

Jenilee is acting up and throwing tantrums, which she almost never does, and I see Daniel and Francis watching her. They are clearly puzzled by her behaviour. I can't find the courage to look them in the eye. What will they do if they find out?

Leon suggests a walk by the river and I agree. Anything to get Jenilee away from the others.

My daughter runs ahead on her fat, sturdy little legs; happy now, falling down and shrieking with laughter. I look at the soft crown of her hair and as always I marvel at how clever God is to make the back of a child's head look so vulnerable. Love me. Protect me. Keep me from harm.

The sun is starting to set and the horizon looks like a fresh wound. And this is when we come upon the swan. It has snagged its wing on a piece of wire netting and struggles desperately, tearing the wing ever more and staring at us with a crazed, black eye. There is a lot of blood. *Jenilee draws in a terrified breath and her hand tightens in mine.*

Later that night as I put her to bed she talks about the swan 'screaming'.

'The swan screamed, Mummy.'

I know she is wrong: the swan had not screamed. It had been a silent struggle, the only sound the torn wing slapping at the water. But I know, no matter what I say, she will continue to remember a scream in all its vivid, prolonged agony. Because this, as Bella always tells me, is how memory works. Memory is not photography. Memory is emotion and experience fused together: a neurological flash so brilliant it can leave phantom patterns on the lenses of our eyes. We do not remember facts: we remember what moves our soul.

I am so aware of her: my daughter. I feel the quick pulse of her tiny wrist beneath my fingers. I look into her tear-filled eyes, touch her wet cheek and kiss her button nose. I hoist her in my arms and her breath is sweet against my neck.

I tell her the swan is fine, even though Leon told me the bird had died on the back seat of his car before he had managed to get it to the vet. But Jenilee believes me because I am her mother and she trusts me. Because children know their mothers never betray them.

Jenilee gives a sad, exhausted sigh. Her small hand moves involuntarily on the pillow as her eyelids close. Her bed is safe and warm but outside her window, in the dark, a swan with dream-white feathers utters a long-drawn-out scream that pierces the air.

I watch my child asleep and I wonder what kind of monster I've become.

CHAPTER SEVENTEEN

Jack's earliest memory was of his parents arguing. He wasn't sure exactly how old he was – four, five maybe – but his recollection of it was strong.

It was dark and he had the blankets pulled up to his chin. His parents were trying to keep their voices low but the desperation, passion and mutual loathing came through the closed door of his room as clearly as though they stood right next to his bed.

He had other early memories too – a fragment of remembrance that included a toy sailboat that keeled over as he splashed his hands in the soapy water of the bathtub; the glittering charms of his nanny's bracelet – but the memory of that urgent ripple of sound cutting through the darkness was his Ground Zero memory: the memory to which all other memories were anchored. It was the soundtrack to his childhood and it still played, white noise, at the back of his mind.

He supposed everyone had a memory like that, one that haunted their inner lives. But what if your name was Eloise Blake and you had no origin memory? Or indeed any memories of the defining moments that made you who you are? What happens to you if you lose recollection of your most jubilant successes and painful defeats; if you have no remembrance of those who loved you and hurt you, and whom you loved and hurt in return? Would you be liberated or would you be lost?

Three weeks had passed since he followed Eloise into the house in Holland Park. On that day he had felt like a reluctant actor: an alternate stepping randomly into a play which made little sense because he had joined it in the middle.

Things have changed. His understanding of what was going on has not increased, but his desire to stay involved certainly has. The more he got to know her, the more fascinated he became. The more he got to know her, the more of a riddle she appeared to be.

How to gain her confidence? Going on the assumption that the best strategy would be a roundabout one, he decided to try and blend in with her tribe. It became routine to join them for a coffee after a morning run, or to meet up for a drink at the end of the day, chatting outside the pub in the cold chill of early evening.

In particular, Jack knew he would need to stay on Jungles' good side and clamp down on his childish urge to pit himself against the guy at every turn. If he wanted to stay close to Eloise, it was crucial that Jungles be comfortable with his presence.

In this he had some success. They were not exactly best mates, but at least Jungles was tolerating him. Once, he even nodded his approval after Jack managed a tricky drop jump, and Jack felt a thrill of accomplishment. He did not want to admit it, but he was gaining a reluctant respect for the man. He was starting to understand why the others were so fond of him. It wasn't just his parkour prowess that made Jungles the leader of the pack. There was a solidity to the guy: a sense that even if there were a shifting of tectonic plates he would remain standing.

So far, so good. To be sure, he did not have much opportunity to be alone with Eloise but, little by little, he was getting to know her likes and dislikes; her gestures, the way she moved.

He was becoming familiar with how she used both hands to push back her hair when puzzled. He knew how she threw back her head when she laughed, exposing the lovely curve of her throat. He knew the way her eyes changed with her moods. When she was feeling hesitant, her head would droop to her shoulder. Her favourite colour was blue. She preferred non-fiction to fiction. If she could afford it, she would have roses next to her bed every day. She liked rainy days as much as sunny ones.

So many questions. So many secrets. He sometimes wondered what she saw when she looked in the mirror. When she stared into those off-kilter eyes, did she wonder if she had inherited them from her mother? Her father? When she hummed her favourite tune, did it have the taste of habit? There was a birthmark on her wrist, which looked like a flower that had been pressed between the pages of a book. Did she wonder if anyone had ever touched his lips to it? When she undressed at night, did she try to remember if her skin had been caressed by lovers in the past? Did she still sense their presence, however ghostly? Who gave her the name Eloise? Did she choose it herself? And, above all, why had she not gone to the police, searched for help when one day she noticed that her world had utterly changed and she had lost her compass?

Fugue state. It sounded like music – but the notes of this composition were written in an alien key. His research told him the condition was rare. The most high-profile sufferer was Agatha Christie, who was thought to have entered a fugue state when she inexplicably vanished for eleven days. Classified as a dissociative disorder, a fugue state involved the sufferer establishing a new identity and often engaging in unplanned travel or wandering. The majority of sufferers regained their memory after a short episode. Those who recover always manage to regain the lost memories of their original identity in full. Memories created during the fugue state, however, would vanish – never to surface again – the new self killed off in one sudden, irreversible instant.

The idea filled him with unease. If in Eloise's place suddenly came a woman whose favourite colour was peach, not blue, who liked pansies and couldn't even remember once preferring roses, she would be someone wholly unfamiliar to him. She would no longer be the woman who had the resilience to start her journey anew even though behind her were no footprints to mark where she had walked. She would no longer be the girl who could be as hard as nails one moment, throat-catchingly vulnerable the next. If Eloise Blake suddenly disappeared, to be replaced by Jenilee Gray, he knew he'd feel her absence as keenly as though she had died.

Eloise. She is lying on her back in the park, enjoying the sun, loose-limbed and sprawling. Her eyes are closed, her long lashes silky black against her cheek. He watches the soft shadows at the corners of her mouth, the sweet curve of her bottom lip. How can any mouth be so defenceless?

She is gearing up for a run, her slight body tense, and now her mouth is uncompromising and sharp with concentration. She jumps, reaches for the ledge. As her fingers hook over the edge, her sweater rides up against the slender V of her back and he sees that the skin peeping from beneath is white as cream. She glances triumphantly over her shoulder and her smile is daring: the smile of a buccaneer.

Eloise. She was the first thought in his mind when he woke up, the last as he closed his eyes to sleep. And she was invading his dreams. He would wake up in the middle of the night with the sheets in a knot, his skin damp. He would go over to his window and open it wide; the chill night air cooling his flushed body. For a long time he'd stand there listening to the city breathing. And he'd wonder if she too might be at her window, staring into the darkness.

Barone had appointed him sentinel but as the weeks went by Jack failed to notice anything sinister that would substantiate Barone's dark presentiment that someone was out to harm Eloise. He wasn't able to keep an eye on her continuously, of course, but as far as he could determine, her daily life was uneventful. Parkour, working at the flea market, socialising with the tribe.

He wondered if she had indulged in yet another bit of book thievery. The unwelcome thought had crossed his mind that maybe she and Jungles were pawning off stolen volumes on the side – the flea market would be a good base for that kind of thing – and he had indeed spotted a box filled with second-hand books among their wares. But one browse through the damaged paperbacks made it clear to him that this box contained no treasures and certainly not a black leather-bound copy of *The Seven Sermons to the Dead*.

Still, all was not well with her. Once, when the group had gathered to watch video footage of themselves at play, he suddenly noticed she had left the room. When he went in search of her, he found her sitting by herself, her head cradled on her arms, rocking back and forth. He touched her shoulder and she looked up.

Her eyes were wild. The amber eye had darkened so much, it seemed black. The green eye looked livid. Her lips were moving. She was … counting?

He dropped to his knee so that their faces were level. 'Eloise?'

'Don't!' she said fiercely. 'Don't you dare feel sorry for me!'

She slammed her palms against her face and started rocking again.

He stared at her, stunned, but the next moment Jungles shouldered past him and pushed him out of the way. His large hands careful, he steered Eloise into the next room and closed the door behind them. Jack could hear her cry and then came Jungles' rough voice, gently soothing.

Something moved behind Jack and he turned around. Tracy was standing a few steps away. Their eyes met and she lifted her eyebrows in an 'I told you so' expression.

He turned back to the door. The sound of Eloise's weeping made him clench his hands. He stared at the smooth wooden door and felt powerless.

CHAPTER EIGHTEEN

He did not see Eloise again until a week later when Jungles unexpectedly asked his help in delivering a vintage crystal decanter and companion whisky glasses to one of Jungles' repeat customers who lived in a flat off Marble Arch. The box was not heavy but awkward to carry.

'The guy has emphysema and hugs an oxygen tank but he's also a lecherous arsehole.' Jungles looked Jack straight in the eye. 'But he is one of my best customers and, unfortunately, he's taken a shine to Eloise. He made it clear he wouldn't buy this piece unless she delivers it in person. I can't go with her – I have another delivery – so I want you to stay with her and stop the guy from trying to feel her up, OK?'

Jack nodded. 'I'll guard her with my life.'

'And don't tell Eloise I sent you along as a babysitter. She won't like it.'

'Gotcha.'

The drop-off at the Marble Arch flat went smoothly, although the disappointment on the guy's face when he found Jack standing behind Eloise as he opened the door was almost comical.

Afterwards, they walked unhurriedly down Oxford Street together. Eloise was smiling. He looked into her eyes – clear green and light hazel today – and the troubled girl he had heard crying behind a closed door only a few days before was nowhere to be found.

They passed a specialist chocolate shop, its window filled with cellophane, ribbons and pretty paper cones brimming with dainties.

'Salted caramels,' she read, her voice dubious.

In the sunlight her dark hair glimmered with light. The top button of her white blouse had become undone and, looking down at her, he could see the hint of lace and the swell of her breasts.

He took a deep breath and tried to concentrate on the shop window.

'It sounds weird, no?' He felt her glance at him. 'Salt and sweet. '

'Come on.' He took her by the hand and opened the glass door. They stepped inside and she looked around the tiny shop, her eyebrows rising at the prices.

'My treat.' As the words left his mouth, he grimaced. She probably thought he was acting the rich boy again. But she made no comment. She pulled out a black lacquered chair next to one of the miniscule marble tables and waited for him to place their order.

He returned to the table with two cappuccinos and a cellophane bag filled with truffles dusted with cocoa powder.

She popped one into her mouth. 'Oh!' Her eyes opened wide like a child's.

'Nice, huh?'

For an answer she dipped her hand into the bag again.

He smiled. The cocoa powder had stained her fingers and there was a streak of dust next to her mouth.

At a table on the other side of the room were a young mother and a little girl in a frilly dress. The little girl was eating a piece of cake, liberally smearing both herself and her immediate environment with icing while her mother watched with an indulgent, adoring expression.

He looked at Eloise, who was just about to tackle her third truffle.

'What?'

'I'm just wondering who has the most chocolate on her face: you or Shirley Temple over there.'

'Oh.' She blushed and moved her hand clumsily, leaving a fresh streak of chocolate in its wake.

'Allow me.' He leant over and brushed his thumb across her cheek. 'There.'

She blushed again. Probably in an effort to mask her embarrassment, she nodded at the little girl and her mother. 'I bet you and your mum used to do things like this all the time. Go to fancy chocolate shops. Or take trips to toy shops.'

'I take it you did not.'

'Well, my mother was always working. And it was difficult because she'd lock herself into boxes.'

'Excuse me?'

'She was a contortionist.'

'A contortionist.' Eloise was looking him straight in the eye, her face guileless. 'I see. She must have been a very supple woman.'

'Oh, yes. And she had a head for heights too. The trapeze was her second home.' She bit into the truffle and chewed slowly.

'She worked in the circus.' He was trying not to laugh. 'You grew up with the smell of sawdust?'

'Indeed. My mother would strap me on her back when she practised in the big top – trapezing, that is – not the contortionist thing, of course.'

'I don't think "trapezing" is a word.'

'Oh, it is.' She nodded sagely.

'And your father?'

'Juan. Knife thrower. Handsome as the devil. He got his talent from my grandmother: she was a knife thrower too. In fact, she was his partner.'

Eloise paused dramatically. 'But there was a family tragedy. Juan's aim was off one night and he took out my grandmother's eye. After that, she had to wear a patch. It became her trade-mark, you know. One-eyed Annie.'

'Miss Blake. You tell a good story. But I think you're fibbing.'

'Do you?' She smiled disarmingly. 'OK. I'm lying about the eye patch. I admit.' She leant back in her chair. 'Your turn to share.'

He shrugged. 'My father is a pirate.'

'A successful one?'

'Very.'

'And he sails the seven seas in search of fortune.'

'Sails hedge funds and international markets. But a plunderer nevertheless.'

She tilted her head and he realised his voice had sounded alarmingly harsh.

'Sorry.' He tried to smile. 'When I talk about my father I tend to get angry. Boring for you. Apologies.'

'He's still alive?'

'Oh, yes.'

'And your mother?'

'She was an alcoholic who wrapped her car around a tree when I was fifteen years old.'

He couldn't tell from her expression what she was thinking. After a moment she asked, making it sound like a statement. 'You blame your father.'

'My mother was a watercolour artist: she painted lovely, gentle pictures. My father belittled her talent and she stopped. She was tongue-tied but he would drag her to functions and social events where he would be irritated by her shyness and humiliate her in front of other people. He cheated on her relentlessly without even trying to hide it. He made her feel small and worthless. My father did not place the bottle in her hand but, yes, I blame him. He's a ruthless son of a bitch – not just where my mother was concerned, but in all his relationships. He trashes his competitors and takes no prisoners. As I said: a pirate.'

'I'm sorry.'

'Yeah. Me too. I wish my father had been a knife thrower. Even one with a wobbly aim.'

Her smile seemed lopsided. 'You can always invent a parent for yourself.'

'Someone like your mother. Who had a head for heights and a facility for getting into small places. Someone to admire.'

'Yes.' She smiled again and this time it was a smile full of sadness. 'Someone like that.'

She had her own Wikipedia entry. *Julianne Gray.* Jack placed his coffee mug on the desk and pulled his chair closer to the screen, feeling a flicker of excitement.

Born in Bodmin, Cornwall on 4 April 1963. Graduated with a PhD from Imperial College, London. Lived with her partner, Lawrence Black, a curator at the British Museum and the father of her child, until he died in a plane crash. After his death Julianne Gray moved to Oxford where she joined Daniel Barone's independent research unit on long-term plasticity and potentiation in the brain. She died after being attacked in her home. Her killer was never apprehended.

At the time of her death she was reputed to be working on a drug that would allow brain cells to increase the voltage of their signals and vastly improve the speed dial connection between protein kinase molecules necessary for creating long-term recall. Even though she died before her research was published, her work is widely considered to be a precursor to the groundbreaking work of the Sackler Laboratory in New York City. It was even rumoured that she might indeed have cracked the puzzle of restoring forgotten memories. But she had never published her research, and her notebook disappeared after her death.

Jack frowned. When he had met Barone for the first time, the older man had called Julianne Gray a great friend, but had said nothing about her being a colleague and a scientist of repute. Strange that Barone hadn't thought to mention it. Even stranger that the two people closest to Eloise before she lost her memory had both been experts on the subject.

He looked back at the screen. The reference to the Sackler Laboratory was highlighted and when he clicked on the link it opened onto a *New York Times* article: 'Brain Researchers Open Door to Editing Memory'.

The article was lengthy. Jack's eyes skimmed the text, which seemed to be a discussion of breakthrough work by a group of scientists on the memory molecule PKMzeta. Not only would manipulation of this molecule help patients suffering from memory loss, but in the foreseeable future it could even offer criminal prosecutors a tool to recover memory traces that are beyond the conscious recall of victims and witnesses: a development as dramatic as the use of DNA.

The article also discussed the Sackler Lab's experiments on another molecule, going by the snappy name of ZIP. If PKMzeta was Superman, then ZIP, it seemed, was Kryptonite. Inject a little ZIP into the neocortex of a rat, and its long-term memories were not just dimmed but completely erased. What's more, the temporary inhibition of PKMzeta did not appear to harm the brain and new, fresh long-term memories could be formed afterwards.

Jack sat back in his chair and stared at the words on the screen. They were setting off a tingling of his palms – a powerful sense of something yet unrecognised but hovering at the periphery of his understanding. Like a shadow under deep water. Like a hologram just before it metamorphoses into shape.

He backspaced to Wikipedia and read through the entry for Julianne Gray again:

... her work considered to be a precursor to the work of the Sackler Laboratory ... rumoured that she might have cracked the puzzle of restoring forgotten memories ... never published her research ... her notebook disappeared after her death ...

The coffee he had brought with him had cooled by this time, forming a thin ring of milk scum on the surface. He stood up and emptied the mug into the kitchen sink. As he watched the liquid disappear down the drain he thought of a time when scientists did not write on computers, but in notebooks: notebooks, which could be lost. And he thought how ironic it was that the one person who might have been able to help Eloise should be the mother she could not remember.

Two days later Jack attended a party celebrating the engagement of a lanky thirty-year-old schoolteacher called Darren. Darren was solemn, intense and took his parkour very seriously. His fiancée was a jolly, rotund squeegee toy who looked as though she wouldn't have the stamina to run around the block – obviously a case of opposites attracting. The room was festooned with paper garlands and coloured lights. Bowls of watery punch stood on one table surrounded by peanuts, popcorn, raw vegetables and a pungent dip. The music was eclectic: a mix of Bruce Springsteen, Shawn Colvin, The Pierces and Arctic Monkeys.

He immediately noticed Eloise as he walked in. She was on the far side of the room and was wearing a scarlet dress made of a shimmery material that clung to her. It was the first time Jack had ever seen her in a dress. And she was wearing heels. He watched her out of the corner of his eye, trying not to stare. When a little later he saw her slip out the French doors and into the garden, he thought of following her, but there had been something furtive in her movements, which suggested she wanted to be alone. He walked to the window instead and looked out.

She had kicked off her evening sandals and was dancing by herself. Her eyes were closed and she was giving herself over to the music. Pale, bare arms but she did not seem to feel the cold.

He knew that from then on, he would dream about it – of the girl with the wonderful eyes dancing in the darkness while he stood inside the house, in the light, watching. He would dream of that moment and how he immediately knew he'd remember it always, because it was the moment he first realised with absolute certainty that he was in love.

CHAPTER NINETEEN

Memory image 10081

If there were memories to sell, what would you buy?
I would buy memories of love.
If there were memories to buy, what would you sell?
I would sell memories of love.
Love is electricity: a neuron that sparks at 200 miles per hour. Love is chemical: a murky torrent of phenylethylamine, kicking the brain into a frenzy as sweet as a needle in the arm. It is the ecstasy of the mystic; the recklessness of a crumpled bed. The bloody umbilical cord between parent and child.
I am four people: the scientist, the mother, the lover, the cheat. Love rules them all.

CHAPTER TWENTY

'I think I need to go to Los Angeles.'

Jack glanced at Esquith, who was jogging next to him, breathing like Darth Vader on steroids. Strenuous exercise was not exactly Charlie's thing but this morning he had woken up with the inexplicable urge to run down the Embankment. They had started off at the pink and white confection that was the Albert Bridge and had now left behind views of the London Eye, the squat bunker that was the Southbank Centre and were approaching Cleopatra's Needle.

'LA? Why?'

Esquith stopped running and leant forward, his hands propped on his knees. 'I read last night that there is a museum where you can go to see petrified mermaids. And miniature paintings on olive seeds.'

'Sounds groovy.'

'And costumed fleas. Imagine.'

'I'd rather not, thanks.'

'Although I'd quite like to see what's inside here as well.' Esquith waved a weak hand at the pedestal that formed the base of the Needle.

'There's something inside?'

'Oh, yes. Two time capsules with multilingual bibles, a box of hairpins, a hydraulic jack, cigars, a baby's bottle and portraits of twelve of the most beautiful English women of the day.'

Jack looked at Esquith suspiciously. 'You're kidding.'

'On my honour.'

'The things you know. Come on.' Jack pulled Esquith by the sleeve. 'If we stop now, you'll cramp out.'

They continued, Charlie dragging but still game, and at last the Millennium Bridge was in sight with its suspended, graceful spikes gleaming silver in the chilly light. As if by common accord, they slowed down and stopped halfway down the bridge's aluminium deck, joining the tourists who were snapping away with mobile phones and cameras.

As views go, Jack had to admit, this one was not too shabby. Upstream was Blackfriars railway bridge with its clattering trains; downstream Charles Dickens's Southwark Bridge with its faded turquoise arches. On the north side of the river the wedding-cake dome of St Paul's soared upwards – airy as spun silk – a perfect foil for the brutalist architecture of the Tate Modern, which faced it on the southern side.

Esquith gave a contented sigh. 'I love London.'

'But you wish to cross the ocean in search of petrified mermaids. You're a restless soul, Charlie.'

Esquith placed his hand on his heart and struck a pose. 'But I always return.'

'Like a pigeon.'

Esquith grinned his appreciation. For a few minutes it was quiet between them. A male cyclist in a white wedding dress cycled past as if it was nothing out of the ordinary to be dressed in tulle and lace. A group of Japanese tourists stared open-mouthed but the locals hardly gave him a second glance. It was true, Jack thought, the British have a boundless tolerance for eccentricity.

A few steps away from him, a girl, her back turned towards him, was leaning against the railing. There was something about her that reminded him of Eloise – something in the unconscious grace of her posture; the soft tendrils of hair curling against the vulnerable nape of her neck.

He suddenly realised Esquith was watching him.

'What?'

'Be careful, Jack.'

'What do you mean?'

'Obsession is never a healthy thing.'

He didn't pretend not to know what Charlie was talking about. But he was not ready to articulate his feelings either.

Esquith nodded wisely. 'Do you know the reason for your obsession?'

'No, oh Yoda. Enlighten me.'

'Because she is fantasy. Only the inaccessible and elusive holds that kind of fascination.'

'You're turning it into more than it is. I find her interesting, that's all.'

'Interesting – always a good word in an emergency. Well, whatever it is you feel, you are losing sight of the main objective.'

Jack looked down at the Thames flowing beneath them. He could smell the petrol on the water. Lurking behind that smell was an older, slyer smell. The smell of decay.

'The main objective. Which is?'

'You haven't been much of a detective. What happened to your plans to take a snoop around her home sweet home?'

'I thought you were against it?' Jack tried not to sound defensive. 'Besides, I haven't had the opportunity.'

Which was not the truth. On the inside of Eloise's combat jacket was a keychain from which dangled a single key. It could only be the key to her apartment. He had seen it many times and it would be easy to lift. She often left the jacket lying around: slung over the back of a chair in a coffee shop, hanging from a peg on the wall of a pub. But the idea now seemed repugnant to him and a totally unacceptable violation of her privacy.

His friend seemed to accept his excuse but later, as they returned to his apartment by cab – Charlie having refused to leg it all the way back again – he warned, 'You do realise, Jack, that at some point Barone is going to ask you for a report on the fair Ms Blake. If you don't have much to give him, he may very well believe you're not taking him seriously and pull the plug on you. Find someone else to take over.'

Jack was silent. It was true. What was he going to tell the man? That she liked to break into houses and steal books? That he had witnessed her suffering a breakdown? It made her sound like a criminal and a headcase. He needed to find something which might place her behaviour into context.

'You're right.' Jack gave a reluctant nod. 'I have to be more proactive.'

He made his move the next morning when the tribe had their usual coffee break. He had brought with him a piece of children's plasticine and when Eloise disappeared into the ladies room, he casually bumped against her jacket where it was draped over a chair. It slid off the back of the chair into a soft heap and he dropped to his knee as though to retrieve it.

The key was cool against his palm. He stared at it for a moment and words like 'betrayal' and 'deceit' flitted through his mind.

He pressed the key deeply into the wad of yellow clay.

CHAPTER TWENTY ONE

There were no names of tenants at the entrance to Eloise's building but she had once mentioned that her apartment was at the very top. A large lift was waiting in the glass-walled lobby, but Jack decided to use the stairs instead. Apart from an old man he had seen pottering outside and who he assumed to be the caretaker, the entire building was eerily quiet. It felt hushed, as though it was keeping a secret: as if behind the closed doors he would find everyone asleep, like those fairy tales where the princess and all around her have been cursed by a witch. Chalky marks against the walls told of water damage and leaking pipes. There was a smell of mould and undisturbed dust.

There was only one apartment on the top floor. He brought out the key, which had been cut the day before. When he had given the locksmith the piece of plasticine with its deep imprint, he was convinced his guilt and nefarious intentions were plastered all over his face. But the man had taken it from him without comment.

The key was shiny and slid easily enough into the lock. When he tried to turn it, however, it felt stiff. Worse, he had trouble removing it. *Great. Way to go, Jack.* She was going to come back after work to find a fat, fake key stuck in her front door. Taking a deep breath, he started jiggling the key around, aware that if he was too forceful, the damn thing might just break in half. He was starting to despair when suddenly, without warning, the key clicked. He was in.

The room was vast and the sparse furnishings made it look even bigger. Generous windows lined one end, flooding the front end of the room with morning light where stood a bed, an attractive dressing table and a few other bits and pieces. But it was the opposite end of the room, the part that lay in shadow, which made him stare. There was no furniture here except for a tall wooden ladder that was pushed up against the wall. His eyes travelled over the smooth expanse of white plaster and he felt the hair on his arms prickle.

Numbers. That's all – nothing more sinister than that. Row upon row of numbers written in a black felt-tip pen. They started high up – she must have stood on the ladder to get that high – and continued all the way down to floor level. Some rows were long: the numbers set off from each other with dashes, forward slashes and brackets. Others contained only a few digits. There was no reason why the sight of these numbers should make him feel as though he were standing on the deck of a listing ship, but it did. There was a palpable sense of desperation – of urgency and fear – that communicated itself to him through the helter-skelter scribbles.

It was so quiet. Dust motes danced silently in the white light. Time felt suspended – almost hypnotically so – and he had to force himself to draw his eyes away from the wall and walk to the front part of the room.

This, clearly, was where she lived. And despite the bareness and the absence of frilly cushions and soft toys, it was a highly feminine space.

The bed was covered by a quilt and a single hail-white pillow. Next to it stood the dressing table in distressed colours. The marble top held a jar of lotion and a fragile-looking Delft cup with a missing handle. Cradled inside were a lipstick and an eye pencil.

On a chrome rail hung her clothes: a few blouses, a towelling robe, a pair of jeans, the backless red dress she had worn
at the party. He knew he shouldn't, but he couldn't help but
run his hand down the smooth, shimmery fabric. On the floor
below were arranged a pair of ballet flats, a pair of trainers
and a worn-out pair of fluffy slippers. Nestled in tissue paper,
in a shoebox, were those exquisite evening sandals she had
partnered with the red dress. They had absurd four-inch heels
and were delightfully frivolous and clearly expensive; she must
have saved up for these for a long time.

His experience with women was that they liked to be surrounded by photographs of themselves: every girl with whom
he had ever been involved had dozens of pictures celebrating
her life scattered around her apartment. But the only picture
around here was a page ripped out of a magazine and taped
against the fridge in the kitchen. It showed an anonymous
parkour runner – a black shape backlit by a red horizon –
flying joyously through the air. Above the kitchen sink was an
old mirror with a bloomed, speckled face.

There was a cat in her life. As he walked into the kitchen
area he noticed a saucer of milk on the floor and a bag of cat
nibbles. He opened the fridge and saw that she was overdue
for a shop. Inside were only a bottle of milk and three eggs.

Flush against the wall, at the far end of the slightly lopsided worktop, were books stacked on top of each other. He
tilted his head and ran his fingers over the titles. There was no
mysterious black book written in Gothic script.

Maybe inside the dressing table? He hesitated but then
pulled open the top drawer of the bureau. It was filled with
pale, soft things: lingerie, a sweater, a nightie with thin straps.
No book.

He closed it, feeling like a peeping Tom, and placed his
hand on the drop handles of the bottom drawer. It slid open
smoothly.

And here it was. *Septem Sermones ad Mortuos. The Seven
Sermons to the Dead*: the same black leather copy he had
examined in the coffee shop. And two other books: a rather

attractively bound volume of *The Compleat Angler* and a bat-tered, coffee-stained paperback edition of *Neuromancer* with a stickered label on the front cover that said MISPRINT.

He flipped through the pages. Maybe there was something hidden inside? He turned over each book, carefully shaking them by the spine, but nothing dropped out. And there didn't seem to be anything pushed behind the elaborate stitching of the Walton book either.

His eyes wandered back to the far wall with its rows of black numbers screaming out from the white wall like distress signals. He pushed his hand into the inside pocket of his jacket and took out his phone. Walking closer, he started snapping away, making sure to record every single digit scribbled on the wall. By the time he was finished, the picture folder on his phone held an additional forty-seven images.

Time to go. But just as he was about to let himself out, he noticed a small terracotta pot in a wire holder. It held a single plant. A rose. This one wasn't blooming and looked cold and bedraggled in its patch of dirt. Tiny thorns stuck baldly from the sides of the stubby stalk.

He stood looking at it and found himself oddly moved. He was thinking, that despite its appearance, the plant would recover and in another few months you'd hardly notice the thorns. A bud would form and then burst into flower. Beautiful and joyous.

Like a wish come true.

CHAPTER TWENTY TWO

Nietzsche said, 'We listen to music with our muscles.' He couldn't argue with this, Daniel Barone thought, as he steered his wheelchair in the direction of the Chopin prelude that was drifting down the passage towards him. He could feel his heartbeat responding to the music's melodic contours; its mathematical perfection.

He stopped his wheelchair at the threshold of the living room. Francis Godine was sitting at the piano, his eyes closed, his long fingers travelling over the keys with practised grace. His expression verged on ecstasy. God, music, memory: to Francis they used to be one and the same.

Francis looked so young. As he watched his friend, Barone could almost believe it was twenty-five years in the past and if he looked over his shoulder he might find the others in the room as well: Leon, urbane and amused, sipping one of his volcanic cocktails; Bella, draped across the sofa with self-conscious elegance; Julianne, throwing him a kiss.

Barone closed his eyes and felt the tears seep from beneath his lids. He so easily became emotional these days.

The music stopped. 'Daniel?' Barone opened his eyes to see Godine looking at him with alarm. 'Are you alright? Have you heard from the hospital?'

'No. Not yet.'

'Don't be afraid.'

'No.' But he was afraid, Barone thought. He was as afraid as he had ever been in his life.

Godine stood up and closed the piano. As he lowered the rounded lid, his finger caught on one of the keys, releasing a forlorn, solitary note.

'Come on.' Francis walked up to him and placed his hands at the back of the wheelchair, pushing it deeper into the room. 'Let's make a fire.'

A few minutes later a cheerful blaze was lighting up the hearth and Barone had a glass of cognac in his hand. It was amazing, he thought, how small rituals and comforts could ease the burden of memory and drive away the shadows.

He looked over to his friend, who was swirling the cognac in the balloon glass cradled in his palm.

'I think it is time we called Jack.'

Godine looked up from the glass, his expression suddenly wary.

'I haven't heard from him since that one email in which he said he had made contact. By this time they should be friends.'

'You know I think you should let this go, Daniel.'

'I know.'

'You know I think she is lost to us.'

'I can't allow her to be.'

Godine sighed. 'Alright. I'll get in touch with Jack tomorrow. But I wouldn't get my hopes up if I were you. If he's anything like his father, he won't exactly be dependable.'

'You still hate Leon. Even after all this time.'

Godine's lips thinned. 'I find him detestable. Even in the days when I considered him a friend, I knew he was a shallow man. To him, *Mnemosyne* was a chance to make money. He was blind to her sacred side.'

Barone smiled, a smile full of regret. 'You once accused Leon of not understanding the spiritual dimension of our work. Do you remember what his answer was? An old Chinese saying.'

'He who carves the Buddha never worships him.' Godine nodded. 'I remember. But that was just Leon being glib. Bella always said Leon interacts with the world in a way that strips it of its mystical power. That was one thing, at least, on which I agreed with her.'

'Why can't you forgive them, Francis? I have.'

'I know. What I don't understand is how.'

The bitterness in Godine's voice was so strong, Barone fell silent. But as he watched his friend lean forward and stoke the embers with nervous vigour, he was thinking that forgiving others was not difficult. It was forgiving yourself that was impossible.

CHAPTER TWENTY THREE

The girl who opened the door was a dead ringer for Lisbeth Salander. Eyebrow ring, kohl-blackened eyes, tattoo tendrils curling from underneath a flimsy tank top onto scrawny, pale-as-death arms.

Before Jack could introduce himself, she spoke. 'You Charlie's friend?'

'Yes. You must be Serena.'

She didn't answer but blew a large, perfectly formed bubble with her gum before opening the door wider. 'Come on in.'

He followed her into the apartment, which smelt overpoweringly of patchouli. The decor was minimalist: uncarpeted plank floors, a grimy-looking futon and a long bench with several computer monitors and other computer detritus. The only homey touch was a floor-to-ceiling poster of a one-eyed, leather-clad Kurt Russell as Snake Plisskin.

Jack wondered how Esquith knew the girl. His friend had been surprisingly coy on the subject and became increasingly evasive when Jack tried to probe. Suspicious. And intriguing. Jack hadn't thought Charlie's taste ran to techno-goth females who did a little off-the-books hacking on the side.

The computer screen showed scribbled figures and Jack recognised them as the numbers on the wall in Eloise's apartment. At Charlie's suggestion, he had forwarded the pictures on his mobile to Serena two days before. 'I have a friend who knows her way around code,' was how Esquith explained it. 'If there is a hidden meaning in these numbers, she'll find it.'

The girl took the gum out of her mouth and squished it up against the wall. Opening the drawer, she took out a fresh piece, which she popped into her mouth. She caught his eye. 'Trying to quit smoking.'

And believing in recycling, he thought, noticing several gum corpses littering the wall.

He looked away from the globs of masticated rubber. 'So what are these numbers? Code?'

The girl turned her smudged eyes at him. 'At the moment it's just shit.'

'What do you mean?'

'I have no idea if this is code or soup. Are you sure there is a source alphabet?' When he looked at her blankly, she said impatiently, 'Are you sure these numbers stand for something?'

'I was hoping they did.'

'Hmm. Well, I ran a brute force attack and came up with nothing. If there is an algorithm here, it is unknown to man.'

'So you're saying it's all just gibberish. Crazy writing.'

The girl must have picked up on the disappointment in his voice. She looked at him thoughtfully and blew a bubble.

'There is one more possibility.' Another contemplative bubble. 'This could be the key for a one-time pad.'

When he didn't respond, she sighed, 'You know, like spy stuff. Where the information – the plain text – is encrypted by using characters from a perfectly random key. During the Cold War spies wrote the messages onto these tiny paper pads so the top sheet can be torn off and destroyed for security. One-time pads.' She shrugged. 'It's old school but it works. A one-time pad is impossible to break. The key is completely random and never used again.'

'So what you're saying is you can't break this.'

'I'm saying I can't break this.'

He stared at the screen, feeling impossibly frustrated. But something was nagging at the back of his mind.

'*The Human Factor.*'

'What?' She looked at him strangely.

'Graham Greene.'

'Who's Graham Greene?'

'Never mind. You said spies used one-time pads. Didn't they also use books as their source material?'

'A running key cipher. Yeah. Where the number points to the specific location of a letter in a book. You think that's what this is?' She glanced at the screen. 'Cool. But I still can't break the code if I don't have the book that was used as the source. And not just any copy of the book. The exact edition.'

'Because the layout of every edition is different.' He spoke slowly as comprehension dawned. 'If you don't have the edition that was used by the sender, you may get the wrong location and the wrong letter if you try to match the numbers to the text. Of course. It makes sense now.'

'Do you know which book and which edition was used as the source?'

'Books. Plural. If I'm right, there are three of them: all rare editions with small print runs. One of the books is a misprinted copy.'

'Smart.' She snapped her fingers. 'Misprints are the best. The fewer copies available, the higher the security and the closer you get to a one-time pad.'

She put her head to one side and looked him up and down. 'What's all this about, anyway? Charlie didn't tell me. What's the big secret?'

'I'm trying to help a damsel in distress.'

She lifted a cynical eyebrow. 'How sweet.' Pulling the piece of gum in a long swag from her mouth, she contemplated it carefully before popping it back in again. 'Well, Sir Galahad. Bring me the books and I'll help you rescue your lady. But I need the books.'

And that was going to be the challenge. The possibility of tracking down duplicate copies of the exact editions of the books hidden in the bottom drawer of Eloise's dressing table was slim to none.

He sighed. 'I'll get them for you.'

As they walked to the door, she said, 'I'm not doing this for free, yeah?'

'Sorry, yes. What are your fees?'

She grinned open-mouthed and he saw a metal stud winking from the middle of her tongue. 'No, Charlie and I have an arrangement. Just remind him he promised me three nights.' She drooped one eyelid in which he realised was meant to be a lascivious wink.

Before he could think of a suitable response, his mobile phone pinged. Text message.

'Bad news?'

He pushed the phone back in his trouser pocket. 'I've been summoned.'

CHAPTER TWENTY FOUR

'Jack, good to see you again.' Daniel Barone smiled and pointed his wheelchair in Jack's direction. The chair sped forward smoothly and silently.

Jack shook the hand offered to him and looked over to the other man in the room who was sitting quietly to one side in a deep wing-backed chair. Aquiline nose, trim beard, heavy-lidded eyes. It was the man he had watched drive away in the Jaguar the first time he had visited Whiteladies. And again the man's face stirred a memory. Jack knew they had never met but he had seen this man before; there was no doubt in his mind. He simply couldn't place where and when.

'This is Francis Godine, my oldest friend.'

'Pleased to meet you.' Jack held out his hand. Godine nodded with cool civility.

'Can I offer you a drink?' Barone asked. 'Something to eat, maybe?'

'Thank you. But I had a sandwich on the train.'

Godine was looking at him with an expression as though he had suddenly come across an interesting, but not very appetising, species of lepidopteron.

'You look like your father but your accent is American.' The way Godine said 'American' did not make it sound like a compliment. Jack sighed inwardly. The man must be one of those stuck-up Brits who thought all Americans were Elvis impersonators.

'Francis teaches at Oxford,' Barone said hastily. 'Medieval studies. He is one of the foremost experts in the world on Meister Eckhart. Meister Eckhart was—'

'—a fourteenth-century mystic tried as a heretic by Pope John XXII.' Let no one say he couldn't be erudite too.

Barone's lips twitched. 'Just so.' He gestured at the sofa. 'Please. Take a seat.' When Jack had settled himself, he continued, his voice edged with barely concealed impatience. 'You've made contact with Jenilee. What can you tell us?'

'Not much to report, really. She seems fine.'

'No other accidents or strange happenings?'

'No.'

'Are you sure? I don't want you to become complacent, Jack.'

'Believe me, Mr Barone, I am keeping close watch.'

'And she still remembers nothing?' Godine this time.

'No.'

'Is she happy?' Barone leant forward, his eyes searching.

Happy? In Jack's mind came the image of Eloise running beside him, her face ecstatic, her cheeks reddened from the wind, her movements joyous.

'I think she is. Most of the time.'

Barone's voice was suddenly filled with quiet fury. 'How can she be happy if she is no longer who she truly is? She needs to be here. I need to help her.'

'Daniel …' There was a warning note in Godine's voice.

'Can I ask you something?' Jack looked at Barone, ignoring Godine. 'If I manage to persuade her to return to Whiteladies, how confident are you that you will be able to restore her memory? You were working on some kind of experimental drug before you retired, isn't that right?'

'Yes.' Barone spoke without enthusiasm. 'But my particular expertise lay in weakening memories, not restoring them. My work was aimed at helping addicts forget their learned

behaviour, or helping victims of violent crime. Or soldiers dealing with post-traumatic stress.'

'And Eloise's mother? I understand her research was about
restoring memories.'

For a moment Barone hesitated, and Jack had a strong
impression he was reluctant to answer. But then he nodded.
'Yes, Julianne approached the memory molecule from a different angle. She wanted to help people remember.'

'Would she have been able to help Eloise?'

'Who knows?' Barone suddenly sounded very tired. 'Her
research never came to conclusion.'

'So there's nothing really you can do for Eloise.' In the
truly honest part of him, Jack felt a guilty sense of relief.

'I wouldn't say that.' Barone's voice was stronger. 'I may
not be able to inject Jenilee with a wonder drug, but I believe
strongly that if she receives professional therapy and if we
bring her to Whiteladies where her life is calm and secure, she
may exit the fugue state involuntarily.'

'If this happens, will she still remember her life as Eloise?'
Jack held his breath.

'No. Eloise will be gone. It will be like wiping away a
secondary painting and revealing the original underneath.'
Something must have moved in Jack's face because Barone
continued, 'Keep in mind, Jack: the first painting is the original. The second layer is fake.'

Fake. The girl who dances in the garden at night. Who
keeps a rose next to her bed. Who runs across rooftops.

For a few moments the room was silent. The light from
the table lamp streamed directly onto Barone's face, allowing
Jack to see the network of lines around the man's eyes. Next to
him, Godine's face was thrown into half-shadow by the deep
wings of the chair in which he sat. But as he watched them
side by side, it struck Jack that although the two men did not
at all resemble each other in appearance, there was something
about their bearing which was similar. It would be difficult to
articulate what it was, except to say that both men exuded a
kind of inner stillness and a single-minded focus that told of

discipline, rigour and study. They seemed to belong to another, more formal age, far removed from the white noise and banality of the present.

What happened next was disconcerting. Barone suddenly leant forward. 'Is she happy?' It was the same question he had asked only minutes before. Even the inflection of his voice was identical.

Jack looked at him uncertainly. From the corner of his eye, he sensed Godine stiffen.

'Er … yes, I think she is. Most of the time.'

'How can she be happy if she is no longer who she truly is?'

Jack stared. But before he could respond, Godine was on his feet. 'Daniel. You're tired.' He turned to Jack, his expression remote. 'I think you may wish to retire. I'll show you to your room.'

'Of course.' Jack got up, feeling a little like a kid who was being sent to bed early. He nodded his goodnight at Barone, who was staring at him with a disconcertingly blank expression. Had the man been drinking?

Godine gestured impatiently and Jack followed him out of the room. At the door he looked over his shoulder. Barone was staring out of the window, his profile calm and handsome. But then he turned his head and the expression in his eyes took away Jack's breath. It was the expression of a man who considered himself quite lost.

Jack slept as though dead until two-twenty exactly. What it was that woke him, he didn't know, but when he opened his eyes, the first thing he saw was the illuminated face of the old-fashioned clock on the bedside table.

For a moment, as his clouded gaze wandered over the dark shapes of the furniture around him, he was disoriented, thinking himself to be in his room in Charlie's apartment and wondering with a distant sense of dread why someone had rearranged the furniture while he was asleep.

A sudden, vicious rattle of wind shook the windowpane and shocked him fully awake.

He padded in his bare feet to the window and looked out. The garden below appeared like a bad dream: all black clawed trees and moon-drenched lawn. A long, jagged line of cloud hung above the glassy river.

He turned back to the bed and switched on the bedside lamp. Even though he was now wide awake – in fact, he knew it was going to be impossible for him to drift off again – the sense of unease with which he had woken up was lingering. Not to put too fine a point on it, he was feeling distinctly creeped out.

He looked at the sturdy oak door. There was no key with which to lock it. For a moment he had the rather horrible feeling that there was someone lurking behind it. If he dropped his eye to the keyhole, maybe he'd find another eye staring back at him.

Bloody hell, Jack. Get a grip.

With a sudden movement he grabbed the dressing-gown hanging from the bedpost. Still in his bare feet, he opened the door with a firm hand and stepped out.

The passage lay empty in front of him. The doors flanking the passage were shut but the moonlight shining through the oculus set high into the wall allowed more than enough light to show him the way. At the end of the corridor, open and silent, was the steel cage of the lift which Godine had told him Barone had installed after his accident. Next to it the Queen Anne staircase dropped down into shadow.

Swiftly he descended the staircase into the darkened hall. To his left was the door to the study. It was closed. But his interest was not in the study. When he had arrived at Whiteladies last night, he had noticed Scott wheeling the drinks trolley from the study into the adjoining room. A glass of Barone's splendid Macallan was exactly what he needed.

He turned the handle and pushed open the door. This room was pitch black, the heavy curtains shutting out even the faintest glimmer of light. He moved his hand across the wall, his fingers searching – and then finding – the old-fashioned toggle of the light switch.

For a moment he stood blinking against the sudden brightness. Just as he had hoped, next to the fireplace was the drinks trolley. But the bottle of Macallan was missing: he was going to have to make do with Johnny Walker Blue Label. A disappointment, but better than nothing. He poured himself a stiff two fingers.

Glass in hand, he looked around him. It was a pleasant room. It suddenly struck him that Eloise would have been a frequent visitor. She would have been familiar with its graceful proportions. She would have known how the armchair had a permanent indent in the seat; her fingers would have dialled the keys of the phone resting on the table. The idea of it was jarring, somehow. He couldn't picture Eloise at home here among the flowered chintz, embroidered throws and soft cushions. Eloise with her small, callused hands, her whiplash frame, her reckless smile. But, of course, she hadn't been Eloise, then. In those days she was Jenilee Gray and Jenilee had looked at the world with far less fire in her soul.

A number of photographs were arranged on an incidental table. Jack walked over to take a look. There was Barone, the picture obviously taken before his accident. He looked rakish and handsome in an open-necked polo shirt, his hand on the bridle of a skittish-eyed horse. Next to this picture was a black and white photograph of a smiling woman with an old-fashioned hairstyle. Barone's mother? But it was the gold-framed photograph at the back which made Jack reach out his hand. He picked it up, surprised at its weight.

It was the same group picture as the one in his father's study. The only difference was that this photograph was captioned. In flowing italic script was printed: *The Order of Mnemosyne*. Below it, written by hand, were the following words: *Frater L.E.O., Frater C.U.I., Soror A.V.I.A.F., Soror Q.M.N.M.D., Frater A.V.A.M., Soror N.O.M.*

Latin again. Jack took a gulp of his whisky. *Frater* and *Soror*. The members of the Order of Mnemosyne had referred to each other as 'brother' and 'sister'. The initials, though, were gobbledygook.

But there, staring him in the face, was the answer to the question as to where he had seen Godine before. He was the first man on the left. In the picture he was clean-shaven but it was definitely him. *Frater L.E.O.*

Jack studied the photograph more closely. They really had been a handsome group, exuding the kind of impervious confidence bestowed by wealth, breeding or brains. The men were tall and strong; the women beautiful. The blonde immediately drew the eye with her languid gaze and sensuous mouth. The second girl was lovely too, but whereas the blonde was a sophisticate, this girl was not as wise. She had a heart-shaped face, wispy brown hair and a fey expression. Julianne Gray: Eloise's mother. Behind her, towering over her slight figure, was his father, one hand resting on the girl's narrow shoulder.

Was there something in that gesture? Now that he was paying close attention to the picture, it seemed to him as though his father's hand rested on Julianne Gray's shoulder with more than a little possessiveness. Maybe something not quite platonic had been going on between Brother *A.V.A.M* and Sister *N.O.M*. He once again remembered his mother's frown when he had asked her about the picture, the way her fingers had played over the faces trapped behind glass. *When your father moved to the States he said he lost touch with all of them, except Daniel.*

Jack suddenly yawned uncontrollably. Time to return to bed. As he switched off the light, plunging the room into darkness once again, he suddenly noticed strange flickers of light shining underneath the door leading to the study. At the same moment, he heard voices. He must have been listening to the voices for some time without realising. As his conscious mind focused on the fact that there were voices coming from the next room, he also knew with certainty that the voices had been there all along. It was an unsettling feeling. He stood motionless, straining his ears. The voices were muted, barely within hearing range, but they were there.

He walked over and placed his hand on the door. The light moved jerkily in the gap between the door and the wooden floor, creating crazy shadows on the threshold. He turned the knob.

Sitting with his back to him was Godine. His legs were propped up on a coffee table on which stood the missing bottle of Macallan. It was empty. Godine was sprawling loose-limbed, his head lolling against the back of the sofa. In his hand, carelessly cradled, was a glass. It too was empty.

The light and shadow play Jack had noticed underneath the door was being created by images on a television screen. A woman with a cloud of blonde hair was looking straight into the camera, a slight frown of concentration on her face. She was standing on a patch of emerald-green grass and behind her was a glimpse of sun-struck water. No doubt about it, he was looking at the front lawn of Whiteladies. And he immediately recognised the blonde as one of the women in the group picture. She was the girl with the ripe mouth.

'Are you ready?' Her voice was light and breathy. Without waiting for an answer, she lobbed the cricket ball in her hand in the direction of someone off-camera. There was the sound of the ball striking the stumps, a man's voice cursing and then a whoop of joy from the person holding the video camera. 'Out for a duck! Well done!' It was another woman – this voice sounding strangely familiar. As she spoke the video camera swerved a little.

'Thanks, Julianne.' The blonde girl smiled triumphantly and pumped the air.

Julianne. Eloise's mother. She must be the woman holding the camera. She was now addressing the man, who was still out of range of the camera's viewfinder. 'Pretty pathetic performance, darling.' She sounded just like her daughter: the same low, husky tones.

'I'll show you pathetic!' The man's voice was much closer now and with a shock Jack recognised it. His heart suddenly pounding, he watched the viewfinder jerk wildly as Julianne Gray shrieked with laughter. 'Get off me, you big bully!'

The camera dipped away and there was a confused jumble of images as Julianne dropped her arm and the viewfinder swept aimlessly across the ground. There was a quick glimpse of feet in high-heeled sandals and then a man's legs dressed in chinos. But after a few more erratic swings, the camera steadied itself and focused directly on the man's face: a man with black hair and blue eyes. He was curling one hand into a claw; brandishing the cricket bat menacingly in the other. 'I am coming for you,' he intoned zombie-like, pushing his face closer and closer to the lens.

Godine pointed the remote at the set and hit the pause button at the exact moment Leon Simonetti's features filled the entire frame, monstrously distorted.

'Come in, Jack.' Godine looked at him over his shoulder. 'Come have a drink.' He motioned vaguely at the empty Macallan bottle.

Jack glanced again at his father's frozen face on the screen. *Oh, man.*

'Take a seat.' Godine was insistent. After a moment of hesitation, Jack obeyed. The floor was littered with stacks of old-fashioned video cassettes and he had to pick his way carefully in order to reach the armchair. He sat down, making sure his back was facing the screen. He certainly didn't feel like staring at a close-up of his parent's nostrils.

'Cheers.' Godine lifted his glass to his mouth. He didn't seem surprised to find it empty.

For a long moment there was silence between them. Godine placed the glass on the coffee table and held his head in both hands.

Jack grimaced. Maybe he could slip out again: the man probably wouldn't even notice he was no longer there. But then Godine lifted his head.

'Love is strong as death, hard as hell.'

As conversational gambits go, this one was a doozy. Jack racked his brains for a snappy response. 'Er, right.'

'Meister Eckhart said that.'

'Oh?' Jack was impressed. Pretty rock-and-roll for a medieval mystic.

'Yes.' Godine nodded emphatically. 'Some women should come with warning labels.'

Jack was startled. 'Meister Eckhart said that too?'

'No, no.' Godine waved his hand irritably. 'Now, your father,' Godine pointed at the screen, 'he knew a thing or two about women. Quite the ladies' man, was Leon. Don't you agree?'

He could, but he said nothing. 'But I have to hand it to him,' Godine continued. 'Your father never allowed his heart to rule his head. He kept his eye on the ball. A clever man, your father. Pragmatic. He is not like Daniel.' Godine placed his palm gently on his heart. 'Sweet Daniel.'

Uh, oh. Jack moved to the edge of his seat. Time for him to get off of this ride.

'Do you know what Daniel's motto was? *Credo ut intelligam*: I believe, so that I may understand. Daniel embodied the perfect balance of science and faith. The world was robbed of a great intellect when Daniel Barone closed the book on Mnemosyne. But he will still be remembered as a giant. And as a good man.'

'I'm sure.' Jack placed his hands on the armrest of the chair, readying himself.

'Sit down.' Godine's hand shot out with surprising strength and grabbed Jack's wrist. 'Are you religious, Jack?'

Jack sighed. 'Not really.'

'Do you know what Nanrei Kobori said?'

'Nanrei Kobori? No.'

'He said God is an invention of Man. So the nature of God is only a shallow mystery. The deep mystery is the nature of Man.'

'I see.'

'And what else is Man but the sum of his memories?' Godine tilted his head towards the television screen. 'See that? That is recorded memory. Accurate. Unanswerable. You can watch this footage a hundred years from now and it will not have changed. The brain is not like that. People think the brain is this vast storage room, Jack, and if we can only find the right tool – a drug, a brain scan, hypnosis – we will be able to extract all our memories, flawless and intact, not altered in any way. They are wrong. No.' Godine shook his head. 'No, no, no.'

'No?'

'The brain is not a storage bunker. It is alive. It records, but it also transforms. And that's why our entire legal system is based on a fallacy. We value confident witnesses whose testimony is clear, and rich in detail. We regard such testimony as truthful and we scorn the witness who hesitates, contradicts himself and whose recollection of events is vague. But scientific evidence has shown again and again that the vividness and detail of a person's memories have very little to do with accuracy.'

Well, if that was true, it just about kicked the crap out of every single crime show on TV, Jack thought.

'Julianne believed we could change this. Julianne was convinced we could get people to remember exactly: like a recording on a camera. But she was misguided. Man is not a machine. The brain is alchemy. As soon as a memory enters the mind, it has already changed. The brain fuses reality with our longings and passions. Our mind changes the way we remember and creates a sense of self, which is unique.'

Godine leant forward. If not for his eyes, and the smell on his breath, you would not know he was drunk.

'Only the human brain is capable of this, Jack. This truly is what sets us apart. No other animal has the ability to use memory to create identity. Only Man.'

Godine's face was so close to his own, Jack could see a tiny nerve jumping at the edge of his left eye. There was something about this scene – the man opposite him staring blindly; his father's trapped face on the screen behind him – which made the moment feel unreal, as though he was, in fact, still asleep in his bed and it was his midnight self who had gone wandering.

'But it was a worthy goal, don't you think?' Godine leant even closer. 'To study and understand memory in all its mystery?'

Godine was now nodding his head over and over again as though unable to stop himself: like a bobble-headed doll. It was rather horrible to watch.

'We thought we would do such good in this world, Jack – our little band of brothers and sisters.' Still his head continued its unnerving up-and-down rhythm. 'Our knowledge would help the soldier get rid of the memories that drive him mad; help the elderly ward off dementia; assist those with learning disabilities. We thought … we might even be able to look upon the face of God. Mnemosyne was a prayer.'

He stopped nodding and looked at Jack with feverish eyes.

'A dark prayer. Worth any sacrifice?'

When Jack didn't answer, his hand shot out and again Jack felt the long fingers tighten around his wrist. He could smell the sweat and alcohol coming in waves off Godine's skin.

'Would you say it is worth the sacrifice of a child?'

Jack felt queasy. 'What do you mean?'

But Godine's face had gone empty. His eyes dulled and he sagged back against the sofa.

'What do you mean?' Jack spoke again, louder.

'Go away.' Godine hunched a petulant shoulder. 'Go away. I want to be alone.'

'Talk to me, dammit.' Jack placed his hand on the man's shoulder and shook it. 'Does any of this have to do with Eloise?'

'Eloise.' Godine started to laugh. A long drool of spit trailed from the corner of his mouth. 'Eloise! "How happy is the blameless vestal's lot! The world forgetting, by the world forgot".'

Jack drew back. There was a cold lump at the pit of his stomach. He wanted quite badly to get out of this room and away from the man whose head lolled against the sofa and who was laughing weakly, his face slack.

He got up and, in his haste, stepped on one of the video-tapes. The splintering crack was loud but Godine seemed not to notice. As Jack fled the room, the recorder behind him was switched on again. The last thing he heard as he pulled the door behind him was Eloise's mother laughing and his father's voice saying, 'You know you can't escape!'

CHAPTER TWENTY FIVE

Memory image 12784

Jenilee is starting to resist. Yesterday, when I picked up the video recorder, she slapped at it petulantly. I think she is beginning to realise there is a link between the recorder and 'movie time' and 'movie time' is no longer fun. It is becoming more and more of a struggle to persuade her to cooperate. I have to resort to bribing: a sweet, a cuddly toy, promises that it will all soon end. Strangely, the visits to the laboratory hold no terrors for her. She seems at ease with the needles, the syringes, the sterile whiteness of the environment. But these sessions in the cosy comfort of our living room drive her to tears.

Leon thinks I should not soothe her. If she is distressed, she may remember more. But she is older now, and the relationship between fear and memory is a delicate one. Fear can etch details into your memory banks with the precision of a scalpel – or blind you like a blunt tool.

Jenilee is sitting in my arms, clutching the big pink lollipop in her small fist.

'Look at the lollipop, sweetheart. Isn't it pretty?'

Jenilee nods.

'If light has no age, perhaps time has no shadow.'

Jenilee repeats the phrase flawlessly. By this time she knows it well.

'If you do not know where you are going, all roads lead there.'

Again her voice follows mine obediently.

'If no one looks at the moon, will it disappear?'

Her delivery is again without error but she now sounds drowsy, even though her eyes are wide open. I point the remote at the TV set and the screen comes alive. The front lawn of Whiteladies. Bella and Leon are standing next to each other under the oak tree. I had shot this footage on a zoom setting through the window of Daniel's office without their knowledge. Bella is standing very close to Leon. He is not touching her and I cannot see his expression. I don't have to.

I glance down at Jenilee. Her eyes are watching the flickering images on the screen; her gaze is opaque.

'How does this make Mummy feel?' I ask her.

She answers without hesitation. 'Mummy feels sad.'

I nod. She's right. Mummy feels sad.

I remove the lollipop, which is drooping from her hand. Tears are rolling from her eyes. When I look up, I stare into my own eyes in the mirror on the wall opposite.

Mummy is going mad.

CHAPTER TWENTY SIX

Mr Henderson stopped Eloise just as she was about to enter the building. She was tired and hungry and looking forward to tucking into the Chinese takeaway and the bottle of beer she had picked up at the market. But it was painfully obvious that the old man was lonely. He kept touching her arm, speaking continuously in his soft monotone voice. He was becoming so deaf that it was difficult to have a conversation with him, but she knew it was the human contact he craved. So she followed him into his small, overly heated living room and allowed him to make her tea: 'Your favourite, Eloise.' He always said that. Truth to tell, she had never much liked Earl Grey but didn't have the heart to say so.

He was now telling her how he had called in the police earlier in the day to help him get rid of a rough sleeper. Keeping the building free of squatters was a constant battle and this one had acted belligerent when asked to leave. 'So rude,' Mr Henderson said, his voice quivering with indignation, 'and he had a *hammer*.' She listened without comment but couldn't help but feel sympathy for the intruder. How was she any different? And if this building was ever repossessed and redeveloped, there was no knowing where she might end up.

It was a full forty minutes later before she was able to break away and head to her own apartment. But as she pushed her key into the lock, she hesitated and looked around her, suddenly unwilling to go inside.

It was the blue hour: her favourite time of the day. The autumn chill was decidedly bracing but the dusky sky was beautiful. Maybe she should brave the cold and have her dinner on the roof.

The roof itself was not attractive. It was home to an old meat locker, a rusted bed, an assortment of messy paint cans and empty drums with the bungs showing. But she liked the view. She sat down on the very edge, her legs hanging over the side.

The street below her dangling feet was deserted but the noise of traffic was in the air and if she leant forward slightly and looked to the right, she could just glimpse the high street with its row of curry shops and its frenetic roundabout. The building across the road from her was boarded up but, two blocks away, yellow light lit up a row of windows in a converted warehouse. Jazz dancers were practising on the first floor, their figures shaking with manic energy.

She opened her Moo Shu Pork and twisted open the cap on the Kirin. Tilting back her head, she took a swig. Way up high, a blinking plane was flying in slow motion and behind it a washed-out moon hung against the sky like an airy ghost. It would be a wonderful night to go free running.

Thinking of parkour made her think of Jack. She wondered where he was. She still had the gloves he had accidentally left behind at Jungles' stall and she had hoped to return them to him at this morning's run. But he wasn't there. She had been surprised at how acute the pang of disappointment was when he failed to turn up. She didn't like it. It was not like her: acting like a teenager with a crush.

Even so, there was no reason why she should not let him know about the gloves. She slipped her phone from her jacket and hesitated.

What damage could it do?

He had given her two phone numbers: mobile and home. She dialled the mobile first but the call immediately went through to his voicemail and she hung up without leaving a message. She would try the home number.

The phone kept ringing. She was just about to hang up when there was a click and a voice came on the line. A woman's voice. It was so unexpected, she couldn't react for a moment. Jack had told her he was rooming with a 'buddy', but she had assumed the buddy to be male.

'Hello?' the woman asked again, sounding impatient.

She cleared her throat. 'I'm looking for Jack?'

'Who is this, please?' The voice was young and fresh. Very crisp, very upper-crust.

'Uh. This is Eloise.' When there was no response, she continued, 'We do, uh, parkour together.'

'Oh!' A pause. 'I'm afraid Jack's not here at the moment.' She lengthened the vowel just slightly. *Ja-ack*. Like a caress. 'But I'm expecting him any minute. Can I take a message?'

'No, that's alright. I'll catch him another time.'

'Alright then,' the girl said cheerily. 'Goodbye!' The next moment the phone was disconnected.

She lowered her mobile phone slowly. The girl had sounded young, but casually confident; exactly like the kind of girl she'd expect to find hanging around Jack. Posh. Someone who read *Tatler* and had her nails cared for at the Dorchester. Who did St Moritz in winter and the Cote d'Azur in summer. Delicately tanned. Long legs. She'd wear fun, but seriously expensive, clothes.

So what? What was it to her?

Jack made her laugh. He was sexy as hell. But his world and hers were two separate planets spinning at very different speeds. The chances of her playing Cinderella to his Prince Charming were exactly nil. *And don't you forget it*, she told herself sternly. He was hardly likely to slum it with a woman he must in any case think of as being wrong in the head.

She returned the empty food container and beer bottle to the plastic bag. The evening had suddenly lost its magic.

A sound behind her made her turn her head sharply. It had sounded like something was out there ... slithering?

She peered into the shadows. Since she had finished her meal, darkness had fallen, softening the texture and outlines of objects. The meat locker looked just slightly sinister. But she could see nothing moving except for a moth, which flew straight at her face like a kamikaze pilot. She waved her hand and it veered off.

OK. Time to escape the cold and the creepiness. She picked up the plastic bag and got to her feet.

But inside the apartment it still felt cold. There was no central heating up here on the top floor. When winter kicked in properly it would be even colder. Cheery thought.

She dropped the bag into the bin before walking to the dressing table and opening the bottom drawer.

She did not take out the three books; she simply stared at them longingly. *The Compleat Angler. Neuromancer. Septem Sermones ad Mortuos.* She had read the first two books several times and had even tried to work her way through the third with the help of a German dictionary in the Kensington library, but she was still clueless. These books held the answer but she wasn't even sure of the question.

She looked towards the far end of the room, half-expecting to see a pale-haired woman and three men whispering secrets, their voices like rustling leaves. But there was no one there.

In the early days she had screamed at the figures. There was still a splash mark on the wall where she had thrown her coffee cup at them. It had had no effect, of course. They were like actors caught on a virtual reel of film that could not be stopped. It was a film prepared just for her – but it came without a remote control. No way to fast-forward or rewind. No off button.

And then there were the numbers. The numbers were as close as her soul, as remote as stars in outer space. She did not understand what they meant or why they filled her thoughts. If asked to, she could have recited them by heart, but they meant nothing to her. At first she had written them down on paper but as the digits kept multiplying in her brain, she started filling the walls. At night, in her bed, she would feel them all around her. Even in her sleep she was held captive in the sticky numerical web spinning endlessly from her mind. The same numbers in the same sequence every time.

Madness.

She slammed the bottom drawer shut and heard the books inside knock against the side. A wave of hopelessness washed over her. Ghosts peopling her life; voices whispering in the dark. Numbers marching through her head and onto the walls of her apartment. Books that held the key, except she had no idea where to find the lock.

Well, no use sitting here feeling sorry for herself. She came to a sudden decision and started stripping off her clothes. With firm movements, she wrapped herself in her towelling robe. A hot bath was what she needed. A hot bath with some of the wonderful rose oil to which she had treated herself only the day before. A hot, fragrant bath and afterwards everything would be right with the world again.

The builders had never got around to installing a bathroom in this apartment, but there was one in another unit one storey below. Number 406 was small and boxy but it boasted a finished bathroom and Mr Henderson always made sure there was hot water. The apartment had no light fixtures, only thick coloured wires dangling from the low ceiling, but a long row of scented candles on the bathroom windowsill provided all the light she needed.

To walk up and down between the two apartments, however, required a torch as it was black as pitch inside the stairwell after sunset. She removed the torch from underneath the kitchen sink, tested it and headed for the door.

As she stepped outside, the small circle of yellow probed the dense darkness. It was very quiet inside the stairwell, the sound of traffic reduced to a distant hum by the close, surrounding walls. Her slippers were warm but they were fluffy and awkward, forcing her to walk slowly and to set her feet squarely on every step.

It was as she was turning the corner of the first flight down that she felt the hairs on her arms rise. Her fingertips tingled. There was something – someone – close by.

She spun around and shone the torch up the empty stairs behind her.

'Mr Henderson?'

Her voice bounced off the walls. She listened. The building was utterly silent. She could hear the muted roar of a motorcycle but it was streets away. The immediate air around her was still.

Imagination. If she wasn't careful she would become so paralysed with imaginings she wouldn't recognise real danger when she had to. Breathing through her mouth, she moved forward again, overly aware of her slippered feet making shuffling noises. The torch in her hand moved jerkily.

Something soft and ghost-like brushed against her.

Her breath exploded from her chest in a huge, terrified gasp. The torch slipped from her floppy fingers, fell, and rolled in a madly spinning circle of light, on and on in crazy circles, bumping down the stairs until it stopped – the beam suddenly steady and pointing unwaveringly upwards. It focused on the cat, who was watching her with arched spine and glittering eyes.

For a moment she just stood there staring at it, unable to move. She could hear the beating of her heart in her ears. Her tongue felt furred and there was a sour aftertaste of fear in her mouth.

The tom relaxed its tense muscles and waited for her as she walked down the steps with weak legs, retrieving the torch with still trembling fingers. It stayed close to her side and when she pushed open the door to number 406, she found it following at her heels.

Her heartbeat was evening out. She made her way through the empty living room and sensed tiny pieces of grit pushing against the thin soles of her slippers. Because it had its own bathroom, she sometimes considered abandoning her loft and moving into this apartment instead, but each time the cramped dimensions of the rooms and the horrible spray-painted cement ceiling dissuaded her.

Inside the white-tiled bathroom, she placed the torch on the windowsill and picked up the box of matches. They must have become damp since the last time she used them, because the first two matches refused to strike. But the third match burst into flame and she touched it to the wicks of the seven candles lined up along the windowsill. As she switched off the torch, the cat jumped up and settled itself on the vanity unit, its long tail twitching lazily, its coat pale cream in the glow of the flickering flames.

She closed the bathroom door – not that there was anyone around to disturb her privacy – but the room was chilly. After pouring a generous scoop of bath oil into the bath, she leant over and reached for the hot water tap. The water rushed out and soon a satisfying cloud of fragrant steam filled the room. Moisture beaded the tall mirror and gave a watery reflection to the tiny, winking candles.

She slipped off her robe and lowered herself into the water. Leaning back against the side of the bath, she allowed the rose-scented bubbles to lap at her chin.

Bliss.

When the door behind her opened, she did not so much hear it as feel it. It was only a soft breath of air, but it made the flames of the candles sway and it cooled the back of her neck.

CHAPTER TWENTY SEVEN

Jack arrived at Charlie's apartment feeling tired and thoroughly out of temper. He had left Whiteladies early in the morning after a solitary breakfast served to him by the taciturn Scott – no sign of either Barone or Godine – and had believed he would find himself back in London around lunchtime. A series of signal failures, however, had led to a three-hour wait at Whitley train station, followed by a miserable journey as the jam-packed train moved towards London at a pace any self-respecting snail would have sneered at.

To make matters immeasurably worse, Jack had found himself hemmed in by the family from hell: Mummy, Daddy and four anarchic children. The mother was a fluttery-voiced woman who had no hope of controlling her brood and the father distanced himself from the mayhem by snapping Bose noise-cancelling headphones onto his head and burying his nose in some paperwork. As if the constant bickering between the siblings wasn't enough of an ordeal, the youngest member of the family, a seven-year-old with a brutal haircut, started throwing his toys over the back of Jack's seat like missiles, several of which caught Jack painfully on the head. Each time he turned his head to glare, the kid would stare grimly back at him. It was a battle of wills he had no chance of winning.

It was already dusk by the time he climbed the stairs to Charlie's apartment. But as he pushed open the front door, he realised his day was not yet through.

'Jack!'

Alice unfolded herself from the couch where she had been lounging and flung herself across the room at him. Her arms flew around his neck and she immediately started to squeeze.

Jack gave an agonised look over her shoulder at Esquith, who had stepped out of the kitchenette and was watching his sister with a wide grin.

'How are you, sweetheart?' With difficulty, Jack managed to pry himself from her limpet grip.

'Devastated that you haven't come to see me!' She pouted fetchingly.

'Charlie told me you were in the Bahamas.'

'I got back yesterday! Swimsuit issue! But the weather was foul! I almost froze to death!'

Alice spoke in exclamation marks, which had a certain chirpy charm at first, but became trying very quickly indeed. In her short life, she had flitted from one pastime to another until, much to the dismay of the Esquith family, she decided the modelling world was to be her oyster. The first time they were introduced to each other, she had given Jack an eye-popping publicity photograph of herself flirting with a piece of chocolate. She had autographed the picture with the words, 'You deserve something sweet' – the 'sweet' festooned with hearts and followed by a number of suggestive dots. Alice was kind-hearted and undeniably pretty and had told him he had supplanted David Beckham on her list, which he gathered was the ultimate compliment. But, as he also discovered, to be the object of undiluted adoration could be exhausting.

She was now dragging him to the sofa. 'It is so wonderful that you're here! I brought a bottle of Cristal to celebrate! Charlie!' She waved her hand in a kind of 'go, fetch' gesture. 'Now!' She pushed Jack down. 'Tell me *every*thing!'

Fortunately, it seemed this demand was not to be taken seriously because she immediately launched into a description of her own recent trip, which involved missing luggage, a sullen stylist called Enrique and a shoot, which was 'just *hell*!'

Jack sagged against the sofa cushions and allowed the tide of happy inanity to flow over him. He took the glass of champagne from Charles, avoiding his friend's sardonic gaze, and drank deeply.

Having exhausted her Bahamas adventure, Alice trained her focus on him.

'So, Jack. Charlie tells me you've hooked up with a group of free runners! Wicked!'

He nodded, feeling slightly woozy. His last meal had been at Whiteladies a lifetime ago and the Cristal was going straight to his head.

'You *must* take me with you one day! Oh, I forgot! Someone called for you!'

'Oh?'

'She said she runs with you! But I forgot her name! Silly me!'

He sat up straight. 'Eloise?'

'Could be …'

He reached for his bag and removed his mobile phone from the zipped outside pocket. He had switched it off on the train because the battery was running low. And there it was: one missed call from Eloise Blake. She hadn't left a message.

He lowered the phone. 'Did she say why she wanted to speak to me?

'No! She said she'd catch you later!' Alice looked at him anxiously.

He got to his feet. 'I need to call her back.'

'OK! But don't dawdle! I've made us reservations at Colbert's! And then we're meeting friends of mine at Boujis! I want to show you off!'

He gave a vague wave and headed down the passage to his room. Once inside, he closed the door behind him and hit the return call button. A click. Voicemail kicking in. 'This is Eloise. You know what to do.'

'Eloise.' He paused, at a loss how to continue. 'I'm return-ing your call. Actually ... I need to talk to you. Urgently. Please ring me back.'

He switched off, feeling frustrated. His eyes came to rest on his bag. Opening the top flap, he removed the framed pho-tograph inside.

It was the picture of the members of Mnemosyne. On a sudden impulse he had slipped it into his bag just before leav-ing Whiteladies. It was quite bulky and what Barone would do if he noticed the photograph missing, was another question. But after his dead-of-night conversation with Godine, he was convinced that something about the Order of Mnemosyne was off. Somehow – and the connection was still wholly unclear to him – these three men and two women were responsible for what had happened to Eloise. It made no sense, but he knew it in his gut.

There was a knock on the door and Charlie put his head around it.

'Are you coming?'

When Jack didn't answer, Esquith entered the room fully. 'What's this?' He reached for the photograph in Jack's hands. 'Is this your father?'

'When he was living in Oxford.'

'Who are the hot women?'

'That's Eloise's mum,' Jack pointed with his finger. 'I don't know who the other one is.'

'Hmm. She looks familiar.'

Jack got to his feet. 'I need to go talk to Eloise. Face to face. I have to persuade her to give me those books.'

Esquith dropped the photograph onto the bed. 'You realise you'll have to tell her how you know about the books. You'll have to admit that you spied on her.'

'I know.'

'She may not forgive you.'

'The thought has crossed my mind.'

'And if she tells you she never wants to see you again?'

'I'll tell her that's too bad because I'm not going anywhere.'

Charles sighed. 'Alright, then.'

Jack hesitated. 'Alice …'

'Don't worry. I'll take care of it.' He clapped Jack on the shoulder. 'Go with God, my son. And good luck.' He paused, his face sombre. 'Something tells me you'll need it.'

CHAPTER TWENTY EIGHT

The breath of chilly air against her wet skin made her freeze. The muscles in her back locked.

The scrape of a shoe broke through Eloise's stupefaction. She whipped around, the water splashing violently over the side of the bath.

Too late. He was upon her, his gloved hands on her head, pushing down.

She screamed and the screams bounced deafeningly off the tiled walls, and then her head was pushed down even more forcefully and she swallowed water. She struggled, splashing wildly and managed to struggle upwards. Another lungful of air, another scream before she went under again. As her head disappeared under the surface, she heard the enraged snarl of the cat and saw it explode from its perch in a burst of panicked energy as it sought to escape the room.

Her chest was on fire, her nasal passages burning. The taste of soap filled her mouth. She fought her way upwards, coughing, her head breaking water, and was pushed under almost immediately again.

His hands were now around her throat. He had obviously decided it might be easier to strangle her before drowning her. His hands were large and they were squeezing so hard she couldn't find her voice. Her legs thrashed helplessly. She tried to hook her fingers around his thumbs to break his grip but he was wise to her: his thumbs were balled into two hard knots, digging into the sides of her throat.

'Fuck you!' It came out as a whisper but her fury was suddenly all-consuming. Turning her head, she bit into one of the hands with all the venom she could muster. The hand was covered in a latex glove but she bit right through it. A grunt – she had inflicted damage – but the stranglehold did not slacken. Behind her eyes light throbbed in bright red and yellow pulses. The next moment he pushed her head underwater again. One hand was pushing down on her chest – she felt him roughly handle her breast – the other hand was over her face. His thumb carelessly poked into her right eye and bright pain sliced through her head.

She was tiring. The bath was slippery against her slick, naked skin and she couldn't get enough of a grip on the sides to help her push herself up. Everything was now happening in slow motion. She could hear her heart in her ears but it also seemed to her as though she was tuned into a second heartbeat. His. As if their hearts were somehow connected and his heart was labouring in sympathy with her own sluggish organ.

So tired. She gave one last, despairing scream but her voice sounded weak and faraway.

Her head slid under the water and she knew it was for the last time. She would not be able to fight her way upward once more: the hand on her forehead was too heavy. Through the layer of water she saw him looking down on her, his face under the nylon stocking monstrous. Up high, behind his shoulder, shadows wavered against the ceiling.

The stockinged face was growing dimmer and dimmer and then she could no longer see it. She wondered, feeling quite detached, if it were true that you saw your life flash before your eyes before you die. She did not see anything. She felt only pain and confusion. But she knew they were all around her. The beautiful pale-haired woman and her guilty lover. The two tall men with their whispering voices. They were close – she sensed them powerfully – as they converged on her like gossiping angels of death.

CHAPTER TWENTY NINE

The quickest way to Eloise's place was the Tube but after his nightmarish journey from Whiteladies to London, the idea of yet another train trip was too much to bear and Jack hailed a black cab. Enough was enough.

The traffic was indeed heavy, the stream of cars surging and ebbing futilely as the traffic lights clicked over in slow motion. It looked as though half of London had converged on Knightsbridge: couples holding hands, men in suits talking on iPhones, tourists gawking at the window displays at Harvey Nichols, handsome Arab boys showing off their baby-blue Zondas and yellow Lamborghinis. Soon they would be gone. Charlie had told him these cars were shipped in from the Middle East by their owners at the beginning of every summer, only to disappear when the weather turned grey and they headed back to warmer climes, like exotic birds.

He could feel the tension building up inside of him. The longer he remained in the taxi, the more he started to worry that Charlie might be right and that she was going to slam the door in his face. How do you tell someone that you had befriended her with the express purpose of finding out as much as you could about her private life without it sounding like utter betrayal?

By the time the cab drove down Maitland Avenue with its curry houses, pubs and run-down shops, a full twenty-five minutes had passed since they had left the affluence of the Royal Borough. It was busy here as well, but differently – white vans, far fewer cabs, certainly no luxury supercars – and the pavements showed a mix of young men in tracksuits and hoodies, thick-set women in colourful saris and giggling young girls looking all sparkly and dressed-up. As the cab swung off the roundabout and headed down the long, quiet residential street that would lead to number 322 he realised he was holding his breath. *Smart move, Jack.* Holding your breath was a great way of staving off disaster.

'Here you are, mate.' The cabbie sounded dubious. 'Are you sure this is the place?'

Jack took out his wallet, and glanced out the window. Number 322 was almost completely dark except for the ground-floor lobby, set behind its expansive glass walls. The space seemed vast, over-lit and very bare. The building itself looked squat and strangely sinister, quite different from when he had visited it the first time.

He paid the cabbie and opened the door, taking a deep, steadying breath.

Right. Time to be a man.

But as he walked up the shallow steps and pushed against the large plate-glass doors, they wouldn't budge. The building was locked up for the night. And there were no call buttons or a communication device of any kind on the outside. Even though he knew it was probably useless, he banged the side of his fist against the glass door a few times. Nothing.

On the other side of the plate-glass window, the large lift sat motionless, doors wide open. If he looked past the lift, he could see straight through the lobby and out the other side to what looked like a skip and some building debris and the beginning of a narrow alley that disappeared into darkness. There was a small service door, which would also give access to the building – but how to get there? Besides, there was no guarantee it wouldn't be locked as well.

He took out his mobile phone and called Eloise again. Once more he got her voice message.

It was hopeless. She was probably not even at home. He should simply go back.

But just as he started to turn away, the lift doors suddenly closed and he stopped in his tracks. Chances were, whoever had summoned it was heading for the lobby. It could even be Eloise herself.

He watched the glowing numbers above the doors as the lift made its way up. It stopped on the fourth floor: one floor below Eloise's apartment. So it probably wasn't her. But whoever it was might be willing to show him the way in.

The lift was moving down again. Four, Three, Two, One – a pause and then the black G inside the first disc lit up. The doors opened smoothly.

A tall man in a long camel-coloured overcoat stepped out. He had a black felt hat on his head pulled low and the bottom half of his face was wrapped in a paisley scarf. His eyes were covered in dark glasses and his hands were pushed deep inside his coat pockets.

Jack brought up his hand and rapped his knuckles sharply against the glass door. The man turned his head and looked straight at him.

There was something unnerving about those blank dark glasses, especially in the harsh overhead light. The man's coat looked as though it had been liberally splashed with water: the light camel colour had turned a soggy chocolate brown around the waist.

Jack motioned to the door. 'Can you let me in, please?'

No answer. No movement. Just the blind stare. Then, without haste, the man turned his back on him and started walking away from the main entrance towards the small service door on the opposite side. As he placed his hand on the handle, Jack noticed his hand was wearing a latex glove.

Something was wrong. Jack banged his fist urgently against the door. 'Hey, let me in!'

The man pushed open the door. As he stepped into the outside darkness, he looked back. Despite the shaded eyes and being separated by two sets of glass walls and the vastness of the lobby, Jack felt the weight of his gaze as though it was tangible.

The tall man turned around and disappeared into the alley.

Jack whipped around and ran down the steps, turning immediately left. If his thinking was correct, that alley would lead in somewhere on the next block down. In the distance he could hear the wash of high-street traffic but here it was quiet. He started running and the sound of his anxious feet slapping the pavement was loud in the echoless silence.

He turned the corner. He was right. A tiny black gate stood wide open – the entrance to the alley. It led past a pile of bin bags to the back of 322. Of the man in the camel coat there was no sign.

He didn't spend any time looking for the intruder. His brain was urging him to hurry, hurry. Something was wrong. Something was badly wrong.

The service door gave way under his hand. He stormed into the lobby and towards the lift, only slowing down as he passed through the steel doors.

Which floor? His fingers hovered over the buttons. Five was Eloise's apartment. But the lift had descended from four.

He jabbed his forefinger at number four. The door slid closed and the lift started its ascent.

When the doors opened, he found himself staring into an unlit corridor. The only illumination was the light spilling out of the lift. Gingerly, he stepped out.

'Hello?' His voice echoed down the dark passage.

He started walking, his fingers trailing along the wall. As he peered through black, un-curtained windows, his own distorted image was reflected back at him and it became clear that all the apartments on this floor were empty. He tried a few of the front doors as he passed them. They were all locked.

He was almost at the end of the passage when he noticed something strange. A row of flickering candles – like votive offerings – showed ghostly flames through the frosted glass. The door to this unit was wide open.

His fingers searched for the light switch. It clicked emptily. 'Eloise?'

He walked inside, moving through an empty room with concrete floors. From a door to his left came the faint glow of candlelight.

It was a bathroom. He stepped over the threshold and stopped, momentarily confused. It took another second for him to realise there was something in the bath. *Someone.*

She was staring up at him from underneath a sheet of water with wide open eyes. Her expression was puzzled. One hand rested on her pale breast.

'Eloise!'

He slammed his arms underneath her body and lifted her up. She felt incredibly heavy. Dragging her out of the bath, he laid her down on the tiled floor and placed his ear to her mouth. No breath. He grabbed her arm, but her wrist was so slippery and wet, he wouldn't have been able to find a pulse even if there was one.

Lacing his fingers, he started to compress her chest, forcing himself to count. Thirty compressions. Clasping her nose, he completely covered her mouth with his and breathed gently into her lungs. Once, twice.

How long had she been underwater? Four minutes? Five? Irreversible brain damage occurred after four to six minutes.

As he resumed the compressions once again, he realised he was praying. *Please, God. Please, God ...*

CHAPTER THIRTY

'Francis?'

Daniel Barone steered himself down the long passage to where the door to his friend's room stood ajar.

The house was silent, the only sound the soft whirr of the electric motor of his wheelchair. He stopped at the door and knocked.

'Francis?'

No answer. Leaning from the waist, he pushed the door wide. The room was empty.

Barone struggled to remember if his friend had mentioned that he would be going out. Yes, Francis had said something about going to London. Or had that been last week?

For a moment he closed his eyes tightly as, if by doing so, he could will himself to remember, but his mind remained slippery, without purchase and grip. He sensed the familiar panic welling up inside of him.

He opened his eyes and breathed evenly, the way he had been taught, and after a while he felt his heart calming itself, his fingers relaxing on the large envelope which rested on his lap. And then he noticed that the old-fashioned coat rack, which usually held Godine's coat, was bare. So Francis had gone out, after all.

Barone steered his wheelchair deeper into the room and looked around him. It was a room monastic in its sparseness: a thin metal bed with bleached linen, the corners folded with military precision; a desk, an armchair and a bookcase stuffed with books with faded titles. The only thing in the room which was in any way unusual was the large drawing that covered almost one entire wall. It was a complicated architectural rendition of a Gothic memory palace, replete with galleries, endless staircases, passages turning in on themselves, Escher-esque tessellations and infinite loops; rooms within rooms and inside them grinning gargoyles, oblique symbols and images of dark beauty. Memorising a palace of this magnitude required almost unthinkable mnemonic gymnastics but Barone knew that there was a time when Francis Godine could have found his way unerringly through its labyrinthine ways. Like St Augustine the Blessed, Godine had believed he would find God in memory. Memorise all of creation and you may gaze upon the face of the Great Storyteller himself.

Barone knew that, for Godine, this prayer had long since died. Quests for the divine can be shipwrecked against the rocks of passion, betrayal and blood. The memory palace now existed uninhabited: a discarded masterpiece no longer visited or explored.

Barone felt his heart beating like a tired clock. As he looked at the abandoned memory palace it occurred to him that he should persuade Francis to start his work afresh. After all, life was too short to be little. Bella used to say that. But they were not her words: she had read them somewhere else. It was a quote from … the memory hovered elusively, disappeared. And again he felt his mind contract with panic.

He looked at the large envelope that rested on his lap. He had wanted to share this with Francis because he was afraid. He was becoming like a child, constantly seeking reassurance. Suddenly furious with himself, he savagely tore at the envelope and withdrew what was inside.

It was a SPECT scan: a single-photon emission computed tomography scan of his brain. A week ago he had checked himself into hospital as a day patient and had allowed himself to be injected with a compound containing a minute amount of radioactive material which attached itself to his brain cells. For another fifteen minutes the scanner had slowly rotated around his head, building up a 360-degree image of his brain, highlighting brain activity and blood flow. This was the result.

He peered at the picture with sick fascination. It seemed almost ghost-like: an eerie, phosphorescent organ floating against a background of deepest black.

He wondered what would be the last to go. If he had no more memory left, would he still be capable of feelings of joy and awe? Would he be capable of prayer? Of reaching for something greater than himself? Or would everything be snarled and dead, smothered in plaques and tangles and dementia?

Alzheimer's. The very word was a curse. Why him? He had worked with memory for the greater part of his life, had studied it, familiarised himself with its myriad facets, had felt himself the master of it. Why him? The man who had the power to take memories, now the victim of enforced memory loss. An irony there, or a truth, if only he could grasp it. If only he could *remember*.

And suddenly the memories came unbidden. The way the early morning sunshine had slanted off the windowpanes with terrible brightness. The deep tyre imprint left by the police car on the front lawn, like a wound on the fresh green grass. The forensic specialists cocooned in white, like visitors from outer space. And Julianne – huddled on the tile floor like a broken doll – her skull dented, her lipstick smeared. The image was so vivid it was as though she was there in the room with him. *If I close my eyes, I could touch her. I could touch the blood on her forehead; I could feel the coldness of her hand.*

CHAPTER THIRTY ONE

The amount of water that finally left her mouth was surprisingly little. Jack was still compressing her chest, when Eloise suddenly coughed violently. A stream of fluid left her mouth in a thin, convulsive spasm.

'Eloise?'

She looked at him without recognition. In the light of the candles, her eyes seemed enormous. Her lips moved – she was trying to say something – but then another bout of coughing shook her frame. When she made a feeble effort to push herself upright, he reached for his mobile. 999, that was the emergency number in the UK, he reminded himself. Not 911, 999.

As he spoke to the emergency operator, she kept watching him with the same docile, still gaze. She did not seem surprised or even alarmed. He returned the phone to his pocket and looked around for something with which to cover her. There was a towelling robe hanging on a hook behind the door.

But when he tried to insert her arms through the sleeves, she suddenly reacted violently – pushing against him with panicky strength. She screamed – a thin, high-pitched scream – her arms beating against his chest.

'Eloise! No! It's me!'

He grabbed her face between his hands, forcing her to look at him. Her eyes were wild with fear and her mouth worked convulsively.

'Eloise! Stop it! It's me, Jack!'

For a moment she stared at him, her eyes rinsed of any spark of recognition.

'Jack?' Her voice was hesitant.

'Yes. It's me. You're safe.'

Another long moment of puzzlement before her face crumpled and she let out a hoarse sigh. 'Jack.' And then she started crying, her chest heaving with helpless, exhausted sobs.

'I'm here. You're safe.' He draped the robe around her shoulders and placed his own jacket on top. He sank down next to her and pulled her close, hugging her, rocking her and stroking her wet hair. 'You're with me now. You're safe. I'll keep you safe.' He tightened his arms around her and pressed his lips to her forehead. 'I won't let you go.'

'Miss Blake had a lucky escape.' The A&E doctor looked tired. Everything about him seemed to droop: his shoulders, his wrinkled white coat, his tired eyes looking at Jack behind drooping spectacles. His name tag stated that he was Dr Pembridge. The name tag too hung at half-mast. 'There doesn't seem to be any neurological damage.'

Jack felt his face split into a silly grin. 'She's going to be OK?'

'Thanks to the quality of CPR you gave her. It is fortunate you had lifeguard training. But we'll keep her overnight, just to make sure. Often there are complications that develop later – electrolyte imbalances – or sometimes fluid in the lungs will impair the breathing process hours after resuscitation. Delayed pulmonary oedema or secondary drowning. But she should be fine,' he added hastily as Jack stepped forward involuntarily. 'She's in excellent health. Very fit.'

He paused. 'The paramedics reported that Ms Blake drowned in a bath?'

'Yes.' Jack frowned at the note of scepticism in Pembridge's voice. 'Why?'

'An adult drowning in the bathroom is most uncommon. It is more likely a case of auto-erotic asphyxiation. There is definite bruising around the throat. Did you find anything rigged up around her neck?'

'No!' Jack tried to moderate his voice. 'No. You're wrong.' He took a deep breath. 'I believe this was a case of attempted murder.'

Pembridge looked even wearier. 'The chances are unlikely. If suicidal drowning is not common, homicidal drowning is extremely rare. I think you'll find the police will not give much credence to this idea unless you found someone standing over her, pushing her head underwater. Did you?'

'Not ... exactly.' Jack sighed with frustration. 'But if Eloise tells the police what happened, they will have no choice but to investigate.'

'Ms Blake's story is that she fell asleep in the bath.'

'But—' Jack stopped, confused.

'Excuse me.' Pembridge reached for his beeper as it went off. 'I have to check this.'

'Wait.' Jack placed a hand on the man's arm. 'Can I see her?'

Pembridge nodded. 'Walk with me.'

A few doors down the corridor, he stopped and gestured at an open door. 'In there.' He gave Jack a limp half-salute and shuffled on in the direction of the nurses' station.

Eloise was awake. When he walked into the room, she opened her eyes. They were deeply smudged by shadows.

'Hey.' Jack placed his hand on hers where it lay, motionless, palm up. 'How are you feeling?'

'I'm OK.' She smiled at him with pale lips. 'Just really tired.'

'Eloise ...' He tried to keep his voice soothing. 'Dr Pembridge says you told him you fell asleep in the bath.'

She blinked. 'That's right.'

'You know that's not true.' He paused. 'I saw him. The man who did this to you.'

Her eyelids fluttered and her hand jerked underneath his.

'I want us to talk, OK? But not now. Tomorrow.'

She sighed and moved her head slightly – it was difficult to tell whether in assent or denial.

He leant over and kissed her forehead. 'Now rest.'

Without argument, she obediently closed her eyes.

'I'll come back for you,' he said but she was already asleep.

CHAPTER THIRTY TWO

By the time Jack arrived back at Esquith's apartment it was well past midnight. As he placed his key in the door, he tried to keep the noise to a minimum. Softly he closed the door behind him and tiptoed inside.

He needn't have worried. The reading lamp in the living room was on and Charlie was sitting in his battered leather club chair wrapped in a flowery blanket.

'Tell me you didn't wait up for me, Mom.' Jack hooked his jacket onto the Victorian coat stand and moved his shoulders a few times. He could not remember the last time he had felt this exhausted.

'You look tired, mate. Drink?'

Jack flopped onto the sofa and watched as Esquith uncurled his lanky limbs from the chair and poured him a stiff three fingers.

'Oh, yeah.' Jack took a deep, grateful gulp.

Charlie looked down at him, hands on his hips. 'Let me guess: she told you she hated your guts and you've been wandering the streets of London wallowing in self-misery.'

'No.'

'No?'

'No. Pour yourself one and fasten your seatbelt.'

• • •

Charlie's eyebrows had permanently disappeared into his fringe by the time Jack had finished.

'If you really believe someone tried to drown her, Jack, you should go to the police.'

'I need to talk to her first and find out exactly what the hell happened. She clearly doesn't want the police involved.'

'Which is what concerns me.'

Jack yawned. He was so tired, things were starting to go fuzzy at the edges. But the effort of actually leaving his chair and getting himself to bed was too much to contemplate.

Esquith walked to his desk. When he turned around he had the framed picture of the Order of Mnemosyne in his hand.

'I hope you don't mind, but I took another look at this.'

'And?'

'The method of science, the aim of religion.'

'What?'

'Aleister Crowley. *The Equinox.*'

'Charlie, I love you. But what the hell are you talking about?'

'Aleister Crowley was an occultist who believed that mysticism should be approached scientifically. He—'

'I know who Aleister Crowley was, for God's sake. "Do what thou wilt." Magic, sex, blood sacrifice. What has he got to do with this?'

'Nothing, probably. Except I think the Order of Mnemosyne might have been modelled after Crowley's Hermetic Order of the Golden Dawn. See these initials?' Charlie's long finger tapped against the glass. 'And how they are preceded by *frater* and *soror*? Well, that's typical of the Golden Dawn. Members all referred to themselves as "brother" or "sister" and they used the initials of their magical mottoes as pseudonyms. The idea was that members would write in magical diaries and use their mottoes – usually in Latin – to separate their magical identity from their mundane, everyday identity.'

'Magical diaries? How very hocus-pocus.'

'We're not talking about flying broomsticks, Jack. Crowley expected his followers to use the diaries as a scientific tool. The diaries functioned as laboratory notebooks – chronicling the various investigations into the self as undertaken by the magician.'

'Let me look at that again.' Jack held out his hand. For a moment he was silent as his eyes wandered over the faces in the photograph. How arrogant Leon Simonetti looked. And how possessive his hand on Julianne Gray's shoulder. Arrogance ...

Jack looked up at Esquith, suddenly excited.

'*Frater A.V.A.M. Aut vincere aut mori.* "Either to conquer or to die." My father has a sculpture on his desk engraved with those words. I always thought it was just more of his macho bullshit. But it must be his motto.'

'Well done.' Esquith nodded. 'One down, four to go.'

Into Jack's mind came the image of Godine's feverish eyes, his voice intoning, *The world was robbed of a great intellect when Daniel Barone closed the book on Mnemosyne.*

'I think I know what Barone's motto is.' Jack spoke haltingly, trying to remember. 'Last night I talked to Francis Godine, Barone's best friend. He was drunk and I didn't understand half of what he was saying but he told me Barone embodied the perfect balance between science and faith and took as his motto *Credo ut intelligam*: "I believe, so that I may understand." *Frater C.U.I.*'

'Which leaves the other three. *Frater L.E.O., Soror N.O.M* and *Soror Q.M.N.M.D.* Any ideas?'

'Not a clue.'

'Well, I may not know her motto, but I know who the hot blonde woman is. I told you she looked familiar.'

'So?'

'Bella Wilding. Her picture was all over the tabloids a year or so ago. A wealthy investment banker left her all his worldly goods after he passed away. What is interesting is that there had been no romantic liaison between the two of them. He left her his fortune as a token of his gratitude for helping him write his "memory book",' Charlie's fingers sketched quotation marks in the air, 'after he heard he was terminally ill. It was big news.

Some of the old man's relatives disputed the inheritance but the court found in her favour.'

Jack leant back in his chair. 'It doesn't seem right, does it? Two of the members of the Order of Mnemosyne made out like bandits: my father and this Bella. But Leon Barone is in a wheelchair and Julianne Gray was murdered in her kitchen.'

'Life isn't fair.'

'You don't say. Now, if only we can figure out what all of this has to do with Eloise.'

'Maybe nothing?'

Jack shook his head emphatically. 'Everything. Don't you think it's just a little too coincidental that every member of Mnemosyne was an expert on memory, and here is Eloise suffering from memory problems? Those five people are responsible. I'm going to prove it.'

'Are you sure you want to go there?' Esquith's voice was suddenly quiet.

'What do you mean?'

'You are getting sucked into a world which is outside your ken. I don't want to see you get hurt, Jack. This woman may be …' Esquith searched for a word, 'dangerous.'

'Charlie. I love her.'

There was a long silence. Then Esquith sighed. 'OK.' He leant back in his chair, his fingers steepled on his chest. 'Where will you start?'

'Barone's investigator told me that, before she disappeared, Jenilee used to see a psychiatrist. I think it's time I paid him a visit.'

'Forget it. You won't get anything out of him. Doctor-patient confidentiality.'

'He'll have to talk to me if his patient tells him to.'

Esquith looked sceptical. 'What makes you think Eloise will cooperate? Have you come clean with her? Told her that you knew about her all along?'

'No. But don't worry,' Jack spoke with airy confidence. 'Things have changed. I saved her life, remember.'

'Hmm. I hope you're right.'

Jack got up from his chair and stretched. 'Of course I am. No woman can resist a knight on a white horse.' He flashed a grin at Charlie's dubious face. 'I'll tell her tomorrow and she'll forgive all. You'll see.'

'*Non omnis moriar:* I shall not altogether die.'

—*Horace, Odes 3:30*

CHAPTER THIRTY-THREE

Mr Derek Payne. The letters engraved on the nameplate resting on the secretary's desk were small and formal. They meant nothing to her.

The secretary caught her eye and smiled warmly, as if they were old friends. Eloise smiled back. She had never seen this woman before in her life.

Mr Payne's waiting room was decorated in subdued greys and moss greens. She wondered if this colour combination was meant to have a soothing effect on his patients. Maybe studies had shown them to be particularly effective in calming the seething brainwaves of the mentally disturbed.

She could feel Jack's anxious eyes upon her but she refused to meet his gaze. The truth was she felt embarrassed – no, humiliated. Finding out that he had known all along what had happened to her – had observed her like an insect in a jar – filled her with shame and fury. That he had also saved her life somehow made it worse. She knew she was being irrational, but she hated feeling like this: like a broken, hopeless thing in need of rescue. If she could walk away from him this minute, she would. But she needed him. As she had discovered only this morning, he knew things about her she did not … such as the fact that she used to see a psychiatrist. It looked like there had been bats in her belfry for a long time.

The door to the psychiatrist's inner sanctum opened and a big, round-shouldered man beckoned to her. A stranger.

'Jenilee.' His voice sounded as though it emanated from his boots. 'So good to see you again. Why don't you come in?'

It is dark in the house and I am looking for my mother. I am dressed in pyjamas and I'm holding my teddy bear. The clock on the wall has a fluorescent face and this is how I know it is three o'clock in the morning. There is a door in front of me and light coming from underneath. As I push my hand against it, I smell something. Lemons?

And then ... nothing. I wake up.

Mr Payne stopped reading and lowered the folder.

'I came to see you about a dream? That's all?' She didn't know what she had expected, but this felt decidedly anti-climactic. 'I didn't come to you because I was hearing voices? Or seeing people who aren't there? Or numbers? Did I talk to you about numbers?'

A hint of puzzled concern coloured the deep voice. 'No.'

Mr Payne placed the folder to one side and leant his substantial forearms on the desk. 'You came to me because you had a recurring dream and it was causing you distress. It was obvious to me that you were repressing a childhood memory – in all likelihood, a traumatic one.'

She felt at a complete loss. 'Well ... did I ever manage to walk through the door?'

'Not under my supervision, no.' Mr Payne leant back and spread his hands wide.

Jack spoke. 'Did you try hypnosis?'

'I am not a fan of hypnosis,' Payne grimaced. 'Research has proven that patients under hypnosis do indeed show increased recollection of facts, but they also show increased recollection of fiction. What's more, the patient becomes more and more unable to distinguish one from the other. In other words, you can't always trust what a patient says under hypnosis. But, yes, we did try it. Jenilee proved resistant. It was impossible to put her under.'

'A teddy bear.' Jack was thinking out loud. 'Jenilee must have been very young if she was still playing with teddy bears. Even if you had managed to retrieve the memory, wouldn't it have been a hazy one?'

Payne shook his head. 'This is where children and adults differ. Adults who survive catastrophic experiences – a car crash, fire – very often show deep memory impairment. After the traumatic incident, they have difficulty recalling it in full. Children, on the other hand, seem to suffer very little memory loss. For example, a child who has been subjected to a kidnapping will remember the incident in great detail. The child's interpretation may differ from that of an adult, but the child will have no difficulty recollecting the event itself.'

He turned his head towards her. 'It is just a question of getting you to walk through that door, Jenilee, and you will remember.'

'Oh, for God's sake.' The harshness of her voice startled even herself. 'I can't even remember having this dream. I can't remember a door. I can't remember a clock. I can't remember the fucking teddy bear. I can't remember *you*.'

She had to hand it to the good doctor, he did not so much as blink. But when he spoke again he enunciated his words with a slow carefulness that set her nerves on edge.

'I think you *did* remember. Once – when you were on your own.'

She waited, her stomach in a knot.

'It is my contention that shortly before you disappeared you may have had a breakthrough, which enabled you to open the door. And whatever you saw on the other side acted as a stressor and propelled you into your present fugue state.'

She felt sick. 'Why can't I remember the stressor?'

'Sufferers never do. Not until they revert to themselves.'

'Well, that's just lovely.' She looked over at Jack. 'I'm leaving.'

'Jenilee, wait.'

The fury squeezed her chest tight. 'I'm not Jenilee, and if you touch me again I'll break your hand.'

She got to her feet. Her legs felt wobbly. As he pushed back his own chair, she said, 'Don't follow me.'

He did follow her, of course. In the street outside he grabbed her by the arm and spun her around.

'What the hell is the matter with you?' His face was flushed. 'I'm trying to help you.'

'Please. Do not. Help me.' She tried to break free from his grip but he was too strong. 'Let go!'

People were beginning to stare. A woman pushing a baby in a pram walked by, craning her neck to watch. A man in a suit broke step, but one look from Jack and he continued smartly on his way.

He tightened his fingers on her wrist. 'I told you I'm sorry.'

She pushed her face up against his. 'Was it a thrill for you? Spying on the clueless girl who's funny in the head? Did you discuss it with your girlfriend? I bet you had a good laugh, the two of you.'

'Girlfriend?' He looked dazed.

'How could you? Pretend to be friends! Break into my apartment. Touch my things!'

'I didn't touch your things. Well, I mean I didn't touch them *that* way, for God's sake.'

'And you colluded with that man, Barone. *Conspired.*' She spat out the last word.

'Don't be such a bloody drama queen!' He was now thoroughly angry. 'Daniel Barone is your godfather. He is worried about you. He was the first to realise someone is out to harm you.'

He paused and breathed heavily. 'Have you forgotten about that little detail? Someone wants you dead, sweetheart. And if it weren't for Barone, who told me to keep an eye on you, you would now be a very pretty corpse lying in a morgue somewhere.'

The brutality of his tone shocked her. She swallowed. 'I don't care. I don't trust him.'

'You will have to trust him. He is your best chance of recovery.'

'Don't you understand?' She felt tears and blinked angrily. 'He told me he will take her away from me.'

'Take away who?'

'Take away me. From *me*.'

He stared at her and she saw understanding come to his eyes.

'If he ... cures ... me, I will be gone! I won't remember anything of my life as Eloise. Nothing! I'll become a stranger to myself!' She was weeping now, her tears blinding her, but she could still see that dreadful look of compassion in his eyes.

'Don't pity me!' She screamed the words at him and tried to wrest free again but he pulled her close – so close the coarse wool of his Aran sweater rubbed painfully against her cheek. He folded one arm strongly around her waist and placed the other hand against her head in a sheltering, cupping gesture. She felt his lips move against her hair.

'I don't pity you, you idiot. I love you.'

He could clearly see the bruises around her neck. Like the fingerprints of a ghost. But even before he touched his lips to the abused skin, he could sense her pulse beating strongly in the hollow of her throat. Her hands grasped the bedposts above her head, her knuckles turning white with the strength of her grip. But the inside of her arms seemed so tender and vulnerable.

Shadows, contours, sensuous shapes and long lines. Contradictions. Ankles and wrists fragile but her feet powerful and callused and her calf muscles taut. Skin so soft he was worried his hands were too rough, but strong muscles threading underneath the surface. His blood pounded inside his chest but he forced himself to slowly trace her shoulders with his mouth and follow the graceful line of her arms; to roam without haste across the slim hips, the pale belly, the hipbones. As he eased himself on top of her, she sighed deeply and for a moment her eyes were remote, as though she were looking past him to something he could not see.

Who was she? She was yielding one moment – heavy, languid, utterly accepting – and the next her nails were digging into his back, her thighs straining against his, fighting him. He grasped her head between his hands, forcing her into stillness. Her hair was wet against her forehead. She tasted of salt as he moved his tongue around her ear, and on towards the back of her neck where the hair curled in damp tendrils. She submitted to his caresses but he sensed a humming inside her body, like rampant electricity. He kissed her. A sharp pain, and he tasted his own blood from a cut lip.

Who was this woman? He whispered her name and she smiled. He fell asleep on a cloud of drifting exhaustion, his cheek against her back.

When he woke up, the first thing he saw was the filigree of black numbers against the white wall. They were muting into shadow. The light outside the windows had turned a cold, late-afternoon yellow and long grey fingers crept across the ceiling.

She stirred beside him. 'Are you awake?'

'Yes.'

'I slept like the dead. I can't remember when I last slept this soundly.' She pushed herself up and placed her arms around her knees.

'Good.'

She smiled at him over her shoulder. 'What are you thinking?'

'I'm wondering what made you choose the name Eloise Blake.'

'*Songs of Innocence.*'

'"Little Lamb, who made thee?"'

'That one exactly. My twisted sense of humour.'

He drew his finger down the curve of her back. 'Methinks you have more of the tiger than the lamb in you, Ms Blake.'

'You may be right.'

'And Eloise? From the Pope poem?'

'No. I just liked the name.'

She turned around fully and placed her head on his chest, her breath warm against his skin. Her gaze followed his to the far wall with its spider's web of coded numbers.

She sighed. 'We should talk.'

CHAPTER THIRTY FOUR

Eloise Blake came to consciousness two years and thirteen days in the past. She was standing in a small alcove in a restaurant in Soho and in one hand she held the receiver of a pay phone. The phone was dead. She did not know who she had called or who had called her.

In her other hand was a sheet of paper. On it was written: *To my daughter: in case of need*, followed by the titles and publishing details of three books. She did not know what they meant or why this piece of paper was clutched between her fingers. What she did know was that she was afraid – deeply afraid – stricken by the kind of fear that gives you a metallic taste in the mouth and leaves your fingertips cold. The kind of fear that taps audibly at the door to your mind. *Knock. Knock.*

Nothing around her seemed even vaguely familiar and she felt at a complete loss. But the adrenaline which had flooded her body had also primed her for flight and, after a moment of frozen indecision, she folded up the sheet of paper and pushed it into her inside jacket pocket. She left the restaurant furtively and in a rush, sensing imminent danger.

The next two days were deeply disorienting. At some point – she could not remember exactly when – she realised she did not know her name and she did not know where she lived. She had no handbag on her and no credit cards or mobile phone.

She was, however, fully functional. She could still read and write. She knew what day it was and what year, which political party was in power and what the rate of VAT was. She discovered, by chance, that she could speak French. She knew the name of the author of *Leaves of Grass*. She realised she was computer-literate and that she'd be able to drive a car if she had to. Her skill set, for want of a better word, was intact.

What had disappeared was her entire database of biographical details. She found herself bereft of any markers or personal map. She did not know her age or where she was born or if she had loved ones who were looking for her. The face she saw reflected in shop windows was the face of a stranger and the palms of her hands were unknown territory. There were no faint memory flashes; no tip-of-the-tongue moments; no hesitant crackling or white noise travelling along the synapses of her brain that might indicate a dormant memory trying to push its way through. If there was even one ghostly projection or after-image of her old self still lingering in her mind, it did not register. The void was complete.

Except for the fear. *Knock. Knock.* The fear was constantly tapping its morse code signal inside the grooves of her brain and she must have carried this panicked pulse over from before, to now. And even though she could not put a face to the threat, she knew she had to hide. The knowledge that she was in danger was one of only two things she had carried over from her previous life. The second was a meaningless sheet of paper on which was written the titles of three books.

Not having money was a problem, but the watch on her wrist was a Cartier and the tiny jewelled dragonfly pin on her lapel had the Van Cleef and Arpels diamond-shaped logo engraved on the back. Even though she could not recall where she had acquired these pieces, she had a good idea of their value and was able to extract a fair-ish price from the second pawnbroker she approached. This would hold her for a while.

Should she go to the police? They would surely be able to point the way back to her old life, but what they would not be able to do was restore her memory. And without her memory she was blind. Once out of hiding, and returned to wherever she came from, she would be completely vulnerable – clueless – as to where the danger lay. And if there was one thing in this morass of incomprehension about which she felt absolutely sure, it was that there was indeed danger lurking in her past.

But after two weeks she was in bad shape. As she sat on her narrow bed in the B&B off King's Cross, she watched the lights from the Chinese takeaway flash monotonously outside her window and wondered if she might not have done something terrible, which would explain what had happened to her. Maybe she had committed a terrible crime, an act so heinous her brain had crashed from the horror of it all. Maybe she was on the run from the police. Or maybe someone was hunting her; looking for revenge. And maybe that revenge was justified.

She had almost made up her mind to go to the police, after all, when she started hearing the voices.

If there is some person or cause for whom you would like us to pray, please write a name or brief description on a piece of paper and place it in the box. We shall offer the prayers during worship on Sunday.

She held the leaflet between both hands but had difficulty reading the words because her entire body was shaking as though she had palsy.

'Are you alright?'

She looked up. The man in the black cassock standing at the end of the pew had an old face but young eyes.

She tried to speak but her teeth were chattering.

He looked at her searchingly for a moment and then slid into the pew beside her. Gently he took the leaflet from her unresisting fingers.

'Would you like us to pray for someone?'

She nodded.

He took the stub of pencil from the pew box and looked at her expectantly. 'Name?'

'Eloise.' She realised she was still nodding her head. With difficulty she forced herself to stop.

He started writing, the pencil scratching softly against the paper. 'Is she ill?'

'Yes. She is sick.'

At the front of the church a tall woman in a grey cardigan was removing a length of flower-arranging wire from a large bag. On a piece of newspaper next to her were lilies with long green stems. A muscled man wearing a red shirt and a black beanie on his shaven head was propping a ladder up against the wall. He walked up the ladder with pantherish grace and started to unscrew a light bulb.

'There.' The priest replaced the pencil in its box.

'Thank you.'

'Would you like to tell me what is wrong with Eloise?'

'She hears voices.'

He cocked his head to one side. 'So did Joan of Arc.'

'And look what happened to her.'

'Indeed.' His eyes crinkled. 'Fortunately we don't live in the fifteenth century any more.'

The muscled man had finished replacing the light bulb. She watched as he skimmed down the ladder with impossible lightness. When his feet touched the ground he turned around and his eyes briefly met hers.

'Is there something else I can help you with?'

She looked back at the priest, who was watching her closely.

She clasped her hands together, trying once more to stop the shaking. 'I wonder ...'

He waited patiently.

She tried again. 'I wonder if the way we behave in the present is always linked to what happened in the past.'

'If that were true, then Man would have no free will but be a captive to past memories his entire life.'

'You believe in free will?'

'Of course. The past is not tyranny, despite what Freud said. We all do things and react certain ways and sometimes the reasons do lie in the past. But it is our ability to imagine the future that makes us who we are. It is our willingness to believe we can write fresh pages, despite carrying old baggage. The steps we take to make that future happen are the true indication of self.'

A cloud had moved in front of the stained-glass windows and a shadow descended on the inside of the church. The saintly scent of the lilies mixed with the workmanlike smell of polish and turpentine.

Suddenly she was so very tired. It was time to go. She stood up and moved sideways out of the pew and into the aisle. She held her hand out to the priest but, as he took it, she saw his face crumpling with alarm and heard his voice – far away – calling for help.

Her ears filled with the sound of the blood circulating through her veins and it sounded like the trilling of a bass note on a cello. The last thing she saw before losing consciousness was the man in the red shirt rushing towards her and catching her as she fell heavily to the ground.

CHAPTER THIRTY FIVE

'It was Jungles, wasn't it? The man in the red shirt?'

Eloise nodded. 'Yes, it was. And after I met Jungles things were much better.'

Jack felt a pang of jealousy. 'In what way?'

'In every way.' Her face lit up. 'But mostly because he showed me a way to control the voices.'

'I don't understand.'

'He introduced me to free running. And I discovered that when I run, I don't hear the voices and I stop seeing people who aren't there and the numbers' – she pointed at the far wall – 'recede. Free running saves me every day. As long as I can run, I can hide.'

'But the voices come back.'

'Always. But the day in the church was the turning point. I decided the only responsibility I have is for my future. I truly have freedom of choice: it doesn't matter what may have happened in my past. I can choose to walk away from whatever lies behind me. I can live only in the moment.'

He tried to imagine making a decision like that: to consciously embrace a void. He wondered if he'd have the courage. He knew he didn't.

'You must think I'm insane.' In the gathering dusk, her eyes were bottomless.

'I wouldn't be here with you if I did.'

'Yes? Are you sure, Jack? I want you to be quite clear on this. I see people, right here in my apartment. Even in the street. Ghosts in broad daylight. It's like an old film of past memories running before my eyes – except …' She stopped.

'Except what?'

'They're not my memories. They don't belong to me.'

'What do you mean, they don't belong to you?'

'They are false memories. They belong to someone else.'

'Who?'

'They are the memories of Julianne Gray.'

Jack could swear he felt the hairs on the back of his neck rise. After a few moments he said slowly, 'But you told me you don't remember your mother.'

'I don't. Julianne belongs to Jenilee, not to Eloise.'

He thought how disconcerting it was to hear her talk about herself and her mother as though they were strangers.

'I don't understand. How do you know these memories are not flashbacks to your own life as Jenilee? How do you know they belong to your mother?'

'One of the figures I see is Barone. But in my false memories he is young and he can walk. And he doesn't call me Jenilee, he calls me by my mother's name. You must believe me, Jack – they are her memories. Not mine.'

She stopped, clearly frustrated by the puzzlement he realised must be written on his face. God knew, he was trying to keep an open mind, but it was a lot to take in.

'And the numbers?'

She shook her head. 'They just come to me. The same numbers, in the same sequence, every time.'

She moved to the edge of the bed and reached down. Her fingers searched between the mattress and the base of the bed and extracted a creased envelope.

'This is the note she left me. It is the only thing I have carried over from my previous life.'

He opened the envelope and removed from it a sheet of paper folded into four. The edges were soft from repeated folding and unfolding.

To my daughter, in case of need:

The Compleat Angler. Izaak Walton and Charles Cotton. 1760 first Hawkins edition. Ninth edition overall

Neuromancer. William Gibson. Grafton, 1986

Septem Sermones ad Mortuos. Carl Gustav Jung. 1916, privately printed

She tossed the blanket away from her and walked in her bare feet over to the dressing table. Opening the bottom drawer, she took from it the three books.

'I do not want to be Jenilee again. And therefore I cannot accept Daniel Barone's help. But I *have* to get rid of the voices and the ghosts in my life. When I have these hallucinations, it feels as though I *shatter*. Something inside me fractures. If it continues … I will go mad.'

She placed the books on the bed in front of him. 'The books and the numbers hold the key: I'm sure of it. If I can decipher what they mean, I will understand why I shatter. And maybe I can stop it from happening and move on.'

He picked up the copy of *The Seven Sermons to the Dead.* The leather felt cool underneath his fingers.

He looked at her. 'I know someone who can help.'

CHAPTER THIRTY SIX

Memory image 14377

Tonight we are celebrating. Daniel's research has taken a quantum leap forward. It sometimes happens like that. Long months and years when everything moves at a glacial pace and then suddenly – lightning.

Daniel's voice is passionate as he recounts his triumph. 'Think about it,' he says, his face flushed and happy. 'Beta-blockers, propranolol – they are useful, certainly, but they only soften, they do not take away. The memory of the trauma remains and continues to do its damage. Whereas I will be giving the patient the gift of a clean slate.'

He continues talking. He cannot seem to stop smiling. I look at Leon, who is listening carefully to Daniel telling us that trials may soon begin. Another five to seven years of testing and refining: of playing safe and getting it right.

A long time.

'Scientists are marathon runners, not sprinters,' Daniel says, as he pours champagne into our glasses. 'Isn't that right,

Julianne? You hang in there. Your breakthrough will come too.'
I know he doesn't mean to sound patronising.

'It is the journey that is important,' Francis confirms and I see Leon and Bella exchange looks. I sense their thoughts as clearly as if they had spoken them out loud: not a journey. A race. And the race is always to the swift.

On the sideboard stands a painting shrouded in white. Francis gets to his feet and removes the protective cloth. It is our gift to Daniel to mark the occasion.

It is the kind of painting that would appeal to Francis – and to Daniel, for that matter. The woman's milky shoulders, her flowing hair and diaphanous gown belong to an idealised vision of the feminine. The black water of forgetfulness and the lamp of remembrance are potent symbols in the Romantic tradition. I would have preferred something more modern. Not a lamp but an electric flash. Not water but desert. Not this woman who looks like …

Daniel says, 'She looks like you, Julianne.' But as I stare into the eyes of the woman in the painting I think she looks like Bella.

From the other side of the table Bella smiles. 'I like the lamp. I think I may have it tattooed on my wrist.'

Cool Bella. Glamorous Bella. I already know the tattoo will look fabulous.

Leon raises his glass. 'A toast. To Mnemosyne.'

'To Mnemosyne,' we say in unison.

We open another bottle of champagne, then a bottle of whisky. It is like old times. Except for Francis, who keeps glancing at me. He suspects something, I suddenly think, and I feel my throat closing.

We are all quite drunk by the end of the evening and in no state to drive home. Leon invites us to stay the night. A sleepover at Whiteladies. We had done this before and as always it feels like a cheerful party when we take clean sheets and soft blankets from the cupboard. Francis is to sleep in the guest room. Bella gets the pretty room with the blue wallpaper in the attic. Leon is assigned the sofa-bed in the study. Jenilee, who has long since fallen asleep in Daniel's arms, is tucked away in the small room leading off the master bedroom. And I – well, I share Daniel's bed.

I am staring at the ceiling with my eyes open. Next to me Daniel's body is a gentle furnace. I listen to his breath in the darkness. He always sleeps like a baby, and why shouldn't he? He is a good man. A man worth loving.

Slowly, I ease myself out of bed. He mumbles and sighs deeply.

My feet make no sound in the passage outside. I cast a wary eye at the closed door leading to the guest room where Francis sleeps. I am starting to believe that Francis senses that I am cheating on Daniel and, where Daniel is concerned, Francis is ferocious. I must be careful.

I descend the stairs, quiet as a mouse. The study door is wide open and my eyes search for the sofa and the shape of the man who should be sleeping there. The sofa is empty.

My video recorder sits on the coffee table and I pick it up, feeling its familiar weight. I feel eyes on me and look up. From the wall opposite, Mnemosyne smiles at me; her expression is mocking.

I walk back up the stairs, the recorder dragging in my hand. When I reach the first floor I continue up another flight of stairs. The attic.

Bella always says that memory is like perfume. Without a fixative, perfume loses its scent. Without emotion, memories disappear. I think of this as I approach the door, my heart beating like a drum, the blood rushing in my ears, almost drowning out the sounds coming from within the room. I will remember this moment, I think, for a long time. Until the day I die.

I turn the handle.

They look beautiful together. Her legs are long with impossibly slender thighs. They are entwined with unconscious grace around his back. His skin is dark against the paleness of her legs but his buttocks are creamy. He has a scar on his hip. The first time I saw it, he had explained to me that it was an injury from his childhood. I remember now that I had pressed my lips tenderly to the puckered skin.

Bella opens her eyes and sees me standing in the doorway. She smiles, her teeth gleaming. Leon is thrusting himself into her, oblivious of anything except his own pleasure. She throws back her head, her hair fanning silkily across the pillow. Her mouth is open. Softly she starts to moan, but she is watching me from below her lashes; her gaze remains locked with mine.

I bring the machine up to my eye and press the on button. The whirr as it starts to record is hardly audible.

These are my memories. Sick perfume. For a sick woman.

CHAPTER THIRTY SEVEN

After Jack had given Serena the books, it took another four days for her to get back to them. When she called, Jack's first thought was that he had a heavy breather on the phone. But then she spoke, her voice muffled.

'Sir Galahad.' A kind of smacking sound. 'Good evening to you.'

The reason for the indistinct diction, he realised, was because she was chewing.

'Were you able to crack the code?'

She responded with something unintelligible.

'Serena. Take it out. Stick it on the wall.'

'OK,' she said amiably and then after a bit, 'Better?'

'Much. Hold on. I'm putting you on speakerphone.' Jack glanced over to where Eloise was pouring from a bottle of wine. As she placed the scratched tumbler in his hand he made a mental note to buy her some proper wine glasses.

'OK,' he said to Serena as he positioned his mobile phone on the table. 'Go.'

'Right. I ran the numbers against *Neuromancer, Sermons* and *Angler*. The tough part was figuring out which numbers refer to which book but, once I had that figured out, it was easy. Well, fairly easy. It basically came down to identifying the page, the line, the correct word and the correct letter.'

'Sounds good to me.'

'Except that around three-thirty this morning I realised I was being taken for a ride.'

'What do you mean?' He took a swig from his glass. The wine was tannic.

'I mean, the guy who wrote this code is one devious motherfucker. There is systematic misdirection in the numerical key. Would have fooled most people, except I'm not most people. I'm a genius.' No false modesty for Serena.

'So you solved it?'

'It depends on what you mean by *solved*. I've uncovered what was meant to be hidden. But what it means? No idea. They're a bunch of senseless sentences. But kind of cool, you know? Like Buddhist koans. Do you have a pen?'

He plonked down the glass and grabbed the pad of paper and the pencil that Eloise held out to him. 'Shoot.'

'If light has no age, perhaps time has no shadow.'

'Huh?'

She continued almost immediately: 'If you don't know where you are going, all roads lead there.'

'What—'

'Shut up and write.'

He shut up and wrote.

'If no one looks at the moon, will it disappear?'

'Wait.' He stopped writing. 'This one I recognise. It's a quantum physics riddle.'

'Yeah?' A popping sound. She must have decided to resume her chewing. 'Sounds to me like poetic shit dreamed up by someone who was high.'

'Is that all of it?'

'Two more. The first is a word.' She spelt it out for him.

'Otsworth? What's that?'

'How the hell should I know?'

He sighed. 'Alright. What's the last one?'

'I think it's Latin.' She enunciated each letter carefully: 'N-O-N O-M-N-I-S M-O-R-I-A-R.'

'*Non omnis moriar…*'

'That's the one. Mean anything to you?'

'As a matter of fact, it does: it's a quote from Horace. It means, "I shall not altogether die."'

'Cree-py.' Another pop. 'And now I have some bad news for you. We're missing a book.'

'What! There's a fourth book?'

'Yes, Einstein. There's a fourth book.'

He looked at Eloise. She lifted her shoulders helplessly.

Serena spoke again. 'So you need to get me the fourth book. Otherwise I can't finish the job … Hello, are you still there?'

'I don't know how I'm going to get it to you if I don't know the title and which edition it is.'

'Well, work it out, yeah? And tell Charlie I expect a down-payment about now.' She gave a deliciously dirty laugh and hung up.

Jack looked at Eloise again. 'You have no idea what the fourth book is?'

'The note from my mother only lists those three books.'

'And these sentences?' He glanced back at his notepad. 'Does any of them sound familiar?'

'They do not.' She spoke with exaggerated slowness.

'What about this word: Otsworth?'

'No.'

'Are you sure? Think, Eloise.'

'I told you, I don't know!' Her voice was ragged.

'I'm sorry.' He felt like a bully. 'I'm sorry.'

She picked up his mobile phone and after a moment he saw the Google logo with its cheerful primary colours appear on the screen. As she started scrolling, her lips moved along with her thumb. 'Otsworth … Otsworth Collection …'

'Find something?'

'Maybe.' She didn't look up, her eyes moving over the text. 'It says here the Otsworth Collection is more than two hundred years old and home to some rare writings and original manuscripts.'

'Sounds promising.' He twisted her hand around so that he could see the screen properly. 'It's a library?'

'Looks like it. But no lending services. See – it says here the collection is not open to the public.'

He shrugged. 'No matter. We'll find a way to get in.'

'And then what? '

He was momentarily confused by her question. But it was true, of course. Even if they managed to get inside, they wouldn't have the first idea what to look for.

She dropped the phone onto the table and suddenly pressed her hands against her face. 'Oh, God. We're never going to work this out.'

'Yes, we will.' He placed his arms around her from behind and drew her close.

She twisted sideways and looked up at him. He couldn't put his finger on it, but for just a moment it felt as though she had subtly withdrawn from him. But then she turned around fully and started to undo his shirt buttons. She slipped her hand inside his shirt and he felt her lips against his chest. 'It can wait.'

She watched as he walked his fingers across the calluses on her feet, the scar on her ankle left by something sharp and unexpected in the dark during a night run months ago. He traced his fingers up the inside of her thigh. His hands were warm, but she shivered.

There was a candle next to the bed; the flame was scented and slightly smoking. He had bought it for her. Over the past few days he had been buying her things: roses, a box of fancy chocolates, a new pair of running shoes, a silk shawl with a fringe. She had but to express admiration for something in a shop window and he would immediately want to go in and buy it for her. She needed to tell him to stop. It made her feel … how did it make her feel? The thought hovered in her mind, unformed … slipped away.

The candle flickered. It was the only illumination apart from the necklace of white fairy lights strung around the thick concrete pillars of the room and around the slim posts of the bed. She stared at them over his shoulder. One tiny bulb had gone out: a black hole in a string of perfect symmetry.

He was on top of her now, and she drew her thumb across his collarbone, feeling the savage bone through the skin. He was so beautiful. The muscle definition in his arms and shoulders was strong without being bulky. There was a vein throbbing at the side of his neck, and she placed her fingers against it.

He lowered his head to kiss her and his mouth tasted of wine. She moved her hands to the bottom of his spine, lacing her fingers together. He breathed in and his eyes closed, long lashes sweeping his cheeks.

Yesterday he had asked her about her dreams. 'What do you dream of?' He had leant forward, staring into her eyes as if her dreams might tell of a revelation. She did not dream, she told him. Which was true, as much as it wasn't true. The other night she had dreamed of an old city walled against spear-wielding intruders and of fallow fields where wild orchids grew and ancient armies had fought and died. It hadn't felt real – she knew she was dreaming – and maybe the dream had its birth in something she had read or seen posted on the window of the tiny travel shop around the corner, because she had never vis-ited such a place. Or had she? Maybe she had indeed travelled there: her other self. Perhaps that woman had left fingerprints on the sun-washed stone, leaving tangible evidence of her pas-sage. If so, she had not taken anything with her when she left: no memories of smell or sound, no visual images evoking an emotional response which would signal that these memories truly belonged to her and were not remembered pictures from a magazine.

The other her. The real her, according to the man in the wheelchair. Eloise Blake was the echo; Jenilee Gray the orig-inal sound. Maybe that meant that she could never go back. Because an original sound can produce an echo, but an echo cannot produce an original sound.

His breathing was speeding up, his body tensing. She watched his face – no holding back, completely vulnerable and open to her. When he shuddered and released, she felt tears come to her eyes.

The woman behind him, the woman whose long white fingers now rested on his shoulder, seemed somewhat amused. Hair like pale silk. Wanton mouth. Bare shoulders. A tattoo inked on the delicate skin of one wrist.

The outlines of the room wobbled; the darkness turned white at the edges. As the woman smiled again, she felt her own mouth open in protest.

'No,' she said, and 'No' again – louder – but Jack didn't hear. She watched as he turned his back on her and reached out to the blonde woman. His fingers coiled her silken hair around his fist, and he pulled her towards him slowly; so very slowly …

'NO!' The scream was so unexpected, it felt as though a giant hand had punched him in the chest, sucking the breath right out of him. The next moment Eloise pushed against him and he almost fell off the bed. She was still screaming, her voice high – a keening, insane sound.

Jack slammed his finger against the switch on the wall. The fluorescent lights against the ceiling sputtered; burst into life.

The screaming stopped as though cut by a knife. She flinched and blinked against the ugly, shadow-less glare.

'Eloise!'

He recoiled before the hate in her eyes.

'I'll kill you!' She flung herself at him and he felt her nails rake across his face.

'Stop it!' He grabbed her by the wrists and flung her down on the bed. She strained against his grip and started screaming again. Her face was ugly; spittle flew from her lips.

'Eloise! Stop it! Please!'

She resisted for another moment. Her pupils were huge and dilated. But then she suddenly stopped fighting him and became boneless under his hands. Her sudden collapse was almost as shocking as her attack. And now she was weeping – sobbing – a sound so desperate it made him clench his jaw.

'I'm sorry.' She was shivering, her teeth chattering. 'But I saw her. I saw her. She was right there. I saw her right behind you.'

He tried to moderate his own breathing. His heart was racing like a steam train and he felt slightly sick. 'It's OK. Come to me. It's OK.'

He pulled her into his arms and after a while the shivering stopped and she drew a long, shuddering breath.

'I'm going to make you some tea, OK?'

For a moment she held on to him, but then she nodded.

In the kitchen he switched on the kettle and took a mug from the shelf, adding four big teaspoons of sugar and a teabag. He looked over to where she was sitting on the bed, picking unseeingly at a thread from the quilt wrapped around her. She looked vulnerable. Defenceless. Lost. Wholly unthreatening.

I'll kill you!

He suddenly realised he too was shivering and must be in shock himself. He looked into the small mirror above the sink. She had drawn blood. There were three deep scratches across his cheek.

He handed her the mug. 'Drink up.'

She sipped obediently and when she placed the mug on the bedside table, her hand was almost steady. He reached out again and pulled her into his arms, not saying anything, simply concentrating on holding her close.

He felt the breath from her lips on his skin. 'It's getting worse.'

'The hallucinations?'

'Yes. They felt so real. What if I start having trouble recognising what is true and what's not?'

She reached out a tentative hand and touched his face. 'And look what I did.' Her voice was indescribably sad.

'It's nothing.' He thought desperately of something to say that would comfort her. 'We're going to fix this, I promise.'

'How?'

He couldn't bear to look her in the eyes any longer. He drew her to him again and she leant her head into the curve of his neck like a weary child.

Over her shoulder he could see the bedside table and the pad of paper with Serena's sentences: enigmatic, senseless, maddening.

If light has no age, perhaps time has no shadow.

If you don't know where you are going, all roads lead there.

If no one looks at the moon, will it disappear?

Non omnis moriar ...

She must have sensed his body stiffen because she moved away. 'What?'

He reached for his mobile phone.

'Who are you calling? The loony bin?' She tried to smile.

'Don't be silly. The loony bin is closed on weekends. We'll have to wait until Monday.'

Esquith picked up on the third ring. He sounded sleepy and testy. '*Hello?*'

'Charlie. Explain to me again about Aleister Crowley and his magical diaries.'

'Jack?' There was a rustling sound. 'What the hell? Do you know what time it is?'

'I'm sorry. It's important. You said members used their magical mottoes as names when they wrote in their diaries.'

There was a pause as Esquith tried to gather his scattered thoughts. 'Yes. Crowley expected his followers to use the diaries as a scientific tool. The diaries functioned like laboratory notebooks of the inner psyche: chronicling daily activities and self-reflection. Members used their magical names when writing in the diaries. Why?'

'Never mind. Go back to sleep.'

'Thanks very much!'

Jack hung up. 'This,' he tapped his finger to the page. 'This is the title of the fourth book. It is a unique book. A true one-of-a-kind: the diary of Sister N.O.M. Sister Non *Omnis Moriar*. Your mother.'

She looked at him with parted lips.

'The diary must be in the Otsworth Collection.' He was speaking rapidly now, the words tumbling over each other. 'We must go get it. And then give it to Serena.'

'And the sentences?'

'I don't know. We have to talk to someone who does.'

'Barone?'

Jack shook his head. 'I still believe he has your best interests at heart. But he is too close to Godine ... and that man I don't trust. No, I suggest we talk to one of the other members of Mnemosyne first.'

'Your father?' She brought her hand to her face with the thumb under her chin and the forefinger crooked across her mouth. It looked like a question mark.

'Not my father.' He smiled grimly. '*Cherchez la femme.*'

CHAPTER THIRTY EIGHT

It was a surprisingly mild day for November and the sunshine that slanted through the window and onto Bella Wilding's dressing table was bright. A cheerful sun, she thought. And unforgiving: she preferred a kinder light. She snapped the velvet curtains close together, cutting the wash of yellow to a mere glimmer.

She sank down on the satin pouffe and studied her face. It was still a beautiful face with its patrician nose and high cheekbones; its unexpectedly wanton mouth. But like the petals of a flower showing a fingernail of brown at the end of summer, her features were becoming marked by the passage of time. It showed in the gentle fraying of the skin underneath her eyes, the ever-deepening line next to her mouth, the softening of her jaw. Sometimes she envied plain women.

She wondered how Julianne would have aged if she had lived. Not that Julianne had been plain – far from it – but her beauty was not what had defined her. Her genius made her who she was. Her genius and her neediness. How sad that someone as brilliant as Julianne had been so uncertain of herself and so desperate for love. Julianne could have ruled the world. Instead, she had allowed herself to be ruled by a man who did not have even a fraction of her talent or potential.

It was time to stop daydreaming. They would be here any minute. Nervously, she ran her finger over the gold-capped tubes of lipstick. These days she usually stuck to more decorous shades – pale browns, dusty pinks – which were more flattering to a mature skin. But today – today she needed courage. She unscrewed the top of one of the gleaming tubes and brought it to her mouth. Pirate red.

Only one thing left to do before she faced them. She walked over to the cupboard and opened the top drawer. It was filled with dozens of left-handed gloves. She was known for it: wearing only a single glove. It was not a fashion statement, even though most people thought it was. She pushed her hand into the tight grip of a black leather glove and flexed her fingers.

Her feet made no sound on the soft carpeted stairs. But one flight down, the carpet ended and her heels clicked on bare plank floors. She grimaced at the sight of the ladder and other building paraphernalia, which the builders had left behind before taking off for the weekend. When she had bought the house next door, she had thought it would be a simple matter to knock down the dividing walls and extend the living space, but she was no longer so sure.

One of the walls had a hole sledgehammered into it. Gingerly she drew the polythene sheeting to one side and peered into the long, dark passage behind. It smelt dusty and looked decidedly uninviting – if not downright dangerous – with open gaps in the floor and strange dark stains on the walls. She dropped the sheeting in a hurry and turned around. Crossing the landing to the other side, she opened the doors onto her beautiful, ordered drawing room with a sense of relief.

Here there was no smell of dust, only the scent of lilies. Fresh flowers in the house was something she had become addicted to ever since the summer she first visited Whiteladies. The garden there had yielded the most perfect blooms and Daniel's housekeeper had filled every room with fragrance.

Whiteladies. The scent of freshly mown grass. Sun slanting off the mullioned windows, creating a diamond glitter, which makes her shade her eyes as she turns her head in the direction of a child's laughter. Julianne, video camera in hand, chasing after her daughter who weaves across the lawn like a small, drunken sailor before collapsing in a heap of frilly dress and bruised knees. Julianne scooping the little girl into her arms. Extravagant kisses to stop the laughter from turning to tears. And she, shading her eyes, watching mother and child, and trying to conceal her cold, cold heart.

The sound of a taxi pulling up outside the house, its engine idling, brought her back to the present. From behind the lace curtains she watched as a young man pushed his long legs out of the cab door before hauling himself onto the pavement. As he turned around to assist the second person inside the cab, his profile was towards her – as clean-cut as an etching on a penny. Leon's son. She would have recognised him anywhere.

She turned her gaze to the inside of the cab to where a girl was emerging with head bowed, her eyes on her feet.

Bella Wilding brought her hand to her throat.

'What did she sound like on the phone?' Eloise's face was set.

Jack tried to put his arm around her shoulders but she disengaged herself with a slight shrug. She was as jumpy as a cat. Whenever he tried to touch her, she'd move away as if scared she might suddenly lash out again.

'What did she sound like?' he repeated. 'Sympathetic, I guess. She said she'd try to help.'

'I'm still not sure why you reached out to her. We don't know this woman. We don't know if we can trust her. If she was a member of Mnemosyne, we probably can't.'

'I'm not saying we should trust her. But she may know what those sentences mean. She almost certainly has other information that might help us. Let's give it a chance, OK?'

'Anything you say.' Her voice was tight.

'Eloise …'

'Relax.' Her face was pinched. 'I'll behave.'

They crossed the road. The houses that lined the street were tall and elegant but this area of Notting Hill had retained a touch of bohemia. The cars lining the kerb were an eclectic mix: a BMW, a Volvo, a beaten-up Willys Jeep, an old Herbie Volkswagen with a dirty interior. But the sleek shape of a Porsche was parked further up the block.

On the pavement outside number 71 was a skip filled to the brim with building detritus. The house immediately adjacent seemed derelict and its façade was disfigured by steel scaffolding. He noticed a metal plate hanging jauntily from one of the steel bars: 'MURRAY SCAFFOLDING. CALL ON US FOR STRONG ERECTIONS.' Cute.

They walked up the shallow flight of stairs and Jack placed his finger on the buzzer.

They waited. The house was quiet. The curtains on the ground floor were drawn. After about half a minute he placed his thumb on the buzzer again and tried to listen for sounds coming from within. Nothing stirred. Only a thick layer of silence. But he suddenly had the strongest feeling that there was someone on the other side after all. Someone who had her hand loosely pressed against the door, as if trying to come to a decision.

When the door opened, it was so sudden, he took an involuntary step backwards. Beside him, Eloise gave a sharp intake of breath.

The woman facing them was immediately recognisable as the stunning blonde girl standing next to his father in the Mnemosyne photograph. And yet she seemed a different person. It wasn't the wrinkles around her eyes or the slackness at her throat, but something barely definable. The young Bella Wilding had exuded an air of aloof arrogance: I'm young. I'm beautiful. I know where I'm going. This woman's mouth was not as indomitable.

'You.' Eloise spoke from beside him, her voice high; tension plucking at her vocal cords. 'You ... I see you ... all the time.'

'I know.' Bella Wilding inclined her head. 'Please, won't you come in.'

• • •

She opened the door fully and they stepped inside.

The hallway was filled with things: lamps with rose-tinted silk shades, pieces of velvet-upholstered furniture pushed up higgledy-piggledy against each other, Chippendales rubbing shoulders with Victorian-style armoires, a massive ginger jar, bric-a-brac, fat-cheeked wooden angels, oil paintings leaning against each other like drunken men, something that looked like a mah-jongg set in ivory, and a collection of exquisite Chinese fans, their spines splayed like the brittle bones of a bird.

'Excuse the mess,' Bella waved a vague hand. 'Renovations.'

They picked their way through the clutter to where the curve of a staircase wound its graceful way upwards. Jack was surprised to find that he was starting to feel claustrophobic. There was a rather overpowering scent in the air and he noticed several vases with yellow narcissus flowers arranged on top of a slender bureau that had dolphins' heads for drawer pulls. He glanced over at Eloise, who was looking uncomfortable as well. There was too much stuff. Too much opulence.

The wall next to the staircase was covered in mirrored glass, reflecting their figures back at them as they made their way up the stairs. On the first landing was a ladder, a table with a tray and trowel, and a box of nails. They seemed out of place, as did the dirty plastic sheet, which barely covered an open gap in the wall; the brickwork broken and rough.

Bella noticed his look. 'I bought the house next door. I'm beginning to think it was a mistake.' She gestured at him to follow her into a room to the left. 'It's better in here.'

He didn't know if it was better, but it was certainly luxurious: all silks and velvets and dripping chandeliers. Once again his nose filled with the scent of flowers: lilies, this time. He had already noticed the orange pollen stain across Bella's sleeve. It suddenly occurred to him that a few moments ago she might have been standing next to that bowl of flowers at the window; a furtive watcher.

She sat down in a large armchair and gestured to them to take a seat on the over-stuffed sofa.

For a few moments it was silent in the room. When she had opened the door to them, she had seemed unsure of herself, Jack thought, watching the calm, beautiful face of the woman opposite him. But she had since regained her composure.

She wore a severely tailored white shirt and black trousers, the mannish cut emphasising her femininity. Her hair was silver-blonde and caught in a loose chignon – the kind that appeared casual but which required skill and time to put together.

Eloise broke the silence. 'I know you. You walk through my thoughts. You are inside my house. I see you everywhere. You and the others. I hear you whispering.'

'Yes.'

'Why? I want the truth.'

'There is no one truth.' Bella Wilding stroked the glove on her arm. Black leather, it came up to her elbow where it flared like the gauntlet of a musketeer. Striking, but odd. Jack wondered what had happened to the woman that necessitated her wearing it. Her right hand was bare.

'Do you know what I do for a living?' Bella didn't wait for an answer. 'I am a memory curator: a chronicler of memories, if you will. People come to me – usually at the end of their lives – and ask me to help them recall their past. They want to make sense of their life and who they are.'

'You're a therapist?'

Bella smiled. 'No. The reason people go to therapists is because they have memories that are troublesome and they want them fixed. The therapist usually tries to bring repressed memories to the surface and insists that the patient attempts a completely honest recollection. That's not what I do.'

'I don't understand.'

'When people reach the end of their lives they are no longer as concerned with accuracy. We tend to revisit our glory days and embellish our triumphs. We gloss over painful episodes. It is no longer necessary to think about loved ones or relatives as realistically as we once did. Many of the major players in our lives have passed on and so we allow ourselves to take the edge off hurtful words; to rationalise our own flawed responses. We become forgetful of the sins of our past. And that's fine. I encourage it.'

'Encouraging lies.' Eloise's voice now held contempt. 'And people pay you for this.'

'They're not lies.' Bella's voice was patient. 'We do not keep our memories sealed in vacuum-packed bags in a deep freeze where they wait for us to unwrap them, flawlessly intact. We are storytellers. We build fables, tales about ourselves in our own minds, throughout the duration of our lives. You can't call them lies. Memory is never really about what happened: memory revises itself year after year. This is how we become the people we are. At the end of our lives, we have built this amazing creation in our minds: part myth, part reality. And I believe' – she paused – 'quite *passionately* that this is how it is meant to be. In my experience, people who age the best are not the ones who try to remember the harsh truth and stare it in the face. No. We are meant to forget. We are hardwired this way.'

She looked Eloise directly in the eye. 'Your mother thought differently.'

On the mantelpiece the clock chimed softly. It was an impressive piece, museum quality, and Jack had noticed it immediately when he walked in. Meissen, possibly nineteenth-century, all gilt and heavenly blue and surmounted by two figures: a sinewy Father Time and the caped man with the scythe. But what kept pulling his eyes back to the piece were the frankly lascivious-looking putti on either side holding floral garlands. They were exquisitely modelled but something about their heavy-lidded eyes was disturbing.

'Your mother believed that what was, can never altogether die. She believed memory could be restored, perfectly. It was a religion for her. A prayer. She was *dauntless*.' The word sounded strange, old-fashioned.

Bella turned her head. 'Your father believed it too.'

Jack shrugged. 'If he believed it, it was not because of religion but because he hoped he could profit from it.'

He had managed to surprise her. The pale eyes looked at him appraisingly. 'Yes. Julianne, on the other hand, was an idealist. Her research into hypermnesia – supermemory – was because she wanted to help people. But her ideals got corrupted.'

'By money?'

The angels stared at each other across the bulging clock face with mute lust.

Bella shook her head. 'By love.'

CHAPTER THIRTY NINE

It was a dream breath-taking in its ambition: to map the complex and dizzying maze that is memory and to explore its myriad facets – from science to mysticism. For the young Daniel Barone, it was a calling.

But for the dream to become reality Barone knew he needed help. After careful thought he invited four of his peers to join him in the Order of Mnemosyne. Beautiful, confident and intellectually brilliant, each member approached the memory puzzle from a different perspective.

Barone imagined a world where a learned behaviour such as drug addiction could be cured by a simple injection; where a war veteran's nightmares could be replaced by untroubled sleep, where a rape victim would be able to rid herself of her mental scar tissue forever. A forgetful world.

Yin to his yang was Julianne Gray: intent on finding the key that would allow neurologists to restore those recollections that had become faded or lost. Her goal was to offer victims of memory loss a second chance at remembering. In this quest she was assisted by Leon Simonetti, who also doubled as the group's business manager.

The link between emotion and the hardwiring of long-term memories in the brain was the domain of Bella Wilding, the fourth member and the psychiatrist of the group. And then there was Francis Godine, mystic and visionary, who believed that absolute knowledge and the mastery of memory would allow mortal man to come face to face with God. As the group's conscience, he had the task of keeping the moral compass of the Order of Mnemosyne pointing true. Together, the friends embarked on an ambitious journey of the mind.

'It was a great adventure,' Bella said. While talking, her face had lit up with remembered fervour. 'We were so excited. We thought we were invincible.'

Jack watched her smooth the glove on her arm. It was obviously a gesture from which she derived comfort.

'Why did you model Mnemosyne after the Hermetic Order of the Golden Dawn?'

She gave a graceful half-shrug. 'We didn't – not really. In fact, Francis thinks Crowley was a charlatan. But he approved of the idea of magical diaries in which we recorded our innermost thoughts. He said it would keep us honest. And he believed our work on memory would change us. He wished for us to chronicle our own personal transformation.'

She touched the glove again, a nervous gesture this time. 'You have to understand: Francis is a mystic. He believes in the alchemy of the soul; the transformation of the self. He moulded himself in the image of the memory artists of the Middle Ages who were convinced that memory and knowledge are the closest man will ever come to his creator. To Francis, memory is sacred.'

She ran her tongue over her lips. 'Me? I just thought the whole secret society thing was cool. You know, the idea of having a magical identity separate from a mundane one. Mottoes for names.'

She paused and looked suddenly tired. 'I was young.'
'And then?'
'And then things didn't work out as planned.'
'Why?'

'Passion. Greed. They will always trump science, and even the love for God.'

Eloise leant forward. 'You said my mother was corrupted by love. What did you mean?'

'Julianne was the last member to join Daniel's research unit.' Bella narrowed her eyes as though trying to see more clearly into the past. 'I remember the first time I saw her. She had given birth to you only six months earlier and still hadn't lost the weight she had picked up during her pregnancy. But, God, she was brilliant. Leon saw that from the beginning. He wanted to exploit her talent and turn it into profit. If you consider how many millions of pounds are spent each year on a simple herb such as ginkgo biloba, you can imagine how much people would be willing to pay for a drug that can guarantee them unforgettable memories. Leon was convinced Julianne would be able to do just that.'

'And you?' Jack asked when she didn't continue.

'Money has never been my poison.' She saw him give a quick glance around the luxurious room and shook her head. 'I enjoy luxury but if all of this disappears tomorrow, it wouldn't matter to me. No, I was interested in Julianne's research not because of the money but because I was curious.'

Her lip twisted. 'Such an anaemic word – curious. Let me amend that. I was *insatiably* curious. I was born this way. But my intellectual curiosity has always outstripped my brain power: a case of reach exceeding grasp. Rather sad, wouldn't you say?'

She was still smiling but there was a hint of bitterness there. 'Do you know what my magical motto was?' The smile became self-mocking. '*Quod me nutrit me destruit.*'

'What nourishes me, also destroys me.'

'Exactly. Curiosity feeds the soul … but it leads to temptation.'

She turned towards Eloise. 'I was envious of your mother's genius. And I was fascinated by it; I wanted to know if her research would work. But it takes years to test a drug and get it approved. So Leon and I decided we should push the timeline.

Hard. But it would require Julianne to break the rules and I knew she would never agree to that. Unless …'

Bella looked back at Jack. 'I am going to tell you things about your father which you may not want to hear.'

'Nothing you can say about my father will shock me, believe me.'

She accepted this with a slight inclination of her head. 'Leon deliberately set out to seduce Julianne. It wasn't difficult: Leon had a way with women. He saw to it that Julianne fell hopelessly in love with him. I suggested it.'

'You suggested it.' Eloise's voice was flat.

'Your mother was brilliant, but needy. I recognised the type immediately.'

'The type?' Still that flat voice, but something dangerous lurking underneath the surface.

He placed a calming hand on her arm. 'Alright. Julianne Gray becomes infatuated. My father is in a position to fulfil his dastardly, money-grubbing plans. Then what?'

Bella's voice was without emotion: the voice of an academic. 'The basis of learning and memory in the human brain is molecular and cellular in nature. If we were ever going to strengthen potentiation, chemical intrusion would be necessary. A drug. Julianne called it DE7.'

A pause.

'We tested it on rats first, of course. We injected it into their neocortex and the results were astonishing. But we knew it would be far more valuable to try out DE7 on a human test subject. Jenilee was five years old. The optimum age. Any younger and we risked infantile amnesia. But at five the hippocampus is fully operational and a sense of identity is in place. Perfect.'

It took him a moment to grasp the implications. 'You injected her in the brain?'

The outrage in his voice had the effect – shockingly – of making her seem deeply bored. 'The brain has no pain receptors. These were tiny procedures. The child did not suffer.'

He looked at her calm features and felt like slapping her. But this time Eloise was the one who reached out a restraining hand. 'To what purpose?'

'DE7 strengthens the speed dial connection between the molecules that are involved in creating and maintaining recall. It lifts neurotransmitter receptor expression and enhances synaptic connection strength. In layman's terms, we managed to turbo-boost your memory. We vastly increased your capability for recollection.'

'Let me guess,' Jack said. 'It didn't end there.'

'No.' She glanced away from him and looked down at the floor. 'Leon decided we should try to add additional memories to Jenilee's memory bank. Memories that were not her own.'

'Why, for God's sake?'

'Leon foresaw a future where people would be willing to buy and sell memories. Glamorous memories. Exciting memories. Memories of film stars. Or star athletes. Even politicians.'

He stared at her, dumbstruck.

Bella made an impatient gesture. 'It's not such a wild idea. Gossip magazines sell like hot cakes. Imagine if people could buy the memories of superstars. It could even be considered a kindness. It would allow dull people with dull lives to live vicariously. They may even find themselves transformed by those memories: become less dull and more stylish and daring themselves.'

'Whose memories were added to mine?' Eloise's voice was very quiet.

'Don't you know?'

'My mother's.'

Bella nodded. 'Julianne made video recordings of events seen from her own perspective. She played these to you under hypnosis and imprinted on you her own emotional response. It was fascinating: an adult frame of reference implanted on an almost virginal matrix. And she continued to dose you with DE7. It was thrilling: we were in effect retooling the engram factory itself.'

Thrilling. The woman didn't seem to understand how grotesque she sounded.

Jack found his voice. 'Was Godine involved in the experiments you did on Jenilee?'

'Hardly.' Bella gave a short laugh. 'When Francis found out, he was furious. Self-righteous prick.'

The obscenity shocked, as did the sudden glimpse of unplumbed venom behind the poise and elegance.

'Did Daniel Barone know what was going on?'

'No – thank God. And he is still in the dark. Francis never told him. Francis wanted to shield Daniel against the ...' she took a deep breath, *'disappointment.'* The word hung in the air, clearly inadequate. 'Daniel is an idealist. He would have considered our actions the greatest betrayal. And it didn't help that he and Julianne were a couple.'

Jack looked up sharply.

Bella nodded. 'Daniel was very much in love with her. Obviously, she kept her affair with Leon a secret from him. Daniel would have been destroyed if he knew she not only used her child as a guinea pig, but had also cheated on him. Francis wanted to spare him the pain of ever finding out. Francis is very protective of Daniel.'

'So this explains why Barone is still friends with my father.'

'Yes. If he knew the truth, I doubt the friendship would have survived.'

Jack frowned. 'If Barone was in the dark, why did he end Mnemosyne?'

'Because of Julianne's murder. Daniel simply couldn't cope with his grief. And then, shortly after she died, he had his own accident and was paralysed. He lost heart, I think.' Her eyes darkened with remembered regret. 'Leon went to the States. Francis moved in with Daniel to take care of him and I started a new life.'

'Why did you and my father not continue with the research? Just the two of you?'

'We tried. But Julianne was the only one who knew the exact formula for DE7. And she took it to her grave. We never found her notes.'

Long seconds of silence passed without anyone speaking. Then Eloise said, 'Why are you being so helpful? You didn't have to tell us any of this.'

'Would you believe me if I told you I am trying to make amends?'

'Why wouldn't I? You've shown such remorse.'

Bella winced. 'I am a scientist. I can't help but be excited by possibilities. But I also wake up in the middle of the night and I know what we did was wrong. If I can help you, I will.'

'In that case,' Jack took his notebook from his inside pocket and handed it to her. 'What are these?'

CHAPTER FORTY

Memory image 21776

I want to please him, the man I love. But I don't trust him, the man I love.

I need to protect my daughter – just in case. Just in case something goes wrong – not today, or tomorrow, but far in the future. Just in case there comes a time when I am no longer around to help her, should she need me.

How?

I must devise a talisman for protection. A tool she can use to render undone the memories I've imprinted in her brain. A failsafe.

Leon is aghast when I tell him, but this time I am strong. I am adamant. Even though she may never need the failsafe, Jenilee should have the option. One should always have the option of going back.

How?

A key.

A mental on-off switch.

A code word.

Simple.

CHAPTER FORTY ONE

'Do you know what they mean – these sentences?' Jack pushed his notebook at Bella. 'You said you wanted to help. Here's your chance.'

The sunshine outside the window of Bella's house had disappeared. The elegant room was filling with shadows.

'*If light has no age, perhaps time…*' Bella stopped reading. 'So you *do* know.'

Bella touched her lips with hesitant fingers. 'When Julianne imprinted Jenilee, it was done under hypnosis. These were the sentences she used to put Jenilee under.'

She glanced at Jack. 'They're also one half of a key.'

'A key?'

'Julianne wanted to make sure there's a failsafe; a way to get out of it. If the imprinted memories ever became trouble-some, Julianne wanted to give Jenilee a way of blocking them. These sentences,' she gestured at the notebook, 'give her that option. But only if they are used under hypnosis in combination with a code word.'

A code word.

In Eloise's eyes, Jack saw hope, which was starting to touch his own mind as well.

'Do you know what the code word is?'

'Julianne never told us. She knew we did not like the idea of a failsafe and I think she realised that Leon, in particular, would do anything to keep her from ever using it. She may have been in love with Leon, but she didn't trust him. She certainly did not trust me.'

'Why am I not surprised?' He was staring at her unseeingly, but he could feel a bubble of excitement rising inside him.

'If we can find the code word, Eloise can free herself of the hallucinations. Isn't that right? We will have found the cure.'

'There is one thing you have to understand.' Bella's voice was low.

Jack frowned, not liking the tone of her voice.

'Using the code word was supposed to be an uncomplicated process – like turning a key in a lock. Open. Close. But Julianne could not have foreseen that Jenilee would go into a fugue state.'

A pause. 'The fugue state has complicated matters.'

He waited, his sense of excitement starting to ebb.

'Eloise's identity is now linked with Julianne's: the two memories have become integrated. This means that if you use the code word to get rid of the imprinted memories, the chances are you will kill off the fugue identity as well. Block one, and you delete the other. Eloise will almost certainly go back to being Jenilee again.'

'You mean I won't remember anything as Eloise?' Jack felt Eloise's hand tighten on his. 'Not even this conversation?'

'No. You will pick up your life once more as Jenilee. Probably from the moment you first lost your memory.'

'Will I remember Jack?'

Bella looked at her with something like compassion. 'You will not.'

The expression on Eloise's face was so raw, Jack felt his insides twist.

'So what you're saying is, I'm stuck with the voices, the madness.'

'If you keep on living your life as Eloise, yes. And I'm afraid the voices may grow more intense over time.'

In the silence that followed, the soft ticking of the Meissen clock was like the heartbeat of a fourth person.

Eloise got to her feet. 'I have to go now.'

'Please stay.' Bella's voice was urgent. 'Please. There is still much we have to talk about.'

'I don't think I should.' Eloise's voice sounded almost conversational, as though she was declining the offer of a cup of tea. Her face was calm. Her eyes blank. But then Jack saw a vein pulsing at her temple. She was angry, he suddenly realised. So furious, she was blind.

Bella too had picked up on it; he saw her grip the arm of her chair. For a moment something hung in the air – something dense and dangerous.

Eloise turned and walked out of the door without looking back.

The clock ticked anxious seconds into the silent room. There came the sound of the front door opening and closing.

Bella's face was stricken. 'I'm sorry. I—'

He cut her off. 'Tell me this. If Eloise becomes Jenilee again, will she remember the stressor that pushed her into the fugue state in the first place?'

'Almost certainly, yes. But, Jack, you need the code word first. And the code word is in Julianne's diary. She hid it from us. I don't know where the diary is.'

'I do.'

'What!' Her voice shot up. 'Where?'

The greed in her eyes was shocking. She caught the expression on his face and flushed. 'Julianne's diary not only holds the code word. It also contains the formula for DE7.'

'And you want it.'

She didn't respond. He stood up, now wishing only to get away from this woman with her beautiful face and her avid mind; this room with its sickly scent of lilies. 'You and my father. While he was romancing Julianne Wilding, he also had an affair with you, am I right?'

'Leon and I enjoyed each other physically. It wasn't serious.'

'What a lovely, cheating bunch you were. My father cheating on Julianne, Julianne cheating on Barone and you cheating on everyone.'

Her features seemed to flatten out, her cheeks sagged. He suddenly knew what she would look like as an old woman.

'What you, my father and Julianne did to Eloise was child abuse. From where I stand, you are nothing but a criminal. What was it you said earlier? As one grows older, one tends to forget the sins of the past? Well, good luck with that.'

She spoke with a voice that held no energy. 'I am trying to atone, Jack. Forgive me.'

'Find a priest. I don't give absolution.'

She said something very softly; it could have been, 'Wait.' But he didn't stop. In his urgency he almost walked into the ladder straddling the landing outside the door, but he didn't stop. He hastened down the stairs as though he was being chased and hurried on into the shadowed hall with its baroque angels, its jumble of furniture, its pots of flowers and opulent knick-knacks. He breathed deeply as though his lungs were labouring under the assault of the overly fragranced air. It wasn't until he placed his hand on the door knob that he looked over his shoulder.

The staircase was empty.

But as he stepped outside, he looked up at the window on the first floor and thought he saw a hand in a black glove draw the curtain aside for one split second.

Flick.

CHAPTER FORTY TWO

Memory image 32985

I walked in on Bella today as she stood looking at herself in the mirror. Vain Bella with her rapacious mind. She has only two loves and I often wonder which is the greater.

'Come to see the freak show?' She turns around and gestures at her arm. The dressing only came off yesterday and I have no idea what her hand looks like now. She is wearing a glove that comes up to her elbow. It looks strangely glamorous.

When I think about the fire, I find it difficult to concentrate. An electrical fault in Jenilee's playroom, which spread with terrifying rapidity. Strange how long ago it feels – years, not months – but Bella tells me this is commonly the way adults process trauma. I can't remember much, but what I do feel is guilt. It should have been me, rescuing my daughter. But Bella was the first on the scene, and if it hadn't been for her actions, who knows if Jenilee would be alive today?

I watch, feeling detached, as she slowly takes off the glove. The flesh appears melted and marbled, like the fat on a rancid piece of steak. The image of Mnemosyne's lamp, which was tattooed on her wrist only a week before the blaze, is distorted, drooping like something from a Dali painting.

I know I should be thanking her but instead I ask: 'Did you run into the room because you wanted to save Jenilee or because you wanted to save a research project?'

She smiles. So beautiful. So heartless. She walks towards me and brings her face close to mine. 'Does it matter? One day, when we are both old, my motive will be long forgotten. We will remember only that, if not for me, you may have lost a child.'

She leans over and kisses me hard on the mouth. 'And you will be grateful.'

Her lipstick is smeared. She walks back to the mirror to make repairs. I wonder what she'll say if I tell her about the dreams I have. Dreams where I kill her and Leon. Violent, messy dreams of blood and a shiny axe and body parts. Mad, insane dreams.

'It's over, Bella.'

'What is?' She lowers the lipstick and lifts her eyebrows enquiringly, her eyes meeting mine in the mirror.

'I am leaving Mnemosyne. I am taking Jenilee with me.'

She whirls around and her face is suddenly white. 'You can't do that.'

'I can. She is my daughter.'

She looks as though I have punched her in the stomach. She is quite undone. I smile.

'Does Leon know?' Her voice is actually trembling.

'He is still in Edinburgh. By the time he returns, I'll be gone. You must tell him, Bella. He will take it better coming from you.'

'Are you trying to punish Leon and me – because we sometimes enjoy each other? Is that why you're doing this?'

'I am doing this because he wants to turn my daughter's brain into a shopping centre.'

'Your notes—'

'They are safe. But you will not find them.'

She takes a deep breath and I can see her struggling to calm herself. 'Julianne, don't do anything rash. Let's talk about this.'

'The only person I will talk to is Daniel.'

'No!' Alarm disfigures her face. She doesn't look so pretty any more. 'You mustn't tell Daniel. You cannot! He'll end Mnemosyne!'

'Francis always says confession is good for the soul. The time has come for me to confess. Tomorrow I will tell Daniel everything.'

'You selfish bitch.' Her mouth is a red slash in her face. 'It will destroy him.'

'Goodbye, Bella.'

'I won't allow it!' She is screaming.

I walk away. Enough. My new life starts tomorrow.

'Science continues to be a channel for magic – the belief that for the human will, empowered by knowledge, nothing is impossible ...'
　　　　　—*John Grey,*
　　　　　　The Immortalization Commission

CHAPTER FORTY THREE

The Otsworth Collection, according to its minimalist website, was more than two hundred years old and home to some of the rarest writings and original manuscripts in the world. Its original founder, a certain Lord Delvin Otsworth, was described on the site as a 'visionary who wished to create a place of safe-keeping for works of scholarship which straddle the divide between spirituality and empirical science'.

From further googling, Jack learnt that 'visionary' might be an overly generous description for a man who had clearly been a raving lunatic. Otsworth had lived in a crumbling pile in the Chilterns, conducted moonlight séances and orgies in true Hellfire style, painted the inside of his mansion with some rather eye-popping erotic paintings and scryed angels with a fervour that would have put John Dee to shame. But despite his proclivities, he was blessed with a discerning eye and had managed to build up a collection of bona fide high-quality literature dealing with that borderline world where science and mysticism shake hands. Upon his death he left the collection in trust and endowed it with enough money to ensure the archive not only survived, but could, indeed, be expanded. Judicious purchases were made from time to time but new manuscripts were typically donated. As far as Jack could make out, the archive functioned as a kind of vault for manuscripts deemed too private, too controversial or too dangerous to be perused by the general public.

All of which led Jack to expect the collection to be housed in a flamboyantly turreted edifice resembling Hogwarts but, no, the archive had its home in a large Victorian house situated at the end of a discreet cul-de-sac in residential Richmond. Miniature ivy and climbing roses, their white petals rusted by the chill, covered the red brick walls.

But the place did have an enigmatic air about it. Three storeys high, it faced the street squarely and was set behind a curlicued wrought-iron gate and a twelve-foot-high wall. Ruby velvet curtains hugged the mullioned windows that flanked the imposing wooden door. An intertwined O and C were carved into the green, lichen-stained flagstones of the driveway.

Jack pushed through the gate and started walking towards the house at a crisp pace. Although access to the collection was restricted, he had been granted permission to visit and for this he had Charlie to thank – or rather Charlie's father – it helped if you were one of the most influential men in the City. A phone call from Esquith Sr had opened the door to the archives – albeit only a fraction. Jack would be allowed to read from the diary but would not be allowed to make notes. And he could not do any photocopying of any kind. Still, simply to be allowed inside was a major concession.

Of course, it did involve a little fibbing and an identity swap. Lionel Esquith was under the impression that he had arranged access to the archives for his son, not his son's friend. Therefore, inside Jack's wallet now reposed two of Charlie's credit cards and a doctored driver's licence, courtesy of Serena. Esquith Sr, thankfully, was happily ignorant of this state of affairs. Just as well. Jack had met Charlie's father once before: a man as choleric and fierce as his son was languid and laid-back.

It was only four o'clock in the afternoon but it had clouded over so much it was almost dark. There was a strange purple haze in the sky that promised nasty weather, and the flagstones underneath his feet were already spotted with a few fugitive drops of rain. Jack jogged up the front steps and tugged on the old-fashioned bell pull. It pealed deep within the house.

A surveillance camera was angled above his head. Someone was watching. But when the door clicked open, there did not seem to be anyone on the other side. He pushed the door open and stepped into the lobby.

A young woman in a cherry-red suit and high heels was sitting behind a slender Hepplewhite desk on which rested nothing except a vase of flowers. No papers, no pens, no computer. Just a telephone and a surveillance screen. He was in the presence of the gatekeeper.

She watched him coolly and with a kind of detached interest. One slender eyebrow moved slightly, which he took as a sign that he was meant to approach. He stepped forward and gave her his most winning smile. 'I'm Charles Esquith. I have an appointment with a Mr Cole?'

'Yes.' She frowned a little. Either she found his attempt at a British accent troubling or the idea that he was to be allowed inside these hallowed halls did not rock her boat. 'Identification, please.'

He handed over the credit cards and the fake driver's licence. If she was impressed with his rakishly handsome image smiling at her from the little plastic card, she did a heroic job of keeping her admiration in check. But at least she didn't query its validity.

She handed the cards back to him. 'May I have your mobile phone?'

'Excuse me?'

'Your mobile phone.' She spoke in the patient tone of someone dealing with a not-too-bright child. 'And do you have a camera? I will need that as well.' She opened the slim desk drawer and removed a clear cellophane bag. 'You are allowed to take with you your keys and wallet, but please place them in this bag.'

Right. So much for his plan to use his mobile phone to sneak pictures of the diary's pages.

'Shoes?' he asked nastily.

Another miniscule lift of the eyebrow.

'Should I take them off?'

His attempt at sarcasm made no dent on her glacial composure. 'That will not be necessary.'

Plastic bag in hand, Jack followed the ice queen as she walked with a measured tick of her high heels across the entrance hall and down a creaky passage where the walls were covered in a depressing-coloured William Morris print. It was very quiet. Jack wondered how many other members of staff worked on the premises.

At the end of the passage was a lift, its doors open. The ice queen gestured him inside.

'Mr Cole will meet you downstairs.' Without entering, she leant forward and pressed a button marked with a B before stepping back. The doors closed.

The lift hummed and then stopped with a slight bump. After a moment the doors opened slowly.

Jack walked out and stopped, surprised. He had expected long, depressing metal shelves and a bunker-like atmosphere or else scarred wooden desks, battered leather chairs and dusty volumes. But the room in which he found himself was unlike anything he had ever seen.

Pale limestone floors and walls. A breathtakingly lofty ceiling. A small number of slim desks and matching anorexic chairs were arranged in a semi-circle in the middle of the room. From each desk a small halogen light sprouted like an alien eye. But it was the collection of books that made him draw his breath.

The books were sequestered behind a glass wall, but seemed to float. Housed not in shelves but hanging instead from wires thin and glistening as strands of nectar, they seemed ghostly. Each volume, or sheaf of papers, was encased in its own acrylic box. Their otherworldly appearance was even more pronounced because of the violet-coloured light in which they were bathed – to keep the pages from fading, Jack guessed. The rows of boxes stretched upwards, the last row practically touching the high ceiling.

The keeper of the archives was the biggest surprise. No stooped academic or druid-like figure this. Bulky and squat with a block-like face which showed eyebrows and hairline in close proximity and ears resembling cauliflowers, he looked like a wrestler who had seen bad days in the ring. But his voice, when he spoke, was soft and cultured.

'Mr Esquith.' He held out a ham of a hand. 'I am David Cole.'

Jack gingerly took the hand, but the man's grip was gentle.

'I understand you would like to examine a volume from our personal diary collection: The Diary of Sister *Non Omnis Moriar*, of the Order of Mnemosyne.'

'I would, yes.'

'Follow me, please.'

As they started walking, Jack gestured at the hanging books. 'This is very impressive. But what happens if you have a malfunction? Do the books stay marooned up there?'

'We do have back-up – of the old-fashioned kind.' Cole pointed to a tall metal rod with a steel hook hanging from the wall. 'It hasn't let us down yet.'

'Are all these manuscripts restricted?'

'Some are available for academic research. Others have time stamps as to when they may be released to the public. We have papers in our keeping which will not be released for another century. ' He glanced over at Jack. 'As I am sure you are aware, the collection houses not only papers on empirical science but also research within a more mystical frame of reference.'

'Pseudo-science.'

Cole's voice was indulgent. 'Mr Esquith, the line between pseudo-science and science is a shifting one. Many scientists, even though they denounced superstition, were closet magicians. Newton. Bacon. Edison tried to create a telephone that would connect the living with the dead. Science is never wholly innocent. It is never completely stripped of the fingerprints of religion or prayer. This is still true today.'

'Huh.'

Cole lifted a quizzical eyebrow – or, at least, Jack surmised he was doing so. With his bushy brows and hairline being such near neighbours, it was difficult to interpret the shift and play of expression.

'Scientists of the twenty-first century are often magi,' Cole continued. 'After all, only those who believe humans have powers which outstrip the science of the day are willing to devote their energy to give us what faith and magic promise: the expansion of consciousness, the knowledge of self, even life eternal.'

He became brisk again. 'Please take a seat. And would you be so kind as to wear these while you are examining the material?' He pointed to a pair of thin white gloves.

Cole stepped over to a device with a LED crystal display set into the wall. Jack watched as his thick fingers tapped the virtual keys with the utmost delicacy.

Far above him, one of the boxes started to descend, looking like a spider travelling down its strand of silk. When it reached the bottom, the sealing rubber of the hermetically sealed doors of the glass cage opened with a soft hiss. Cole stepped inside and retrieved the box, which bore the number '1592' affixed discreetly at the top right-hand corner.

'The diary of Sister *Non Omnias Moriar*.' Cole placed the box on top of the desk. 'I do believe you are the very first of our visitors who will be reading these pages. No one has ever asked to examine it before.'

'Is there any chance you might reconsider and allow me to make notes?'

Cole shook his head firmly and pointed to a red sticker. 'As your father has personally vouched for you, you are allowed to read – but that is all.' Cole nodded at the box. 'I'll leave you to it.'

Jack watched as Cole sat down at a computer behind a glass partition. The partition provided a semblance of privacy and the computer was at the far side of the room, but it was clear that he was not going to be left on his own.

Jack turned his attention to the box. It had a flip top and was made of a shiny but opaque acrylic: he could just make out the outline of an outsized volume reposing within. Slipping his hand inside, he gently slid the diary from the box. It had the feel of a scrapbook: large and dictionary-thick with ragged-edged paper. The cover was brown hessian and stamped upon it in gold was the outline of an oil lamp with a flickering flame. Embossed beneath the lamp were three raised initials: *N.O.M.*

He opened the cover. On the very first page, written in a female hand, was the inscription: *To my true love, A.V.A.M – the one who walks with me on this journey of discovery.* She had used a fountain pen – the kind with a real nib. It had trailed a hair and there was a slight drag mark to the words 'my true love'.

A.V.A.M. Aut vincere aut mori. The initials his father had used as a member of Mnemosyne. She had called him her true love: this man who had manipulated her feelings; who had damaged her child.

How could love be so blind? And criminally stupid?

He started paging through. The front half of the book appeared to be filled with tabulations, maths equations and daunting formulae. As his gaze travelled uncomprehendingly over the unintelligible figures, he realised with a slight shock that these entries must be what Bella and his father so desired. The Holy Grail. But to his eyes as impenetrable as runic script.

But to his great relief, the second half of the book was composed of entries of a personal kind. Each entry was labelled 'Memory Image' and written in plain English. Unfortunately, though, Julianne Gray's penmanship left a lot to be desired. Not only were the words written in a small hand that was impossibly difficult to read, but they followed each other in such close succession and the sentences covered the pages so densely, they made him go cross-eyed. If he had to read through the entire book, he was going to end up blind. All he was really interested in was the code word, of course, but unfortunately she had not been thoughtful enough to highlight the word or draw an arrow with 'X marks the spot'. It was going to be up to Serena to find it. But how he was going to get this book to Serena was the six-million-dollar question.

The object of the diaries, according to Bella, had been to keep the writer honest: Francis Godine had insisted on it. It looked as if Julianne Gray had taken his words to heart. In fact, as Jack started reading at random, the emotions were so keen, the observations so anguished, he felt like a trespasser. This was not a book meant for prying eyes.

My compass is spinning, Francis. I am sorry, but I am in a twilight place where I am losing myself and what I know to be right. It is a body of black water that threatens to swallow me – and the only reed I can grasp at is the certainty that I am in love.

Even though he knew he would never forgive the woman whose most intimate thoughts he now held in his hands, it was impossible not to feel a twinge of compassion for her. As he continued reading, it became ever clearer that Julianne Gray had been in torment.

Goya had chosen the wall above his dining-room table as the most suitable place for his fresco of Saturn devouring his son. The artist would eat at the table with the mad god gazing at him with amazed eyes, as if astonished by his own monstrousness as he feasts on the body of his child.

Another entry: *In Roman times, an aphrodisiac would be prepared from decaying fish entrails. It seems appropriate. Love makes us sick.*

One entry merely read: *I am in hell.*

There were several blank pages before the last entry.

My plans are made. This is the last time I will write. I will send this book to a place of safe-keeping, away from Leon and Bella's grasping hands. I have imprinted Jenilee for the last time. Along with the solicitor's note I am leaving her, she will have all the clues she needs in case I am no longer there to help her – in case things go wrong. The numbers have not been committed to paper but are safely hidden in the grey-white grooves of her brain: hers alone.

But nothing will go wrong. I intend to grow old and watch my daughter become a beautiful, strong woman. A gifted woman, with a memory like a shining sword. A flower growing out of black soil.

Tomorrow I will confess to Daniel and Francis. I will confess to corrupting our work. Francis will not forgive me for the darkness I have brought to Mnemosyne, but I know Daniel will.

But science is one thing. Love is another. Will Daniel forgive me when I confess to him the other thing? When I tell him about Leon and me? Maybe. I hope so. After all, love is strong as death, hard as hell.

The entry was numbered Memory Image 31198 and dated Thursday the fifteenth of August. Jack felt his heart beat faster. On Friday the sixteenth, Julianne Gray's body was found bludgeoned to death in her kitchen. She had not had her chance to confess, after all.

'Mr Esquith.'

Jack looked up to find Cole at his desk. He had not even noticed the man approaching him.

'I'm afraid we will be closing in fifteen minutes.'

Jack glanced at his watch. Difficult to believe, but almost two hours had gone by. Reluctantly, he pushed back his chair.

He watched as Cole carefully returned the diary to its box and walked to the glass cage where he hooked it onto its wire carrier. A few taps on the pad and the box started its ascent, sliding smoothly into place; once again bathed in that otherworldly violet glow.

Suddenly, everything went black. The lack of light was so absolute, he couldn't see his hand in front of his face. He heard Cole make an annoyed sound and then the air was all at once shattered by the hysterical sound of an alarm.

Cole's voice shouted from somewhere on his left. 'Mr Esquith! Please wait here!'

Jack sensed the man make his way slowly towards a door on the other side of the room. The door swung open, and the gloom lifted slightly as a wash of greyish light filtered in. Then the door swung shut again and Jack was left to himself.

He was feeling disoriented. The alarm was deafening and even though his pupils were adapting to the darkness, it was still stygian.

Suddenly – the alarm fell silent. The unexpected quiet was a shock.

The air felt thick and there was now no sound at all. Slowly Jack shuffled over to the glass cage which was standing open, the doors wide apart.

Such an opportunity. For a moment he entertained thoughts of brandishing the steel rod and hooking the diary from its resting place high above. How he was going to accomplish this feat in the dark was the question, of course, but – if successful – he might just be able to smuggle out the diary underneath his jacket. But before he could put this wild plan into action, the door opened again and Cole walked in with a torch in his hand.

'My apologies, Mr Esquith. We had a power cut, which automatically triggered the security alarm. I had to disengage the system.' Cole held the door open. Jack had no choice but to follow him into a narrow stairwell.

'Don't you have back-up power?' Jack asked as they started to ascend three flights of metal stairs with only the torch providing light.

'I am embarrassed to admit we don't. But we have, in fact, just passed a budget which makes provision for the installation of diesel generators. We'll also be upgrading our system of sprinklers and smoke detectors. Fire, as you will understand, is our biggest concern here at the Otsworth. Another few months and we should be shipshape.'

Back inside the house everything was dark except for another wavering torch in the lobby where the ice queen was listening to her mobile phone with an irritable expression on her face. When she spotted Cole she rested it on her shoulder.

'The entire street is down. The electricity company can't say when power will be restored. Probably not for several hours.'

'In that case, you should go home. And Linda too.'

Cole continued walking to the front door. As he opened it, Jack blanched. The cloudy skies and spitting rain of the early afternoon had turned into a full-blown gale. Rain poured from a dark sky and the trees swayed in the relentless wind.

Cole's voice was dubious. 'Are you parked close by?'

'I'll be alright. Thanks.'

The doors closed behind Jack and he headed towards the gate. Within moments he was drenched, his hair plastered against his head and his feet sloshing wetly inside his shoes.

Halfway down the driveway he turned to look at the building behind him. Inside that house was the diary and inside the diary reposed the second half of the key. He had held the book in his hands; he might even have read the code word itself, oblivious to its true power. If he could smuggle the diary to Serena, she might be able to work her magic. But how was he going to pull it off? The house, with its shuttered windows and sturdy door, appeared impregnable in the driving rain.

Except ... the place was without power. No lights. No alarm system. No security cameras. Maybe the gods were trying to tell him something.

Jack continued down the driveway but, before reaching the gate, he stepped swiftly behind a hedge of star jasmine, which ran parallel to the high boundary wall stretching along the length of the property. He waited to see if his stealthy move had been spotted, but no one charged through the front door asking him to stand and deliver. Dropping to a half-crouch, he kept his shoulders low to ensure his head did not pop up above the hedge and shuffled back in the direction of the house. By the time he reached the side wall, his thigh muscles were quivering and he was wet all the way to his underwear.

Next to him on the ground floor was a window covered with bars and curtains drawn tight. But there was another window on this side of the house as well, a simple casement window devoid of burglar bars, fronted by a small stone balustrade. Promising, except for the fact that it was set three floors up, at attic level.

Jack lowered his head once more and edged cautiously towards the back. One look was enough to make him realise that there was no point of access here. The windows were all shuttered or barred. There was a back door, which looked as though it would take a bulldozer to knock it down, and even from a distance the lock appeared depressingly high-tech.

It was going to have to be that attic window, after all.

He cupped his hand over his eyes and looked up. It was high. He could use a ladder, of course, but first he'd have to get it past the front gate, which was certain to be locked at night. And the idea of trying to manoeuvre a ladder that tall over a spiked gate set into a twelve-foot-high wall was singularly unappealing.

There was a drainpipe running up the side of the house. Jack blinked the rain out of his eyes and contemplated it for a moment. It did not look too vintage, but would it support a man's weight? And if he did manage to shimmy up three storeys of pipework, which he was by no means convinced he would be able to do, how was he going to reach the window, which was at least two arm's lengths away? It would require the skills of a Ninja.

The rain was now coming down with a vengeance. Jack pushed himself against the wall where the overhang of the roof provided some scant shelter, and brought out his mobile phone.

'Eloise? We need Jungles.'

CHAPTER FORTY FOUR

It felt like several centuries before Jack spotted the glowing headlights of Jungles' van. By this time it had stopped raining but the wind had increased in strength and he was chilled to the bone. He slapped his shoulders and jumped up and down like a boxer about to enter the ring.

The van stopped quietly. After a few moments the door on the driver's side opened. Jungles, dressed all in black, stepped out.

Jack abandoned his pathetic shelter at the side of the house and jogged over to the gates, not bothering to hide his presence. Cole, the ice queen and another woman had left the house almost an hour earlier and, as far as he could tell, there was no one left on the premises. His one fear had been that the power would be restored before Jungles' arrival, but everything was still dark and not one light shone from any of the houses lining the street. Their luck was holding. So far.

Jungles had his hands wrapped around the railings of the gate.

'It's locked.' Jack found he had difficulty speaking. His teeth were chattering too much. 'You'll have to jump the wall. Can you make the run?'

'Take this.' Jungles pushed a slim backpack through the railings. Then he moved off to the side, out of Jack's line of vision.

A slight sound above and to his right made him turn his head. Jungles was on top of the wall, his figure more sensed than seen. Soundlessly he dropped down on the other side in a perfect roll.

'Where to now?'

'Here.' Jack led Jungles in the direction of the house.

By some mysterious sleight of hand, Jungles was suddenly holding a torch. It was small, but the powerful beam did a good job of illuminating the drainpipe, which now looked to Jack to be a lot less substantial than when he had examined it earlier.

Jungles placed his hand on the pipe and gave it a shake. If he was feeling anxious he didn't show it. Still, as he turned the torch on the window, it seemed to Jack there was a rather thoughtful expression on his face. The window was a simple casement window set deep into the wall and fronted by a shallow balustrade fashioned from a row of curved ornamental stone shells.

Jungles rubbed his hand over his shaven head. 'You do realise the only way I'm going to get in there is to smash that window?'

Jack nodded.

'That's breaking and entering.'

'I know.'

Jungles looked at him with hooded eyes. 'Let's do it.'

Rummaging inside his backpack, he took from it a pair of long-sleeved gloves. Further rummaging produced a coil of nylon rope, which he wrapped around his chest and shoulder. He took off his shoes and pulled one of the gloves over the fingers of his right hand, returning its twin to the pack along with the discarded shoes. Then he started to climb.

Jack watched with fascination as Jungles edged his way up the wall. He was using the quoins – the corner bricks that stood proud of the walls and which wrapped around the corner of the building – to provide grip for the fingertips of his right hand and the toes of his right foot. The quoins were laid in an alternative pattern of rectangles and were substantially larger than the rest of the brickwork, but using them for anchorage was still an extremely dicey proposition. As Jungles moved upwards, his left hand grasped the drainpipe, while the blade of his left foot sought what little purchase it could find in the shallow mortar bedding.

The wind chilled the lenses of Jack's eyes but he did not look away from the figure inching its way agonisingly slowly up the wall. He hardly blinked, as if by simply keeping his eyes on Jungles, he could somehow will him from toppling backwards.

Jungles was level with the window. With infinite care he turned his head and moved his right hand from the edge of the wall to the drainpipe. A few slow moments later and he brought his right foot over as well. The drainpipe was now supporting his full weight. Jack held his breath.

Jungles stretched out his left arm, clearly trying to judge how much distance there was between the tips of his fingers and the window. Bending his knees, he placed his feet flat against the wall. The next moment, he launched himself sideways at the window ledge, pushing away from the wall, his hands letting go of the pipe and reaching – fingers splayed – for the balustrade.

Jack's heart jumped into his throat. For one horrifying split second he thought Jungles had missed his target. But the next moment the man was hanging from the ledge by his hands – his fingers clutching, his body a dead weight.

Slowly, slowly, his feet found purchase against the wall once more and he pulled himself up to where he could hook first his left, then his right, elbow over the coping. For a few moments he simply stayed like that. The toll on his shoulders must have been enormous.

The sound of breaking glass as Jungles drove his gloved fist through the pane was surprisingly quiet. Jack watched as Jungles unhooked the catch before swinging the window wide.

The next moment he had pulled himself over and disappeared inside.

Jack let out his pent-up breath. But it was too early yet to open the champagne.

The rope snaked down and he stepped forward to tie it around his waist. Focus. Stop the damn shivering. If he continued vibrating like a broken spring, he was never going to make it. He started walking up the wall, simultaneously pulling himself up the rope, and hoped to God Jungles had secured the other end to something solid. Very solid.

The rope remained taut. Halfway up the wall, Jack was sweating and he could feel the strain on his shoulders. As he reached the open window, he felt Jungles grasp his arms in an iron grip, hauling him inside.

The torch showed a room which was obviously used for storage. A row of old-fashioned filing cabinets lined one wall. Numerous cardboard boxes were stacked on top of a massive refectory table. Jungles had fastened the end of the rope to one of its chunky legs.

Jack walked across the room and opened the door. A long passage stretched ahead of them. The smell up here was musty, as though the air seldom circulated.

He spoke over his shoulder. 'I don't think this part of the house is used very often. With luck they may not even spot the broken window straight away.'

Jungles picked up the rucksack and shouldered past Jack, the torch playing over the walls, creating long shadows. The floorboards protested underneath their feet as they made their way down the passage.

They stopped at the staircase and peered downstairs, the torch a wavering spot of yellow picking out the ground floor in the inky darkness below.

Jungles dropped his voice. 'You're sure there's no one around?'

'As sure as I can be.'

They made their way down the three flights of stairs and walked carefully along the creaking passage. All was still.

'Over there.' Jack pointed to the small side door through which Cole had led him earlier in the afternoon. Just as he was about to open it, his foot clipped a big brass pot, which looked hefty but was not. The pot flipped over and clanged hollowly against the side of the wall, making him jump a foot.

If things continued like this, his adrenal glands were going to explode like grenades. Feeling weak, Jack motioned to Jungles to follow him down the metal stairs. The library door was straight ahead.

It was locked.

For a moment he stood there, feeling desperate, but then Jungles touched his elbow and pointed to a hook on the wall. A hook from which hung a single key.

The key slipped into the well-oiled lock and Jack pushed the door aside, allowing Jungles to enter first.

It was black as Hades in here. Jungles played the torch over the hanging boxes and Jack heard him give a soft grunt of surprise. In that quiet, black room, the suspended books in their opaque boxes looked deeply surreal.

'Where is it?'

Jack took the torch from Jungles and pointed it upwards. 'There – fourth box – second row from the top.'

He could sense Jungles staring at him in the dark. 'How the hell do you expect me to get up there?'

'Don't worry. No acrobatics required.' Jack unhooked the large steel pole with its curved hook from the inside wall. 'This should be easy.'

It was not easy. First, the pole was surprisingly heavy. Second, because of its length, it was hard to manoeuvre. And when he finally managed to slip the hook inside the clip, it refused to budge.

'Bloody hell.' Jack wiggled the hook but the box remained stubbornly in place.

'Let me try.'

'No. I have it.' Jack tugged viciously at the clip. The next moment the box swung free, but instead of staying attached to the hook, it crashed heavily to the floor, almost taking down two other boxes in its wake. At that exact moment, the lights came on.

For a moment he and Jungles stared at each other wide-eyed: Lot and his wife.

'We need to get out of here.' The box had a deep crack at the bottom but was otherwise intact. Jack took out the diary and turned to Jungles. 'Did you bring it?'

Wordlessly, Jungles extracted from the rucksack a large volume in fake brown leather. The title was stamped on the spine in gilt letters: THE GOURMET COOKBOOK.

'A cookbook?'

Jungles shrugged. 'Eloise said you needed a thick book with a brown cover. That's all I had.' He shrugged again. 'Chances are no one will open this box any time soon.'

'I hope you're right.' Jack slid the cookbook inside its new home and flipped the top shut. 'Now to get it back up there again.'

Jungles reached decisively for the pole, obviously intent on avoiding a repeat crash performance, but Jack stopped him. 'We can use the lift.'

He walked over to the keypad and keyed in the numbers that were typed on the label affixed to the corner of the box: 1592. The empty carrier second from the top started its descent. When it reached the bottom, Jack clipped the box in place and pushed the enter key. Abracadabra. The box moved steadily upwards and slid into position.

He turned around to find Jungles holding the diary, looking at it intently.

'Bag it.'

'Wait.' Jungles' voice was very quiet.

'Jungles. We have to go!'

'This.' Jungles touched the diary with tentative fingers. 'This can bring Eloise's memory back.'

'Yes.'

'But then she'll forget again.'

'Yes.'

'She'll forget free running. The tribe. She'll forget me.' A pause. 'She'll forget you.'

For a moment they stared at each other, knowing exactly what the other thought.

'What is best for her?' Jungles' eyes were black as space. 'To be Jenilee? Or to be Eloise?'

Jack spoke slowly. 'We can't make that decision for her.'

A long silence. Then Jungles gave a nod that spoke of defeat. He slid the diary inside the backpack. 'Let's get out of here.'

CHAPTER FORTY FIVE

Bella Wilding pushed the off button on her mobile phone and slipped it into the pocket of her shirt before reaching once more for the cut-glass whisky decanter. Champagne used to be her tipple but lately whisky seemed to do the trick more efficiently. She brought the glass to her mouth and emptied it in one deep swallow before immediately filling it again. Glass in one hand, the half-empty decanter in the other, she stepped onto the staircase.

The house was dead quiet. The builders had left hours ago. The sky outside the window was black and gusty, but at least it had stopped raining. The storm had been so strong earlier in the evening she had wondered if the scaffolding outside the house might fall down.

She walked up the stairs, feeling almost gay from the alcohol and humming under her breath. The mirrored glass on the wall next to her glimmered in the light from the wall sconces and she smiled at the blonde woman reflected in its depths. In this light she could convince herself she was still the Bella Wilding who turned heads whenever she walked into a room.

She continued up the staircase and felt herself sway a little. The glass in her hand tilted, a few amber drops spilling onto the carpet, and she hastily righted it again.

As she reached the top of the staircase a sound from below made her stop to listen. Hugging the decanter and glass to her chest, she walked to the balustrade and leant over, peering into the well that stretched down two floors. The well receded and expanded under her gaze and she suddenly felt vertiginous.

'Anybody there?' Her consonants slurred just the tiniest bit. It made her giggle. No doubt about it, she was tipsy, tipsy. *Better get to bed, Bella, and sleep it off.*

Inside her bedroom she placed the whisky on a side table next to her armchair before looking around her, momentarily at a loss. *Oh, yes. Music.* She pressed her finger on the power button of the CD player and Joan Sutherland's achingly pure voice filled the room.

Slowly she tugged the black glove off her hand. Then she began to undress, slipping into a white nightdress with lace at the neck and wrists. As she was about to drop her blouse into the laundry basket, she felt the outline of something hard underneath her fingers. Her mobile phone. She took it out and placed it on the side table next to the whisky.

The bright light inside the bathroom made her wince. Her sleeping pills were on the second shelf of the medicine cabinet. A nice, full bottle. She had it filled only last week. It helped if you were allowed to write your own prescriptions.

Returning to her bedroom, she sat down in the armchair in front of the fireplace, lifting her feet onto the quilted foot-stool. She would have two of her pills and one more glass of whisky and then she would go to sleep with beautiful music playing and a soft lamp burning.

Taking a sip from the glass, she closed her eyes as Sutherland's soaring voice gave poignant life to the mad Lucia.

Splendon le sacre faci, splendon intorno...

The liquid Italian words floated through her mind and she felt tears seeping from her closed eyelids.

Al fin son tua, al fin sei mio,...
'At last I am yours, at last you are mine,'
Del ciel clemente un riso la vita, a noi sarà...

The music swelled and ended. She opened her eyes and smiled at the man who was watching her, only a few paces away.

'Francis.' She smiled again, suddenly so grateful for his presence. 'I'm so glad you're here. I was feeling very lonely tonight.'

'I'm sorry to hear that.' He walked over and sat down in the chair next to hers. She was struck anew by how quietly he moved for such a powerful man. It was one of the first things she had noticed about him all those years ago when they first met.

'How is Daniel?'

'Not good. He has Alzheimer's.'

The shock cut through the alcohol daze like a scalpel.

His voice was impersonal. 'It is not yet noticeable to others but it will soon be.'

How terrible, she thought, feeling suddenly so sad. How terrible to become a man without a story. And Daniel, of all people.

'And you?' she asked. 'How are you holding up? It must destroy you to watch him lose himself day by day. I wonder how you can stand it.'

His face was pale and stern, like a judge. 'Love is strong as death, hard as hell.'

'Meister Eckhart.' She smiled in remembrance. 'You still believe in love, then.'

He didn't answer, just looked at her with eyes that had seen much on the journey without gaining any compassion.

She suddenly frowned. 'How did you get here from Whiteladies so quickly? I called you only ...' She paused and looked at the mobile phone on the table, trying to concentrate, '... only an hour ago.'

'Not that long. Forty minutes. I was in London, as it happened.'

'You said you were coming tomorrow.'

'I decided to come tonight.' He leant forward and picked up her hand, gently rubbing the deformed fingers, his thumb coming to rest on the melted lamp seared into the flesh of her wrist.

'This was your finest moment.' He looked up and into her eyes.

She didn't answer; merely reached for the glass and took a deep swallow.

'Although in retrospect I rather wish that day your courage had failed you.'

She hadn't been this close to him in years. He had aged well. He had always been an attractive man with those deep, dark eyes and elongated face. The short beard was new but it made him look all the more like a figure in an El Greco painting.

He sighed deeply. 'Bella. What did you tell them?'

'She doesn't look like Julianne, Francis. But she is beautiful too. And Leon's son. So handsome.'

His voice was no longer soft. 'What did you tell them?'

The hard edge sharpening his words made her blink nervously. 'We need to help her remember who she is, Francis. It is the only way she can be saved. If we don't help her she'll go mad with the voices inside her head.'

'Are *you* mad?' His anger was like a whip. 'She is broken. She cannot be saved.'

'I know you don't like me, Francis. I know you have never forgiven me for what I did to Mnemosyne. But I am trying to make amends. Surely you, of all people, understand the concept of redemption.'

The look in his eyes made her cringe. 'You and Leon.' He spat out the words. 'And Julianne. The three of you brought a cancer to Mnemosyne. You befouled Daniel's legacy.'

And suddenly she was furious too. Banging her glass on the table, she leant forward, pushing out her chin. 'Did you kill her, Francis? I've always wondered. Was it an intruder who killed Julianne, or was it you?'

She knew she was being reckless but she didn't care. 'Did you kill her because you knew Daniel loved her and you were jealous, or did you kill her because she betrayed Mnemosyne? You – so pious. A man of God. Did you bash her head in?'

'You fool.' There was spittle on his lip. '*I* didn't kill her. Daniel did. And the child saw him. *Now* do you understand?'

She stared at him, her brain stupid. 'You're lying.'

In her mind's eye came an image of Julianne as they had found her, with her skull crushed and wet. 'No,' she said. 'Daniel was the best of us.'

'Even the best men can lose their minds when they learn they were betrayed not once, but twice. Julianne told him what she had done to the child. And then she told him about Leon, how she would take him to her, even when Daniel was in the same house; even in his own bed. Daniel is not a saint, Bella. He is a man. He lost himself for only a moment: but it was a moment too far.'

His sweater was a deep inky blue. A small crimson flower was embroidered right above his heart. It looked as though something had pierced his chest, Bella thought. As though he was dripping blood.

A sudden thought made her feel sick. 'So Daniel knows about me ... how Leon and I ...' She stopped, her throat closing. Somehow the thought that Daniel had known of their treachery all these years was even worse than knowing he had killed Julianne.

'He forgave you both. He said he could hardly not do so, considering what he was guilty of.' His eyes flickered away from her face as though he could barely stand to look at her.

'The child ... you said Jenilee saw him. Why did she not say anything?' But even as she spoke, she suddenly knew. He saw the recognition in her eyes and nodded.

'Yes. Daniel made her forget.'

'But it didn't last.'

'Unfortunately, no. When he made her forget the murder, Daniel thought he had also suppressed the memories Julianne had managed to imprint on the girl. But those imprinted memories kept pushing their way into her consciousness. Relentless.

Like … like underlying writing on a palimpsest.' The words exploded from his lips. 'I think the process of remembering the imprinted memories also led the girl to remember how her mother died.'

A long silence.

'She called me.' Godine paused. 'She had her breakdown in a restaurant, of all places. She told me,' he lifted his voice into an unpleasant falsetto, '"Uncle Daniel is a murderer." A murderer! How dared she! I told her to wait for me, but when I arrived she had disappeared.'

The fury in his voice made Bella blink. 'What would you have done if you had found her?'

'Reasoned with her. Tried to explain.'

'And if she wouldn't listen? If she had wanted to go to the authorities?'

He cocked his head. His eyes were blank.

'God help you.' Her lips were stiff. 'You've become as bad as the rest of us.'

'I am willing to carry that burden to protect a superior man.'

The palms of her hands were sweating. She rubbed them against her nightdress. 'You got lucky, didn't you? The shock of remembering Julianne's death pushed Jenilee into a fugue state and all her memories of the murder were wiped clean.'

'Lucky.' He nodded slowly. 'Yes. But it may not last. She may snap out of it at any time. I cannot allow this to happen.'

'Francis, it doesn't matter. No one will believe her. She was five years old.'

'It could be enough to reopen the investigation. There will be talk, gossip. Daniel will be associated with a murder, not remembered for his genius. I cannot stand by and let that happen. Do you really think I would allow anyone – *anyone* – to sully Daniel's reputation? Daniel Barone will go down in history as one of the greatest minds of all time. He is a good man and he will be remembered as a good man. There will not be a whiff of scandal clinging to his name!'

'It's too late.'

He frowned. 'What do you mean?'

'They know about the code word. It is in Julianne's diary.'

'It doesn't matter. The diary is lost.'

'Jack has found it.'

He drew in his breath with a sharp hiss.

Something inside her was enjoying his discomfiture. 'So you see,' she added spitefully, 'it is just a matter of time. Once they have the code word, she will become Jenilee again. And she'll remember how Julianne died.'

For a few moments he watched her unblinkingly. Then he sighed and reached into his coat pocket, his movements unhurried. When he brought out his hand, he held a pair of gloves.

'What are you doing?'

He pushed his fingers into the gloves and picked up her mobile phone. 'I think we should text the girl to come over, don't you? We'll tell her you know what the code word is, but that you will only reveal it to her if she comes alone.'

She looked at him stupidly. 'I don't know the code word. I told her so.'

'She will think you lied. And thought better of it.'

'No.' Bella shook her head. 'She won't come. Besides, I don't know how to reach her.'

'Don't worry. I do.' His thumbs moved quickly across the keys. 'There.'

He replaced the phone on the table and stretched out his hand to the bottle of sleeping pills. 'Having trouble sleeping, Bella? Bad dreams?'

Unscrewing the top, he upended the bottle so that the capsules inside cascaded onto the table. In the same leisurely fashion he lifted the stopper from the whisky decanter and filled the glass to the brim.

The mobile phone beeped. Godine glanced at the screen. 'She's on her way.'

He looked back at her. 'We can do it the hard way or the easy way, Bella. You can swallow the pills and they will find you tomorrow, looking as beautiful as ever. Or you can hang yourself over the balustrade and they will discover you with your black tongue sticking out of your mouth and your eyes bulging. Your choice. Either way, they will think it suicide.'

She stared at the shiny capsules with their pretty, multi-coloured skins. When she spoke again she was dimly surprised at the steadiness of her voice. 'Will you turn on the music again, please? I always like to go to sleep with music.'

'Of course.'

She picked up the first capsule and held it between her thumb and forefinger. 'Brother *Laborare Est Orare*. "Work is prayer." Do you think of this as God's work, Francis?'

'I changed my motto years ago.' He spoke in the hushed voice of someone sharing a secret. 'I have since taken the name of Brother *Pecavi*.'

He held the glass of whisky out to her. 'The one who sinned.'

CHAPTER FORTY SIX

The rain had stopped but tiny waves of water were still rolling down the tall windows, turning the world outside into a blurred nothingness. The wind moaned around the corners of the building. The sound was getting on her nerves.

She had been waiting for what felt like hours. Each time she tried calling Jack or Jungles, their phones went straight to voicemail. Which was not, of course, a sign that anything was wrong. A ring tone interrupting stealthy business was certainly to be avoided. It made sense for the men to have switched off their mobiles.

She grasped her arms with her hands. She was cold. But maybe it wasn't cold she was feeling. Maybe it was fear. Fear of the decision she would have to make.

So what you're saying is, I'm stuck with the voices, the madness.

If you keep on living your life as Eloise, yes. And I'm afraid the voices may grow more intense over time.

Insanity. Unless Jack and Jungles retrieved the diary.

And then what? Swallow the magic pill and wake up the next morning a stranger who does not even recognise the man she loves?

The phone buzzed. The unexpectedness made her freeze for a moment but then she grabbed at the phone with eager fingers. *Jack. At last.*

It wasn't Jack. The sense of relief vanished. She scrolled down the text message, cautiously pushing the words around in her mind.

I have the code word ...

Step into my gingerbread house, said the witch. Step inside and I will give you a treat.

Come alone ...

Come to my gingerbread house alone, said the witch. And I'll show you my oven.

Perhaps she should wait for Jack to go with her.

But then she felt irritated at herself. Bella was a pampered, middle-aged woman. Hardly someone who would have the strength to push anyone into an oven. She didn't need Jack to hold her hand; she could handle this on her own. And if she was quick about it, she might even be back before the men returned. Ironic that, after risking life and limb, they could arrive to find her holding the prize. But then, life is full of ironies. And bad jokes.

On my way. She pressed the send button without hesitation.

At the door, she turned around. There were her clothes, the lovely dressing table Jungles had given her, the roses Jack had bought. But the room seemed suddenly as if from a dream. The neon light outside blinked pink and green and washed watery ripples of colour across the pale bed sheets. The fairy lights strung around the bedposts made the bed seem suspended, as if held aloft by stars. The numbers on the wall looked like magic writing. She had lived in this room for two years, but she suddenly felt like a trespasser. Another woman would return at any minute and wonder who this stranger was and what she was doing here.

She shook her head sharply and closed the door behind her.

Number 71 was dark except for weak light shining through the fan-shaped window above the door and, at the very top, a sliver of light peeping through a small gap in the heavy curtains. The house next to 71 looked strangely sinister with its steel skeleton of scaffolding. The street was empty and gleaming with wet.

She walked up the shallow steps of Bella's house and noticed that the front door was ajar. And now she could hear the music. A faraway soprano voice was spiralling upwards, a lament coming from deep within the house.

She placed her finger on the bell. She waited but when a vicious gust of wind chilled the back of her neck, she pushed the door open and stepped inside. Closing the door behind her, she shut out the distant sounds of traffic and the night.

'Miss Wilding?'

The entrance hall was much as she remembered it, but this evening it was lit by light seeping through the rose-coloured shade of a tall lamp. There was the same overpowering smell of narcissi dripping their scent into the room. Some of the oil paintings that had been stacked against each other had been moved and turned face-out. A girl with dark eyes and a Spanish riding hat looked at her askance. Behind her was a winter landscape – all dramatic shadows and gloomy trees.

Facing the staircase, she stood quietly for a moment, listening.

'Miss Wilding? It's me. Eloise.'

The Spanish girl seemed to be smiling. From far above, the soprano's voice ran dizzyingly from note to note.

She started to walk up the stairs, her feet making no sound on the carpeted treads. She dragged her hand across the mirrored wall. It reflected her image back at her: a phantom figure at her elbow.

The first landing was in shadow. This, too, was how she remembered it. A ladder and builder's tools pushed to one side and, on her left, plastic sheeting covering a rough-edged hole in the wall, the gap behind the opaque sheet dark and unlit. To her right were the two slim doors with drop handles that led to the drawing room where she and Jack had talked to Bella during their visit. The doors were closed.

She rapped her knuckles against the wood. 'Miss Wilding? Are you in here?'

No sound, except for the soprano who continued to sing her heart out. She suddenly had the feeling that someone was watching her and looked sharply over her shoulder. But the plastic sheeting behind her hung motionless. Turning her back on it once again, she twisted the handles of the door in front of her.

One look was enough to tell her that the room was empty. No light shone from the chandeliers and the only presence was the ticking clock on the mantelpiece with its angels staring blindly into the darkness.

She was beginning to feel apprehensive. Slipping her mobile phone from her pocket, she pressed the speed dial button for Jack's mobile. Two short rings and his voice came on the line, inviting her to leave a message.

'Jack. I'm at Bella's house.' She paused, uncertain how to continue. 'Call me, 'she said finally.

She turned and started to ascend the staircase once again. The soprano was trilling like a mad angel, her voice much closer now.

And then she was on the top floor and the room in front of her had its door wide open. She could see a dressing table, the foot-end of a bed covered by a silky blue throw and two armchairs facing a fireplace filled with big flower tubs brimming with gypsophila. Someone was sitting in one of the chairs, the high back shielding the sitter from view, but with one arm dangling over the side. There was pretty lace at the wrist but the hand itself was grotesquely deformed. On the small side table was a glass and a decanter containing amber liquid. An empty pill bottle lay on its side.

'Miss Wilding?' She had to raise her voice against the music. 'Are you alright?' She started walking towards the chair, a sense of foreboding hammering at her brain.

Bella looked asleep. Her eyes were closed, her mouth a little slack. When Eloise touched her shoulder underneath the thin nightdress she could feel the warmth of skin.

'Please wake up! It's me. Eloise.'

The body in front of her sagged underneath the shaking of her hand. Bella's breast, she noticed, did not seem to move. Fighting a feeling of revulsion, she brought her palm close to Bella's lips. She picked up the deformed hand, trying to find a pulse amidst the folds of lace.

The music stopped. The sudden quiet was so unexpected, her breath caught. She whirled around and saw for the first time the man watching her from the corner.

He stepped closer towards her. 'Hello, Jenilee.'

CHAPTER FORTY SEVEN

Francis Godine. At the same moment she recognised him as the man standing next to Daniel Barone in the Mnemosyne picture, as the man whose younger self sometimes walked through her mind, she also realised that the woman whose slack wrist she held between her fingers was either dead or dying. She pushed her hand into the pocket of her jeans and took out her phone.

'Don't!'

The urgency in his voice was such that she involuntarily stilled her movements.

He said something again but she suddenly found she had difficulty concentrating. Her surroundings, she noticed with sick surprise, were sliding out of focus. It was only for a moment, but as she stared at the man facing her it was as though the outlines of the room around them wavered for a second before snapping back into sharp relief.

'I'm sorry.' She blinked. 'What did you say?'

'I said: she is at peace.'

The platitude sounded ugly. 'You don't understand.' She spoke carefully, not liking the expression in his eyes. 'We need to get help.'

'And you don't understand. I won't allow you to interfere.'

He stepped forward and she stepped back in response. Something was very wrong.

'I won't interfere.' She swallowed and tried to keep her voice calm. 'I am going to leave now.'

And then scream her head off for help once she was outside and safely out of range of this nutcase, who was looking at her with the strangest expression on his face.

'I can't allow you to leave.'

The silence hung between them like a living thing. And there it was again: a softening of the outlines of the room; the edges of her vision turning white.

'I can't allow you to leave because I cannot allow you to remember. The reputation of a great man is at stake.'

'What do you mean?' Her fingers tightened on the phone in her hand. The dread inside her was growing.

'Your eyes.' His voice was wondering. 'I had forgotten how strange they are. Do you know, if you had been born in medieval times your mother might have drowned you?' He cocked his head quizzically, as if sharing a humorous anecdote. 'She might have thought you were possessed.'

She didn't respond. The room had – blessedly – settled back into hard-edged focus, but if what she suspected was about to happen, she needed to get out immediately.

Would she be able to run past him? She had speed on her side, but he had bulk and power, and he was standing between her and the door: neatly blocking her exit.

'I am sorry for you.' He sounded sincere. 'I am sorry Julianne was your mother. They say when a woman has to choose between duty and her heart, she always chooses duty. Your mother proved the exception. She sacrificed her child to please her lover.'

He gave a step forward and spoke again but she was no longer paying attention. If he thought she was going to stand here listening politely while he backed her into a corner, he was dead wrong. In one swift movement she brought up her hand and threw the mobile phone at him with all the strength she could muster. Bull's-eye. It caught him squarely on the forehead right between his eyes. His hands flew up to his face and a surprised grunt of pain exploded from his lips.

Even before her arm had completed its downward swing, she was making a dash for the door. She felt his hand grasp wildly but a twist of the shoulder and she was past him and out of the room.

She started running down the staircase, taking the stairs two by two, her hand clutching the balustrade, the blood rushing in her ears. *Hurry. Hurry.* She could sense him coming after her but she didn't look back. *Hurry. Hurry.*

But as she approached the landing of the next floor down, it happened again. The stairs underneath her feet turned liquid; the walls shifted and wavered as if another world were trying to push its way through. And above the beat of her heart she heard the soft whispering of voices like menacing ghosts.

Oh, God. No! Not now.

Shatter.

Jungles' van had no heating. Jack shivered. A chill was spreading through his legs and he felt about a hundred years old. He caught a glimpse of his reflection in the window and turned away hurriedly. He didn't only feel a hundred, he looked it.

'I should call Eloise.' He searched his inside pocket. 'Let her know we're OK.'

From behind the steering wheel, Jungles nodded without taking his eyes off the road. His face, too, was drawn. Two tired men. Their mission had been successful and they should have been basking in the glow of a job satisfactorily completed, but instead they both looked as though they were getting ready to meet the reaper grim.

Jack switched on the power button on his mobile and it immediately started to ring. Someone had left him a message. He brought the phone up to his ear.

'Something wrong?' Jungles glanced over at him.

'Eloise.' Jack listened, baffled. 'She's visiting someone. Let me check if she's still there.' He speed-dialled her number.

'She's not answering.' He glanced over at Jungles. 'Do you think you could drop me off at this woman's house? It's not far.'

'Sure.' Jungles shrugged. 'Who is she?'

'Someone who knew Eloise's mother. In fact,' Jack opened the zip of Jungles' backpack and removed the diary from inside, 'she may be able to help us with this. Identify the code word, maybe.'

'So it's all good, then.' Jungles did not sound as though he thought it was good at all.

'Yes,' Jack said wearily. If possible, he sounded even more depressed than Jungles. 'It's all good.'

'Jenilee.'

She squinted. She was standing on the first-floor landing and Godine was only a couple of paces away. He was not alone. Behind him were three other figures: two men and a woman. Their features floated in and out of focus. Then blurry, then clearly delineated. Their lips moved and she heard their voices whispering.

From somewhere in the house, a mobile phone started to ring, the raucous vocals of Steppenwolf bursting forth with tinny vigour. '*Looking for adventure ...*' Vaguely she recognised the ring tone as her own. She realised the sound came from the room where a dead woman was sitting in an armchair: the same woman who was facing her only a few steps away, smiling, with smeared mouth and distorted eyes.

Her heart shuddered. Her head felt as hollow as an echo chamber. Upstairs, the mobile phone stopped ringing.

Godine's voice was soft. 'Don't make this hard on yourself.'

'Why? Why are you doing this to me?' She stretched out her hand to the wall to steady herself, but it slanted off at a distance.

He spoke in the same quiet voice. 'Do you realise Daniel could have taken his own drug and blocked out his memory of killing your mother? I urged him to do it, but he refused. He felt it was his punishment to relive that night every day of his life. Wouldn't you say that is noble, Jenilee? Wouldn't you say it is the most courageous thing you've ever heard?'

'I am not Jenilee.' Did she say it out loud? 'I am not Jenilee,' she said again. The sound of her voice shocked her into some kind of awareness.

Move!

She grabbed the tall ladder beside her with both hands. As she pushed it over, he brought up his elbows to shield himself but the ladder still toppled down on him with a satisfyingly heavy crash. But now her escape route down the stairs was blocked. Without hesitation she turned, driving her way blindly through the sheet of polythene covering the jagged gap in the wall in front of her.

She pushed through into the inky passage behind. It was dark here and the floor was unstable, with wide gaps between the planks. She carried on, her feet slapping loud against the bare floor. In her haste she stumbled over a bucket, barely visible in the gloom. Some kind of liquid splashed onto her foot.

She heard a rustle behind her as Godine too pushed through the plastic curtain and she felt the floor underneath her feet sag with his weight. She wanted to scream but the scream caught in her throat. Keeping her hands outstretched in front of her, she stumbled on in the darkness, mouth soundlessly open. And keeping pace beside and behind her were those airy figures with their rustling voices saying, *Jenilee. Jenilee. Wait for us…*

'Is this it?' Jungles double-parked in front of number 71, keeping the engine idling.

'Yeah.' Jack opened the van door. 'Do you want to come in?'

Jungles hesitated; shook his head. 'I think Eloise wants *you* with her. Not me.'

'Jungles—'

'It's OK.' But as Jack stepped out the van, he said, 'Promise me …'

Jack waited.

'Promise me you will never abandon her. No matter what.' Jungles gestured at the diary in Jack's hand. 'Whatever she decides to do.'

'You know you don't have to ask me that.'

'I am not doubting your feelings for her. But I don't know if you have it in you to go the distance.' Jungles rubbed his hand over his face. 'She has been tested. You … have not.'

'I will be there for her. Count on it.'

For a moment their eyes locked. Then Jungles leant over and pulled the door shut. Jack watched as the van bumped its way to the end of the street.

He walked up the stairs and placed his finger on the buzzer.

The sound of the doorbell sounded a million miles away. She stopped and heard the man behind her pause as well. For a moment they both listened, their breaths loud in the silence. She looked back and sensed their eyes meeting in the darkness.

'Jenilee.' His voice was just above a whisper. 'Don't run.'

She reacted as though he had cracked a whip. The plank floor underneath her feet felt decidedly unsafe but she was past caring. His footsteps were more hesitant than hers – he was probably worried the floor might give way under his bulk – and she knew her only hope was to outpace him. She ran past a bathroom – caught a glimpse of a white bath, ghostly pale in the darkness; then on past another room, small and bare as a monk's garret, and yet another littered with what looked like rubble and soiled drop sheets. The rooms all had some kind of protective latticework covering the windows, and none had doors. She wanted to hide, but there was nowhere to hide.

The passage was ending and she could see a large room opening in front of her. The entrance was barred by a flimsy wisp of orange 'KEEP OUT' tape stretching from one side of the door to the other. She broke through it without another thought.

There was light here. It came from the red warning lights attached to the scaffolding outside. A breath of wind stirred long strips of wallpaper, weeping from the walls.

Another gust of wind and the wallpaper rustled again. The wind was pushing through a tall sash window hanging at half-mast.

An open window. With scaffolding on the other side.

Her breath exploded from her lips in relief. She stepped forward, but her right foot slid on a loose piece of plastic sheeting. There was a cracking, splintering sound and pain skewered through her leg as her other foot went straight through the rotten wood.

Jack brought his finger to the buzzer once again and this time he held it there.

Still no response. He frowned. A growing sense of unease was starting to nag at him.

There was a brass letterbox in the front door: the kind with a flap allowing access to the inside. As he speed-dialled Eloise's number again, he leant forward and pushed his hand through the letterbox's brass mouth. He caught a glimpse of marbled floor tiles and the corner of a painting. And now he could hear faintly – very faintly – the sound of Steppenwolf. 'Born to be Wild.' Somewhere inside the house her phone was ringing. But she didn't answer and, after a few seconds, her voicemail message came on.

His unease had turned into outright alarm. He allowed the brass flap to fall back into place and leant over sideways to try and ease open the sash windows flanking the door. Predictably, they did not budge. Windows at street level tended to be locked.

Walking back, he looked up at the house. Every window was dark except for a thin sliver of light escaping through a gap in the curtains on the very top floor.

He tried to remember the layout of the house. There was the entrance hall filled with all that stuff, the staircase, the first landing leading to the drawing room and …

In his mind's eye he saw the rough brickwork and clumsy gap in the wall where a hole had been broken through to give access to the building next door. Renovations, she had said. The two houses becoming one.

He retraced his steps and turned to his left, continuing until he faced the derelict house next door. He peered through the steel framework of the scaffolding covering its façade. And what do you know? On the second floor, one of the sash windows was open.

He placed his hand on the bottom rung and pulled himself up. That's when he heard her scream.

CHAPTER FORTY EIGHT

She tugged at her foot and screamed at the pain, which drove through her ankle like a giant corkscrew. Her foot felt broken. If it was, it would be months before she could do parkour again. The thought made her angry.

Taking a deep breath, she gritted her teeth and pulled on her ankle again. Don't. *Pull*. Be. *Pull*. Such a baby! *Pull*! She felt the skin on her leg rip as she dragged her leg free from the splintered gap.

Too late. He was inside the room.

For a moment they simply stared at each other. The red warning lights outside flashed on and off. The light played across his white shirt and stained it a watery pink like a blood-soaked ribbon.

He stooped and picked up the plastic sheeting on which she had slipped, flexing it between his hands. He moved slowly and the expression on his face was almost one of pain. How odd, she thought. He is finding this difficult. He is finding it difficult to kill me.

She tried to push herself to her feet and her leg gave way underneath her. But her movement seemed to be the trigger he had needed to catapult him into violence. He lifted his arm and struck her hard – so hard, her head whiplashed with a sickening jolt. The next moment he had stepped behind her, slapping the plastic around her face and twisting it into a tight knot behind her neck.

It was like looking through glycerine and felt as smothering. She tried to tear the sheeting from her face but her nails scrabbled uselessly against the slippery surface. Convulsing herself backwards she grabbed at his legs, but he merely tightened his grip. As she opened her mouth to scream, she felt her lips press wetly against the plastic and her voice disappearing into the stifling folds.

She realised she was weeping and her nose was running. Not good. She was doing an excellent job of helping him suffocate her. Her eyes ached. Her mouth tasted of dirt. She couldn't hear anything. No air.

Her mind was snapping in and out of consciousness like an electric current cutting out. Jack giving her roses. His voice saying, 'I think you have more of the tiger than the lamb in you, Ms Blake.' Bella stroking the black glove on her arm: 'We are meant to forget.'

The grip behind her head relaxed. She gave a shuddering breath and tore the plastic off her. With furious haste she scrabbled away from him, the floor creaking menacingly. Propping herself up into a sitting position, she pushed her back against the wall.

Jack was standing inside the room, at the window. 'Get away from her.'

The red lights flashed behind him. On. Off. Hypnotic.

'I said: get away from her!'

'She is a monster, Jack. An aberration. No longer fashioned in the image of God.'

At the window Jack placed one foot in front of the other, then stopped at the soft, crumbly sound of sifting rubble.

'I can't let this continue.' Godine was speaking in an almost conversational tone. 'Mnemosyne was hubris. We were like Icarus, flying too close to the sun. I see that now.' He turned his head towards her. 'And you – you are sick. I will be doing you a kindness.' He stepped forward.

'No!' Jack launched himself away from the window.

There was a massive thump as the two men hit the floor, a shout of pain, followed by the sick groan of rotting wood as the men fell straight through into the room below, their arms around each other.

She crawled forward and looked down into the blackness. As her eyes adjusted, she saw one of the figures below pushing himself off the man beneath him.

It had not been a long drop to the cement floor below. Not a long drop at all. Surely not enough of a fall to kill. But as she looked down, feeling nauseous, she could tell that the huddled figure with its legs sprawling and its arms outstretched in a giant hug was quite dead.

CHAPTER FORTY NINE

Memory image 1

They say that on our deathbeds we do not remember poetry, or the thoughts of great men. We do not remember the things that move our soul: they are drowned out by a terrible exhaustion, by the undignified struggle of our bodies fighting the great catastrophe. And then, nothing.

I do not believe it. In the end, what is a life about? Memories of my mother's voice calling to me; memories of my own daughter playing in the twilight with the scent of burning leaves in the air; a Bach cantata; the feel of my lover's body and the sound of his breath in the darkness. Memories of friendship and laughter, of what it means to share a dream, an ambition, a magnificent quest. I am sure I will remember these moments – they will come to me unbidden as I cross over.

They say we live on in our children. This I believe to be true. My daughter is of me and I am of her. When the blood in my veins turns to dust, I will continue to live inside her and I shall not altogether die.

CHAPTER FIFTY

The revolving door swung and swished and Jack watched his father walk across the hotel lobby, followed by a porter carrying a suitcase. His father spoke briefly to the desk clerk before turning around, his eyes searching the lounge area.

A fern-like potted plant shielded Jack from direct view, and at first his father's gaze went straight past him. In those few unconscious moments he had the opportunity to study his parent.

Leon Simonetti looked tired. He had allowed his barber to cut his hair too short and the cropped hair made his neck look thin and vulnerable. The lines from his nose to mouth seemed overly pronounced.

His gaze came to rest on Jack and he lifted a hand. Jack got to his feet.

'Jack.' His father gave him an awkward slap on the shoulder.

Close up, the fatigue on his father's face was even more noticeable. Behind the aggressive spectacles there were dark smudges under his eyes.

'Sorry I'm late. We had car trouble on the way back.'

Jack nodded. His father had flown in from New York the day before but had immediately headed for Whiteladies, where he had spent the night.

'Wouldn't you like to check in first?'

'It can wait.'

They sat down opposite each other.

'How is he?'

Leon Simonetti sighed and slid a finger between his tie and collar. 'In shock, I suppose. He and Francis were like brothers. I fear Daniel will be lost without him.'

'How is …' His father hesitated.

'Eloise.'

'Yes.'

'She'll be on crutches for the next eight weeks but she's fine.'

'Good. Good.' His father pursed his lips. 'I would like to see her. Talk to her.'

'That's up to Eloise. I doubt she'll be interested.'

'You must persuade her. I can help her, Jack.'

'Really? How so?'

'If she gives me Julianne's diary, I am sure we can figure out the failsafe. Along with the formula for DE7, I am confident I may be able to reverse her memory loss. Restore her to her old self, so to speak.'

'Maybe she is no longer interested in her own self.'

'Don't be foolish.' His father's mouth drew down. 'The longer she stays in the fugue state, the more she is at risk. Especially as, from what you told me, the fugue identity seems to be integrating with the memories Julianne had imprinted on her.'

His father raked his hand through his hair; a gesture familiar to Jack – it always signalled extreme impatience. 'It is important for you to understand that, the more often she recalls the imprinted memories, the stronger those neural networks will become and the stronger and more durable the memories themselves. But they will never be her own memories, which means they may tax her sanity in the same way the schizophrenic patient is challenged by delusional episodes. There may already be anatomical change to the brain and the growth of new branches on the nerve cells. The quicker we interfere, the better. Otherwise she may experience a complete psychotic break.'

'I'm hearing an awful lot of "mays". Can you state with one hundred per cent certainty that she will indeed go into the kind of meltdown you describe?'

'Nothing in life is one hundred per cent certain, Jack. But are you really willing to take that chance? Is she?'

'Eloise is no longer under the same stress as she was before. She tells me she is convinced she will be better able to cope with the episodes now that she knows *everything*.'

His emphasis on the word 'everything' did not go unnoticed. His father cleared his throat and looked suddenly uncharacteristically unsure of himself. 'Has she decided if she's going to take this further?'

'You mean, is she going to go tell the authorities about Mnemosyne? No. You can rest easy.'

Leon Simonetti's voice was defensive. 'You're angry.'

'Perceptive of you.'

His father's lips thinned. 'You have no right to judge.'

'She is the woman I love. You decided to play God with her life and she is paying the price for your arrogance.' Jack leant forward. 'You're damn right I'm angry!'

A waitress, who had been heading in their direction, stopped and gave them a troubled look. Jack waved her away and tried to moderate his voice.

'What I don't understand is your sudden concern for Eloise. You're the one responsible for all of this.'

His father placed his fingers on both sides of his nose and closed his eyes for a moment. 'That is unfair. I could not have foreseen she would be witness to a murder, and that the trauma would lead to identity loss. If not for that complication, she would have been fine. In fact, she would have been more than fine: she would have been gifted … instead of damaged.'

'And damaged goods need to be fixed.'

'Don't be so fucking melodramatic.' His father never swore. 'Give me the diary and let's get on with it.'

'That's what it's really all about, isn't it? The diary. This is not about Eloise. You just want to get your hands on Julianne's research.'

'Her research may lead to a quantum leap forward in the way we use our brains. Not something of great significance to you, perhaps.'

Jack heard his own voice as if coming from a long way away. 'Do you believe in hubris? Before he died, Godine said you were all guilty of hubris. Do you agree?'

'Francis was a sanctimonious fool.'

'What about divine justice? Do you believe in that?'

His father looked at him as though he were deranged.

'Think about it. Five members of Mnemosyne. Three died violently. One is living with his brain literally falling apart. And then there's you. The last little Indian. Don't you sometimes wonder what is waiting for you down the road?'

His father stared, his mouth slightly open.

Jack pushed himself to the front of his seat. 'I'm leaving.'

'Well, let me tell you what is waiting down the road for *you*.' Leon Simonetti's face was ugly. 'Eloise Blake could become completely paranoid and delusional. Everything will seem like a threat. I hope you like living with a woman who has brains like scrambled eggs.'

Jack felt his fingers tighten into fists. 'I never realised it. You're a vulgar man.'

His father flushed brick-red. 'Or you can let me help her and she will become the person she used to be: Jenilee Gray. But you don't want that, do you? Because if she does, she'll forget you. You accuse *me* of ulterior motives? *You* are the selfish one.'

'You're wrong. It is her decision to make. I told her so and I meant it.' Jack got to his feet.

'You forget one thing.'

Something in his father's voice stopped him.

'Let's say she doesn't become delusional. Let's say she manages to control the episodes and the two of you walk off into the sunset hand in hand. She could still snap out of the

fugue state on her own, you know. In fact, most patients suffering from dissociative disorder do. It could take years. It could
happen tomorrow. But you'll be living with the knowledge that
she could open her eyes one morning and look at you and have
no idea who you are. Can you live like that? I don't think you
can.'

The eyes behind the spectacles were calculating. 'You're
feckless, Jack. You've never been able to stick with anything in
your life. Frankly,' his father stretched out his legs in front of
him, 'I don't think you have the balls.'

'As long as I have the heart.'

He turned his back and walked away.

'On the first page
That is the chapter when
I first met you
Appear the words
Here begins a new life.'
                    —*Dante Alighieri, La Vita Nuova*

CHAPTER FIFTY ONE

The sky was red as wine and stained with the wash of city lights. The air smelt exciting and gritty. Above the conch-shell sound of traffic, he could hear gulls cry and was reminded that somewhere out there in the darkness the Thames was flowing strong and silent, carrying with it the smell of mud, rotting algae and a hint of spring. It was still cold but in Marks and Spencer's they were selling daffodils for a pound a bunch and, in Hyde Park, snowdrops were blooming.

Jack placed his hands on the cement ledge and peered over the edge of the rooftop, looking down on the light-spattered street below. The door to a restaurant burst open to the smell of kebabs and the convivial sound of voices. A young man in a leather jacket and a young woman with flowing hair exited together. He saw the flick of a gold bangle as she placed her hand on the man's lapel and drew his head towards hers.

He felt Eloise's hand on his arm. 'They're in love.' Eloise's mouth tilted up at the corners.

'In lust, anyway.'

She drew a face. 'You're such a romantic.' She stepped back, rolled her shoulders and flexed her fingers. She was dressed in a black sweater and black trousers and looked lithe, supple and strong. 'Are you ready?'

He nodded. This was her first run since she had broken her ankle and he personally would not have chosen a rooftop run for her comeback, but by this time he knew better than to argue if she had her mind set on something.

'Before we go ...' She looked at the book, sitting where she had placed it earlier, perching precariously on the ledge. 'Did you bring it?' She held out her hand.

His fingers searched and found the box of matches inside his trouser pocket.

'Eloise ... Are you sure?'

For a moment she didn't answer. The expression on her face was almost absent-minded. Then she said, 'I'm sure.'

'If nothing else, the diary is a keepsake. Don't you want to have something of your mother? To remember her by?'

'I do have something to remember her by.' She pushed up her left sleeve. On her inner arm were tattooed the initials, N.O.M., the black ink stark against the white of her skin. She rolled back her sleeve and held out her hand once more.

He placed the matches on her palm but kept his hand on top of hers. 'It's not too late. We can still take the diary to Serena. If you burn this book, you will never know the code word. You will go past the point of no return.'

'I have no wish to return.' Still that abstracted look. 'Besides, I don't need a shoebox of memories to tell me who I am. I know who I am.' She suddenly touched her other hand to his face – her fingers soft as petals against his cheek. 'And I know I love you, Jack. What else is there? Isn't that enough to live a life by?'

She drew a match and he smelt the sharp tang of phosphorus. As she brought the match to the book, the flame crept hesitantly across the thick brown hessian, very slowly turning to black the gold-stamped Mnemosyne lamp, the raised initials of *Soror N.O.M.* The flame curled the fragile pages, flicking to life with greater urgency as it burnt through the cool, passionless tapestry of formulae and numbers. By the time it reached the pages with its anguished words and tear-stained images, it was blazing out of control. Silently they watched as the diary consumed itself in a ball of orange and black heat until only ashes were left.

She scooped up the ashes into both hands and a fugitive breeze swept the pale dust from her palms. Where would it end up? he wondered. In a garden square? On the gilt wings of an angel in a dimly lit church? Maybe on a windowsill where impatient hands would sweep it away, leaving behind nothing.

She smiled at him, her mouth dauntless. 'Let's run.'

He followed her slender figure as it flitted across the dark rooftop. The city was all around them, inhaling and exhaling with giant breaths. She was outrunning him, leaving him behind. Ahead of them, in the diminishing distance, a fat, swollen moon hung low in the sky and it looked for all the world as though she were trying to run straight at it.

She had reached the end of the roof. To reach the next building required a jump across open space. She didn't hesitate, but threw herself across the opening. For a moment she hung suspended, weightless.

Her feet touched down on the other side with perfect control. He stopped at the edge of the roof, breathless.

She looked at him across the gap, her face vivid. 'Are you coming?'

The gap was not that wide – he had leapt gaps easily more ambitious in distance. But he hesitated, staring into the well below. It was dark and deep.

He looked up and across at her once more. Her bright eyes were unfocused, as though she was looking into another world. And then she gave a small, secretive smile.

'I'm coming!' He reached out his hands towards her and jumped.

AUTHOR'S NOTE

In my fourth novel, *Season of the Witch*, I explored the strange and wonderful world of medieval memory palaces and examined the question of whether modern man's memories are becoming shallow and if we are all increasingly incapable of internalising knowledge. *Witch* was a research-intensive novel and, by the time I finished the book, I thought I had finished with the subject of memory.

But a chance reading of a *New York Times* article, titled 'Brain Researchers Open Door to Editing Memory', drew me back to this subject matter. I was fascinated to learn of the discovery of the memory molecule, PKMzeta, by researchers at the Sackler Laboratory, and the implications of the manipulation of this molecule.

Imagine if scientists could erase traumatic memories by merely changing a single substance in the brain. The war veteran will no longer suffer from PTSD; the rape victim will no longer be tormented with excruciating memories; a learned behaviour such as drug addiction will be cured. But if we are able to rid ourselves of troubling memories, would this perhaps tempt us to persist in destructive behaviour or immoral acts because we can now simply swallow a pill and forget about them? And how will tampering with memory impact on our sense of identity?

As I began to research the subject of memory anew, I came to realise that I had always believed that somehow, deep in our brains, memories are perfectly stored—almost as if vacuum-packed. If only we had the right drug, scan or hypnosis at our disposal then surely we should be able to access these memories exactly. But this is not the case. Man is not a machine. The brain is not a camera. As soon as memory enters the mind, it is already changing. The brain alters the way we remember, fusing actual events with our wants and desires and thereby creating a sense of self, which is unique.

And so I decided to write *Dark Prayer* as a story about one of the twenty-first century's greatest remaining challenges: the mystery of memory as the key to who we are. We think of memory as the story of our lives, but how many of these mental images and emotions we summon are accurate and reflect what has truly happened? And does it matter? Maybe this fusion of what is true and invented is central to the human condition: the natural state of what remembrance truly is.

ACKNOWLEDGEMENTS

So much of what we do, we do alone, that writers tend to think of themselves as islands. But if we are lucky—and I am—we have family, friends and associates who form a support network without which we would simply be unable to function.

Thanks to Deborah Schneider, my agent, for keeping the faith.

Thanks to Jane Hammett for her meticulous editing of the manuscript.

Thanks to Lizzie 'Terror' Doyle for sharing with me her knowledge of parkour and its philosophy.

Thanks to Carlos Andrade, who taught me to keep my chin down and my fists high.

Thanks to Gaynor Rupert for always reading my manuscripts with a generous heart and an eagle eye. Thanks to fellow scribes Dianne Hofmeyr and Sonja Lewis and to Catherine Gull, a good friend and a gifted reader.

Thanks to my brother, Frans, for never hesitating to share with me his unique brand of bracing common sense, and my sister-in-law, Catherine Peters, for her heart-warming habit of making all her friends read my books. Thanks to my amazing nephew, Carl, whose imagination takes my breath away. Thanks to my brother, Stefan, for my innovative website and for being my tech guru. Thanks to my mother-in-law, Joan Mostert, for her enthusiasm and unwavering support.

My husband, Frederick, is extraordinary. I cannot imagine my world without him.

Creativity is sometimes described as the courage to turn your back on certainties. My mother, Hantie Prins, is the most creative person I know. I dedicate this book to her.

ABOUT THE AUTHOR

Natasha Mostert is a South African novelist and screenwriter. She grew up in Pretoria and Johannesburg but currently lives in London, United Kingdom.

Educated in South Africa and at Columbia University, New York, Mostert majored in modern languages and holds graduate degrees in Lexicography and Applied Linguistics.

She has worked as a teacher in the Department of Afrikaans and Dutch at WITS University, Johannesburg, and as project coordinator in the publishing department of public television station WNET/Channel Thirteen, New York. Her political opinion pieces have appeared on the op-ed page of the *New York Times*, and in *Newsweek*, the *Independent* and *The Times* (London).

Mostert's fourth novel, *Season of the Witch*, won the 2009 World Book Day: Book to Talk About Award.

She is an avid kickboxer. Please visit her website to find out more about her involvement with the CPAU Fight for Peace project, which teaches Afghan women how to box and feel empowered in their lives.

Future goals include writing poetry, executing a perfect spinning crescent kick, and coming face to face with the ghost of Edgar Allan Poe.

ALSO BY NATASHA MOSTERT

THE MIDNIGHT SIDE

THE OTHER SIDE OF SILENCE

WINDWALKER

SEASON OF THE WITCH

THE KEEPER
A MARTIAL ARTS THRILLER
(published in the US as *KEEPER OF LIGHT AND DUST* by
Penguin Dutton)

CONTACT NATASHA

If you would like to contact Natasha, her Facebook page is where she leaves regular updates and where you can leave a message.

On her website at www.natashamostert.com, you can read synopses of her books and her author's notes, play her games and find questions for book clubs. You can also gain access to her YouTube videos.

Please sign up for her newsletter to receive updates, news of competitions, free copies and more. Your email address will be kept strictly private and will never be shared with a third party.

Lightning Source UK Ltd.
Milton Keynes UK
UKHW010048170223
417092UK00013B/693/J

9 781909 965201